SKY BURIAL

MAX McNABB

Beloved Captive Trilogy Book 3

Max McNabb is a writer from Lubbock, Texas, and the editor of TexasHillCountry.com. He grew up on the family farm near Ropesville. He's the author of the Beloved Captive Trilogy: *Far Blue Mountains*, *Deathsong*, and *Sky Burial*. Contact him at maxmcnabb.com.

Dedicated to my parents

Scott & Amy

And grandparents

Ronnie & Sandra McNabb

Bill & Gwen West

This novel was inspired by the real events of the Fimbres Apache conflict of the 1920s, a latter-day frontier war between the last free Apaches and a Sonoran rancher. May the spirits of the dead find peace in eternity.

TABLE OF CONTENTS

THE STORY SO FAR

Sonora, Mexico, spring 1927—rancher Jubal McKenna takes in a young Apache girl with an injured ankle. She's a member of the last free Apaches, the band that refused to surrender with Geronimo decades earlier, and they live in the high solitude of the Sierra Madre where they keep the old ways. The McKennas call the dark-eyed girl Dolores. She's welcomed into the family by Jubal's wife Sara, their son John Russell, and baby Claudia. When Dolores's ankle heals, she wishes to return to her people. She finds the Apaches camped in a cave. Gouyen the wise woman is like a grandmother to the girl. She tells Dolores they've been watching and they've seen that she has a home in the valley, far safer than the wild sierras where life is brutal and short. Gouyen tells her she must go back for her own good and if she ever sets foot in the blue mountains again, she'll kill the girl herself. Heartbroken, Dolores returns to live as McKenna's adopted daughter.

An eye for an eye, blood for blood. November 1928—Apaches ambush the McKennas on the trail home from Nácori Chico. Gouyen cuts Sara's throat as warriors carry John Russell away. Later an Apache named Matzus shows John Russell a scalp covered in fresh blood and tells him it's his father's. In truth the scalp is old and the blood is Sara's. Believing his entire family has been killed, John Russell is carried off into the Sierra Madre with the raiders.

While Jubal readies his vaqueros to chase after the kidnappers, Dolores tells him a hard truth. He must wait until the boy is accepted into the band, until John Russell believes himself an Apache. Otherwise, if Jubal attempts a rescue too soon, they'll simply kill the boy. Only when he's become a beloved captive will it be safe. Jubal can't bear to hear it. He leads out his vaqueros on the chase. They trail the raiders high into the sierras before abandoning pursuit when Jubal discovers a bloody warning left for them to find. He must return to the valley and wait in hope that John Russell's heart will remember.

The Apaches take John Russell to their sanctuary hidden within a labyrinth of peaks and canyons: Pa-Gotzin-Kay, Stronghold Mountain of Paradise. There the boy is stripped of identity, immersed in Apache culture, a world of brutal conflict and strange magic. He meets Ishton, the beautiful older sister of Dolores and favorite wife of Carnoviste the chieftain. Only Ishton shows him kindness and he loves her for it. He meets Nantan the medicine man, Gouyen's twin brother who has a crippled leg, a black star tattooed to his chest, and mystic Bear Power. The boy is forced to work as a slave for the women.

In the U.S. a man called Cain, once a legendary soldier of fortune, is now middle-aged and reduced to working as a strikebreaker. He works alongside his friend Mosby, a veteran of the negro 10th Cavalry. He discovers an item in the newspaper—a young boy kidnapped by wild Apaches in the Sierra Madre. He knows those mountains well. Cain was there with his old mentor, a cavalry officer named Aubrey Eliot, when Geronimo surrendered. He tells Mosby they're done breaking strikes—he wants to be a soldier one last time. In the darkness of Cain's skull a teratoma incubates. Headaches and eerie visions plague him. Old ghosts torment him with the dark secret that has followed Cain like a shadow through all the many wars he's fought. First he practices meditation to suppress the visions, then turns to opium. He sees the ghost of Aubrey, he sees a dead Filipino boy. They call to him, biding him remember.

On Pa-Gotzin-Kay Apaches place wagers on a wrestling match between the captive boy and a Mexican slave his age. The boy defeats his treacherous opponent and wins the admiration of the People. No longer is he a White Eye slave. They accept him into the tribe as a beloved captive and Carnoviste adopts him as his son.

In the valley below, Jubal drowns his sorrow with whiskey.

Seasons pass. The captive boy receives his Apache name. From this time on, he is Denali. He witnesses the medicine man perform many supernatural acts. The People say Nantan is immortal—no warrior's hand can slay him. He makes a friend—Chatto, the son of Carnoviste's rival Zunde. The boys are tasked with protecting the women while they go out to gather wildberries. Denali and Chatto are standing guard when a grizzly rises up from the brush. A white star on its chest, a crooked left hindpaw. The beast falls upon the women and kills Alopay. Denali looses arrows and Chatto fires his Springfield rifle, but the grizzly escapes through a gully hidden in the tall undergrowth. The boys join Carnoviste's hunting party, tracking the killer bear to its feeding place. The grizzly is nowhere to be seen, his trail vanished, but there sits Nantan as though awaiting them. He'd been gathering herbs, he explains, when his Power told him something was wrong and led him there. Denali and Chatto share a look between them—the medicine man has a black star tattooed where the grizzly had a white mark in the shape of a star. Nantan's left leg is crippled like the bear's. Could Nantan transform himself into the grizzly? Denali and Chatto can tell no one of what they suspect. The People love their medicine man too well, for Nantan's Power ensures the survival of the band. The boys resolve to partner together to follow Nantan's movements and seek proof of their dark suspicion.

Jubal spends the summer and autumn of 1929 in a whiskey haze. Late in the fall Dolores tells him it's time—John Russell has surely become one of them by now. Jubal prepares a rescue mission for early winter to search out the camps in the foothills.

Cain descends into dark memory—the ferry crossing of Los Ebanos, Texas-Mexico border, 1870. The boy enters the world with his umbilical looped about the neck of his stillborn twin. His mother Hedda Killcrop dies in childbirth. Otto Killcrop, the boatman, blames the newborn and calls him Teufelkind—Devilchild. Cain grows up under Killcrop's harsh discipline. One day when Cain is fourteen, he spies a body floating down the river. Cain and his father drag the corpse onto the bank and begin looting it, their usual practice, when Killcrop recognizes the masonic insignia of the ring on the dead man's finger. Stricken with fear, he orders Cain to leave the body in the brush. He tells the boy if men with rings like the dead man's ring come looking, he must tell them where they left the corpse. "Never lie to the men with the rings," Killcrop warns. Later while Killcrop rests in a drunken slumber, Cain swims the river and takes the ring from the dead man's hand. He wears it on a twine around his neck, hidden under his shirt. Days pass. Killcrop's rage flares one twilight evening and he hits the boy, knocking him down, and the ring goes spilling out the front of Cain's shirt. Killcrop is paralyzed with sudden terror. For the first time Cain fights back, surprised to discover he possesses the strength of a man. He gives Killcrop a beating which ends with the boatman imparting a dark secret to the boy, the reason why he has a devil in him. The secret will haunt him forever after. Cain forces Killcrop to ferry him across the river, then he rides away and doesn't look back. For a year he wanders Mexico. He comes upon a mass grave in a potter's field on the outskirts of an abandoned mining town. The marker says only *Los Pistoleros Americanos* and the date *1870*. An anchorite in the ruined church tells him the men were death-dealers from the north who tried to rob the payroll of the mine and were killed in a great battle along with their Indio scout. Cain drifts westward. He rides into the village of Carretas on July 21, 1886, the day his life changes irrevocably. He enters the cantina and finds an American cavalry officer drinking with a group of Mexicans. The American's eyes flash to the masonic ring on Cain's finger. The Mexicans refuse to let the officer quit the table. They pour yet another round, promising if he drinks they'll take him to Geronimo's camp, the object of the American's quest in that country. "No help for the widow's son, is there?" the American asks. The masonic distress code means nothing to Cain. One of the Mexicans attempts to intimidate Cain, then the cantina erupts in a gunfight, with Cain and the American the only men left standing. The American introduces himself as Second Lieutenant Aubrey Eliot, on a mission to find Geronimo in the Sierra Madre and convince the Apache to surrender. He allows Cain to join him.

In Denali's life on Pa-Gotzin-Kay small bands are leaving to winter down in the warmth of the foothills. Denali is now fourteen. His best friend Chatto departs with his father Zunde and they won't be returning in the spring. Zunde chafes under Carnoviste's leadership and wishes to stay down below and rustle cattle. Matzus, the brave who presented the bloody scalp to Denali, also leaves with Zunde.

Jubal searches the sierras for Apache camps, for his lost son in that high lonesome country.

A fever strikes the clovenhoofed on Pa-Gotzin-Kay and sickens deer and cattle. The band determines they must journey down to the foothills where the game is still healthy. Ishton becomes pregnant with Carnoviste's child. Denali loves her from afar.

Spring comes. One afternoon Denali goes hunting and wounds a deer with his arrow. He tracks the deer out onto a ridgeside above the warm springs and there he witnesses something shocking. Far down below in the pool of the springs Nantan and Gouyen bathe together. Denali sees them kiss, sees their naked embrace. The taboo of incest is closely linked to witchcraft in Apache belief and Denali knows the medicine man's Power has turned to darkness. He tries to withdraw back into the trees before they can spot him, but his foot sends a loose rock tumbling. He dives into cover before Nantan and Gouyen glimpse him, but now they know someone was watching from above. Later Gouyen searches the ridge and finds the deer lying dead with the arrow in its side. She removes the arrow and studies its craftsmanship.

Denali can tell no one what he saw. Who would believe a captive White Eye boy? He rides with Carnoviste to gather peyote for his vision quest. They discover a cave midway down a sheer cliff face, a hive of honeybees inside. The Apaches lower Denali on a rope into the cave and he goes naked among the bees, gathering wild honey for the People. His Power is strong and the bees don't sting him.

Cain remains adrift on a sea of memory. Following the surrender of Geronimo he joins the cavalry and serves under Aubrey, who initiates him into Freemasonry. They fight together in the Philippines until Aubrey is shot by an insurrecto. A botched surgery paralyzes Aubrey, but Cain blames himself. Aubrey asks Cain to retrieve a potion from a folk healer which dulls all feeling. When Cain does so, Aubrey drinks the concoction and demands that Cain help him commit seppuku—for he wishes to die like the samurai warriors he admires. In great reluctance Cain obeys his mentor, only realizing many years later that Aubrey had been driven mad by despair. Cain becomes a soldier of fortune, wandering continents in search of war.

On his vision quest Denali fasts alone in the woods. He knows that Nantan may come to kill him while he's weak and isolated, but he must find his vision if he's to be a warrior. A thunderstorm rages on the fourth day as the strange beginnings of an epileptic seizure wash over him and Denali is quickened with a profound religious experience. Then all at once his vision is gone and he feels sudden dread. The grizzly rushes out of the darkness in a peel of thunder. The seizure takes hold of Denali as the bear jumps on him and he strikes out blindly with his knife. A lightning bolt flashes down in the selfsame instant. The lightning strikes the bear and envelopes Denali in a bubble of white light.

When Denali awakes, Nantan is lying dead on top of him in a bearskin, Denali's blade buried in the medicine man's eye. The lightning burned the bearskin and Denali is marked with a Lichtenberg figure on his chest, a fractal pattern of branching scars. He's drained of strength from the seizure and the lightning strike and now he's killed the immortal medicine man. It means exile or death. Denali hides on the outskirts of camp. He spies the maiden Jacali and approaches her, asking if she'll take a secret message to Carnoviste. She agrees. Carnoviste finds Denali in the woods where the boy tells him what happened, then the chief determines to help him. They hide Nantan's body in the honey cave.

New York, 1929—Cain escapes his tempest of memory, but he must endure the long process of kicking his opium habit. When he succeeds, Cain and Mosby hire on with the Purple Gang in Detroit. They guard a plant where Canadian whiskey is cut down with water before distribution to speakeasies. When a rival gang raids the plant, Cain pulls the single-shot derringer he keeps hidden under his shirtsleeve. He takes out one gangster with a headshot, then grabs another weapon and kills the others in a close-quarters gunbattle. After disposing of the bodies, Cain shows Mosby an advertisement he found in a pulp magazine—the Douglas, Arizona Chamber of Commerce is calling for volunteer adventurers to rescue the McKenna boy, still held captive by Apaches. He tells Mosby he intends to contact a former client, a wealthy old banker named Applegate, who would be willing to fund a mercenary expedition.

December 1930—Jubal travels to California to meet with elderly investment banker Horus Applegate. The old man wishes to finance Jubal's next campaign into the sierras and outfit him with a squad of professionals led by a soldier of fortune named Cain. Obsessed with eugenics, Applegate seeks to guide man's evolution into god. In return for funding the campaign he wants to use John Russell's story as propaganda to advance his eugenics agenda. Jubal rejects the offer.

Summer 1931—Denali joins Carnoviste on a raid into the valley. Now he regards the chief as his father, thanks to Carnoviste's loyalty in hiding the medicine man's body. The People had mourned the disappearance of Nantan. Some believed the grizzly had taken him, but Gouyen dismissed the idea. She holds back her accusation against Denali, not least of all because if the boy had killed Nantan and spirited him away, then his own Power is formidable. Denali knows she'll seek revenge one day. There's nothing they can do—even the chief can't accuse Gouyen and her vanished twin of incest without proof. And in any case, Carnoviste has need of Gouyen for her Power of Finding Enemies, which allows her to sense the presence of nearby hostile forces.

It had taken Denali a long while to recover from the lightning strike, but over a year has passed and the winter to come will be his sixteenth. Fully divested now of his old identity, he is Apache.

In a valley pasture the raiders attack a group of vaqueros leading a herd of fresh-broke horses to market. Denali joins in the gunfight. Now he can never return to the White Eye world. Guilt overpowers him when he opens the pocketwatch of the vaquero he killed and sees Dolores's cameo opposite the watchface.

The bodies of the vaqueros are discovered and brought back to the ranch. Dolores weeps for Angel, the boy who would have been her fiancé, murdered by Apache raiders. Jubal tells his men he's done chasing ghosts through the foothills—he's going up into the high reaches and he's a taking a man named Cain with him.

CAST OF CHARACTERS

Jubal McKenna: A powerful rancher in the Bavispe Valley, father of John Russell and Claudia, adopted father of Dolores. Widower of Sara.

Dolores/Bui: Apache girl adopted by the McKenna family. At the beginning of *Sky Burial*, she's seventeen.

John Russell/Denali: The young, red-haired son of Jubal and Sara. Kidnapped by Apaches and adopted as the son of Carnoviste. An epileptic. At the beginning of *Sky Burial*, he's almost sixteen.

Cain: Once a legendary soldier of fortune, now a middle-aged strikebreaker who longs for one last war.

Mosby: Cain's right-hand man, a veteran of the 10th Cavalry.

Carnoviste/Apache Juan: The last chief of the unsurrendered Apaches, husband to Ishton, Tsaltey-koo, and Hanlonah. Father of the young boys Neiflint and Oblite. The adopted father of Denali.

Gouyen: The wise woman is the twin sister of Nantan. She uses her Power of Finding Enemies to sense the presence of nearby hostile forces. Childless, Gouyen treated Bui as her granddaughter.

Nantan: The medicine man, twin brother of Gouyen. His supernatural Power ensures the band's survival and grants him authority that rivals Carnoviste's own.

Ishton: The beautiful older sister of Dolores and favorite wife of Carnoviste.

Sara McKenna: Jubal's wife, mother to John Russell and Claudia.

Claudia: Baby daughter of Jubal and Sara.

Wesley: An old ranch hand who works for Jubal.

Hector Cienfuegos: Ten years older than Jubal, Hector is the foreman of the ranch and Jubal's closest advisor.

Angel Ochoa: A young vaquero, later the fiancé of Dolores.

Zunde: Apache warrior, rival to Carnoviste for the chieftainship.

Chatto: The young son of Zunde, he's also Denali's best friend.

Moroni Thayne: Mormon rancher in the Bavispe Valley.

Aubrey Eliot: Cain's old mentor, a daring cavalry officer who convinced Geronimo to surrender peacefully. He died in the Philippines during the war, but Cain is haunted by ghostly visitations.

Estoni: Apache warrior.

Oblite: Son of Carnoviste, much younger than Denali.

Neiflint: Son of Carnoviste, much younger than Denali.

Matzus: The brave John Russell falsely believes is responsible for murdering his father because he showed the bloody scalp to the boy.

Horus Applegate: Elderly investment banker, former client of Cain's.

CHAPTER ONE

Late autumn, 1931

The Americans crossed into Sonora aboard a private Pullman coach. A pair of stockcars carried the horses and packmules they'd use on their journey into the sierras. Applegate had called in a favor and Phelps Dodge agreed to attach the stockcars and the Pullman behind their engine and hoppers. The mercenaries rode the El Paso and Southwestern toward the copper town of Nacozari de García, streamers of black smoke trailing in their wake and fading in the pale sky.

The men sat back in their seats, hats lowered over their eyes, long accustomed to catching sleep when and where it could be found. Most of them had only met for the first time at the El Paso station, but they shared a soldier's view of the world and their place in it. When you signed on for a job, you saw it through to the end.

Cain had spent the last part of the summer assembling his squad, each man chosen on the basis of his own particular expertise. They were veterans of the trenches

1

in ravaged Europe, stripped of any polite myth regarding the truth of their inner nature, survivors of that storm of steel. They were ex-Foreign Legion and soldiers of fortune, a few of them bounty hunters, all experienced in guerilla tactics and wilderness survival. A trainload of professional killers.

Mosby woke from a brief slumber. He looked about the coach, then rose from his seat and walked to the rear door and opened it. Cain stood smoking a cigarette on the narrow platform and pressing the heel of his hand to his forehead. Mosby stepped up beside the sergeant, closing the door behind him, and leaned against the iron railing.

"Another headache, Sergeant?"

"It'll pass," Cain told him.

The Pullman clattered down the rails. It was the final car and they stood on the platform and watched the receding wasteland, the troubled country of their introduction years ago on Pershing's expedition. They'd ridden that hard land chasing Pancho Villa. In those days Cain was an ex-sergeant in the 4th Cavalry turned civilian scout, Mosby a green recruit in the negro 10th.

After a while Cain said, "Ever have one place in your life where you felt like you were really home?"

"I don't know, Sergeant."

"If you got to think about it, the answer's no."

"I reckon the closest I ever had was the outfit."

"That's a fair answer. No shame in it. I thought for a long time the 4th Cavalry was the only place I'd ever belong."

"But you found somewheres else?"

"I knew this woman in Havana. Teresa was her name. She lived with her boy in a little room about half the size of this train car. Why she took up with me, I'll never figure out. I had some money at the time, but if she was lookin for a man, she could've had richer and younger. Better too. One who would've stuck. I had a suite in a fine hotel in the city and I moved her and the boy in there with me. Those were good days. I liked to make that woman laugh."

"Sounds real nice, sergeant. I'm glad you got them good memories."

"Mo, you ever make a woman laugh? Not some polite little chuckle, I mean from the belly."

"Most the women I known, they was serious women."

"Serious women is all the women there is. That's the point."

"How'd you do it? Make that Havana woman laugh?"

"I remember one time we was layin in bed of a evenin and I kindly kicked at the covers with my feet and said, What's that under there? Like I felt somethin down at the edge of the bed. I raised up the sheet and Teresa stuck her head under to take a look. Well, that's when I let rip a big one."

"What'd she do?"

"Jumped out from under there like a cat with its tail on fire and stared at me so cool. Then both of us broke down laughin. She was a good woman. She'd have done anything to take care of that boy of hers."

3

"You mind me askin what happened? How come it ended between you and her?"

Cain smoked and stared out at the country. "I tried to look after em, Teresa and her son, but I couldn't always be who I was supposed to. Then Villa crossed the border. Maybe I figured I owed it to the outfit for the home they gave me when there wasn't no other. Or maybe I didn't think I deserved what I'd lucked into. So I left and went to scout for old Black Jack. Then I met up with your scrawny ass."

Mosby grinned. "You think I should try makin a woman laugh like you said?"

"By doin what, fartin in bed?"

"Yessir."

Cain looked at Mosby, his shirtcollar buttoned to the top, cheeks clean-shaven, standing straight and stiff with his shoulders back and eyes level. The toes of his boots shone. Everything in perfectly circumscribed order.

"I wouldn't advise it," Cain said. "But I won't say no either. Use your own judgement and maybe try it on a whore first."

Mosby took off his glasses. He pulled a handkerchief from his pocket and spat on the right lens and rubbed it with the cloth, then spat on the left and rubbed it as well.

"Polish them specs any harder," Cain said, "they're liable to catch the sun, burn the damn train to a cinder."

Mosby glanced at the man-shaped blur that was Cain. "I like things to be clean."

"You don't allow a smudge on em, do you?"

4

"It's how I got to look out at the world." Mosby pocketed the kerchief and slipped his glasses back on.

"Well. You see clearer than any other man I know."

"Thank you, Sergeant."

"I need you to be my eyes for me, Mo. Watch those men in there and tell me what you see. I knew every man of em, one time or another, but the years can change you. I need to know who'll stick when it gets bad and who's gone soft enough to cut and run."

Mosby remained astounded that Cain had convinced the investment banker to fund the Sierra Madre operation. Cain had telegrammed Applegate's aide with a reminder of the work he'd done for the old man as a private operative, hinting at certain unpalatable secrets he'd discovered in the course of his work, corporate illegalities sure to be of interest to Applegate's many enemies. It was leverage to convince the aide to give Cain what he wanted—enough of Applegate's time for the old man to read a letter and the clipping from *True Cowboy Adventure*. Nothing more, nothing less.

The story of a white boy kidnapped by wild Apaches had been enough to hook Applegate—just as Cain knew it would.

"Maybe it won't be long," Mosby said. "We'll finish the mission, get that McKenna boy back to his family, then we can come home and start spendin Applegate's money."

Cain was silent. He took a long drag. "I'll bet you a silver dollar I can out ride and out gun any of you boys

5

once we get in the mountains. But it's my last strength and I ain't goin to waste it. There's a place for them that die fightin and that's all I want. One last campaign."

It bothered Mosby when the sergeant talked that way. How Mosby looked at it, there were worse things than getting old—and being dead was at the top of the list.

"Come on now, Sergeant. Don't talk like that. Once them Apaches give up the boy, it'll be front page news. Just imagine all the papers callin you a hero. That's somethin to live for, right there."

Cain flicked the cigarette butt. It hit the steel rail in a little burst of glowing ash, then vanished behind them.

"Keep your eyes open, Mo. Help me see this thing clear."

"Yessir, Sergeant."

* * *

Jubal McKenna rode beside Moroni Thayne and they kept their horses to a slow walk on the trail to Nácori Chico and their rendezvous with the American mercenaries. Hector, Jubal's segundo, had gone ahead to the village the day before, taking the packmules loaded with supplies. Jubal chose to linger behind until the last day. He'd wanted all the time he could get with little Claudia and a still grief-stricken Dolores before he told his daughters goodbye. It was uncertain how long he'd be stalking the high reaches.

He thought of the sadness in Dolores's dark eyes.

6

Angel, the young vaquero she loved, had been murdered by an Apache raiding party that had ridden down from the sierras to steal horses on the ranch. Not for the first time Jubal wondered at the life he'd given Dolores when he'd chosen to adopt the Apache girl. If the sorrow she'd found in the valley below wasn't a harder burden than the short and brutal life she'd have known in the sierras with her people.

Jubal had said his goodbye to Wesley too, the old man lying abed with a sickness of the lungs that made each breath sound as though it were a death rasp. Wesley had become steadily weaker over the past months, first with a terrible cough, then unable to climb onto the buckboard, until finally he couldn't walk without assistance. Dolores took his things from the bunkhouse and they'd prepared a room for him in the hacienda where the girl tended him.

Jubal had stepped to the foot of the old man's bed. Dolores sat beside Wesley, gently moving a straight razor over the shaving soap she'd applied to his white stubble.

"You goin on the hunt again?" Wesley asked. His voice was low and Jubal had to strain to hear him.

"I'm headed out to meet the mercenaries in Nácori. We'll hit Apache camps high in the sierras."

"Wait a little while and I'll go with you," the old man said. "Just a little while now."

"You'd better stay and rest so you can get your strength back," Jubal told him.

Dolores wet a towel from the water basin on the nightstand and cleaned the remaining soap from his cheeks.

"It won't be long and I'll join you," Wesley whispered.

"All right," Jubal said to put him at ease.

Wesley had closed his eyes and drifted to sleep.

Now on the road to the village, Moroni turned to Jubal. "When do you expect this Cain and his men?" he asked.

"Late evenin or tomorrow mornin," Jubal said. "Later if they had rough goin in the hills."

Moroni and Hector would be the only non-mercenaries following Jubal into the sierras. The vaqueros were all staying behind. Jubal trusted Moroni to stand beside him if anything went wrong with the Americans. He'd made it clear to the Mormon rancher what he was signing up for—unlike the previous forays, the goal of this expedition wasn't to complete a rescue mission. It was strictly search and kill.

They rode in shadows where the trail led through a stand of cottonwoods.

"I want to thank you again," Jubal said. "I know it's not your fight. You didn't have to come with me, but I'm damn glad you're here."

"I see now it's not just about you and your family. It's all of us, everybody in the valley. The problem has to be put to bed for good and we've got a real chance—"

Jubal raised a hand. "You hear that?"

They drew up and sat their horses listening. Hoofbeats on the trail behind them, coming at a gallop.

Without a word they got down and pulled their rifles from the saddle-scabbards and walked the horses out of view from the trail, hiding in the trees. They waited for the rider to come.

Dolores rode the dapple gray hard, her long black hair flying out behind her like the mane of a beast born wild and ever to remain so.

The men sheathed their rifles. Jubal stepped out into the trail leading Bardo by the reins.

When Dolores saw him, she slowed the gray. She was wearing old jeans and one of Angel's workshirts, the sleeves rolled up. A black armband of mourning. The seventeen-year-old Apache girl stepped the horse up to her father and looked down from the saddle.

Dolores thought Jubal had never appeared so sad to see her.

"Where do you think you're goin?" he asked.

"I'm coming with you," she said.

"You can't change anything."

"I know."

"Claudia needs you. Wesley does too."

"They have Adela."

Jubal stared up at her, saw that her eyes were set. "I can't keep you safe and these aren't good men we'll be ridin with. I don't have any use for good men. Just go home."

9

"I'll take you there. The stronghold on the mountain, the place they call Paradise. I can bring you to it."

He hesitated. "There's goin to be killin," he said at last. "You're young and you'll have to live a long time with the memory of it."

"It's already too late to forget," she told him.

* * *

The mercenaries didn't appear that day or the day following. In Nácori the priest opened his home to Jubal and Dolores, but they chose instead to camp in the village plaza with Hector and Moroni. The villagers saw to it that the patrón and his companions ate well while they waited for the Americans.

Jubal went over their supplies and made sure the mules and the little mountain-bred horses were fed. Most of the horses were out of the mustang herd they'd captured, hearty and sure-footed. The jinete had done a fine job of training them. Jubal stood at the corral watching them gallop circles in their confines, restless, a wildness in their blood yearning for the high meadows of running roses.

He didn't try to make Dolores return home. The last thing Jubal wanted was for her to accompany them, but he didn't see how he could stop her, not after all that happened. If it was true that she could guide them to the stronghold mountain, her presence might make all the difference.

When the Americans arrived on the third day, the village was mourning the death of Oscar Flores, an old hunchback well-loved by all who'd known him. A few centavos and Oscar would let you rub his hump for good luck. There were those who swore by the jorobado's lucky hump and the change of fortune it was said to bestow. Lying in state in the church his body was positioned in such a way that those paying their respects might in passing receive for a final time the hunchback's blessing.

It was late afternoon when a barefoot boy ran up the dirt street. He passed the funeral cortege and darted in front of the priest and cried out that the pistoleros Americanos were coming.

Jubal stepped from the shade in front of the cantina and watched the procession turn at the cemetery gates. The priest's robes billowing in the wind. Sand blowing, pelting the glass bier.

The boy ran on.

"Pistoleros Americanos," he shouted. He hurried toward the patrón. Jubal tossed him a silver dollar and the boy's grin stretched wide.

Now the horsemen rode into sight, coming up the street between the rows of jacales and thatched-roofed casitas, just as the priest began reading in Latin a passage from Ecclesiastes. Jubal stared. The man at their head riding a great black horse could be none other than Cain. A lanky negro rode at his side and there followed eight mounted killers.

They rode past the cemetery. Cain offered the crowd of mourners the barest glance. He drew up in the plaza where Jubal stood waiting and the column of mercenaries halted in a faint cloud of dust behind him.

"Mr. McKenna," Cain said. A voice like a dried snakeskin to Jubal's ears. "I know you from your picture in the paper."

Jubal squinted up at him, but Cain's face was obscured in full shadow, the sun directly over his shoulder. Cain leaned down in the saddle and offered his hand.

Jubal took it.

"My name's Cain," the American said. "If you want to follow me into those mountains, I'll show you how we can force their hand and end this for good. I'm goin to make those reds turn loose of your son."

* * *

A mercenary named Ives walked out a hundred yards into the meadow with an armful of pie melons.

Jubal stood between Cain and Mosby. They'd ridden to the open meadow on the outskirts of Nácori for Cain's demonstration of firepower. Long shadows stretched, evening coming on. Behind them Moroni and the rest of the mercenaries waited with the horses.

A distance from the others, Dolores and Hector stood gripping the reins of their mounts. When he caught one of the Americans eyeing the girl, Hector let his palm rest on the butt of the .45 strapped to his hip and gave the man a cool stare. The merc settled his gaze elsewhere.

Cain held a Browning Automatic Rifle and watched Ives place the melons on the ground in a row.

Jubal studied Cain. Older than he'd expected, his hair more gray than black. He was shorter than Jubal but powerfully built with wide shoulders and a stout chest. His deep-set eyes were dark and piercing, his face smooth, hairless, beneath those jutting cheekbones. A dangerous man to underestimate.

"That Apache girl," Cain said. "She's the one you took in, I reckon?"

"Her name's Dolores," Jubal said. "And she'll be comin with us."

Cain simply nodded at this news. "Her idea or yours?"

"It was her choice. I'm not forcin her."

"She knows we ain't goin up there to count coup?"

"She knows."

"We hunt and kill. That's all. We're not a search party or some kind of posse. I take it you must have a pretty damn good reason to let her tag along."

"The broncos have a rancheria. It's on a mountaintop with sheer walls, only one trail up. Dolores can lead us to it. They stay there for months at a time."

"Where do they draw water?"

"A spring."

"Sounds like a good place to die," Cain said. "Don't it, Mo?"

"I reckon good as any, Sergeant," Mosby answered.

Ives turned and ran back across the grass to stand by his fellows.

Cain released the magazine. He held it and the rifle out for Jubal to examine. "You ever seen a BAR, Mr. McKenna? John Browning's design. The magazine holds twenty rounds. Fire it full auto or ever time you pull the trigger. We've got a pair of Brownings with us and I promise you, those Apaches won't know what hit em."

He fitted the magazine back in. "I don't like to piss away ammo, but I want you to see my point." Cain handed the rifle to Mosby and nodded. "Mo, why don't you show Mr. McKenna how it beats bows and arrows all to hell?"

Mosby shouldered the BAR. He flicked the selector level to the A-position and threw the bolt back and aimed out across the meadow and pulled the trigger. Slow heavy staccato thuds broke the stillness. Empty brass landed at their feet. Mosby kept firing as he walked forward, melons bursting one hundred yards out, .30-06 rounds kicking up dirt, then seconds later the rifle was empty.

Jubal's ears rang. When the dust settled, he could see bright red chunks strewn on the ground.

"What do you think, Mister Jubal?" Mosby asked.

"I believe it'll do the job," he answered.

"A man's head," Cain told them, "is just a watermelon with hair on it."

* * *

14

Cain and Jubal led them out at first light. The mercenaries were freshly mounted on the former mustangs, all save Cain who favored the mount he'd ridden through the foothills and into Nácori, the big horse he called Black Answer. The packmules were heavily laden with supplies and weapons and a great quantity of ammunition, one mule carrying a mortar and arsenal of 81mm shells. A pack of mongrel hounds escorted the riders down the empty street.

If the Americans resented Dolores's presence, none showed it. They'd been noticeably pleased when they watched her spring to the saddle without aid of the stirrups.

Hector rode close alongside her, accepting it as his duty to watch over the girl through the coming weeks. He'd argued with her the night before. Trying in vain to convince Dolores her decision to accompany them was madness. The pain it would surely bring. "I know you're hurting," he told her, "but this can't heal it. Choose another path—you don't want to see what's waiting down this one."

She'd listened to his pleadings, face impassive, and when he finished, she told him it hadn't been her decision at all. That it was simply one more unfolding in a succession of events set in motion long before she'd ever imagined any choice in the matter. No use wishing for some other path because there wasn't any. One path and one destination and she wasn't dragging her heels anymore but riding out to meet it.

At the edge of the village Dolores turned in the saddle and looked back to see who watched their departure. The street remained deserted, the casitas dark. The citizenry kept themselves indoors, weary of killers from the north.

Only hungry mongrels stood them witness.

They climbed the first of the outer ranges. Slopes gashed with floodcarved canyons and covered in bright green bambusa and everywhere scrub mesquite. Catclaw and Spanish bayonet in a garden of needle and thorn. Cloudbanks sailed above the riders and shut out the sun, casting great shadows on the rolling hills like dark armadas.

Jubal rode Bardo alongside Cain on Black Answer.

"That spade bit's a fine piece of work," Cain said. He motioned at the silver bit in Bardo's mouth. "Myself, I was never partial to silver on a bridle or saddle. Not worth the risk, sunlight glarin off it, lettin the whole damn world know where you are."

"It was John Russell's, on his horse when they took him. I used it before, up in the sierras, when we got close to him once."

Cain gave him a slow nod. "I reckon I understand you then. You figure it's got what the reds call medicine or Power. And that Power's tied to the boy. Might could lead you right to him."

It startled Jubal to hear his own unconscious motives articulated, a superstition he'd never admitted even to himself, not until now.

He made no answer, but Cain could tell from the look on his face that it was so. The mercenary didn't offer any further comment on the matter. Except to say, "There are more forces at work in this world than meet the eye, that's for damn sure." Then he changed the subject. "You got any idea how many bands of Apaches are up there?"

"The bands change all the time," Jubal said. "They'll meet up and join each other a while, then some will split off and go their own way. Always movin. Even Dolores can't say for sure how many warriors are left now."

"Can't be many. Squaws and little nits mostly, I reckon. They'll kill you just as dead, you ain't careful. She tell you where this rancheria's supposed to be?"

"Past the third range and across the river. She'll take us there."

"I wisht I had your confidence."

"You don't think she can remember the way?"

Cain twisted around in the saddle, glanced back at the girl. "We keep goin," he said, "maybe she won't want to remember."

Late that evening they crested a prominence and Cain sat his horse looking over the country. In the distance a ridgeline rose and fell and rose again. Like the exposed backbone of a slumbering son of Anak, giant watchman of the gates through which they must pass to the high cordons.

They camped in a rocky place on the eastern flank and made a fire and enjoyed coffee and a warm supper while they could. Days to come they'd keep cold camps and eat for survival with little savor.

Dolores sat near Hector, nestled in a depression in the rocks, and wiped her plate with a tortilla and studied the Americans. Their shadows played exaggerated and weird on the rock wall. Like heroes of old, mighty men of renown.

Endicott walked out into the dark carrying a pair of plates, supper for the men who stood watch over the caballada. Rourke and Ives were guarding the horses and mules where they'd hobbled them down below in a grassy area.

"The sergeant ought to've been back by now," Mosby said. He ladled a second helping of beans from the pot, but he wore a troubled expression. "I wisht he had sense enough to let somebody go with him."

Cain had ridden out in the last light to scout ahead in preparation for the next morning, going alone at his insistence. It had been full dark now for some time.

"He strikes me as capable of lookin after himself," Jubal said. He sipped his tin mug of coffee.

"Never know what you're goin to run into," Mosby said.

"Hell," Slotkin spoke up. "Whatever's out there sooner ought to be afraid of runnin into Cain." He ran a hand through his long gray-blond goatee.

"Reckon you're right," Mosby told him.

"I know I am. Your sergeant's killed at least a dozen men on every continent."

"I used to think he was just made up," Clovis joined in. "I'd hear old mercs talking about him. Always figured they were telling tales out of school, then I ended up serving under him down South America way."

"Knew a Russian in the Foreign Legion," Van Zandt said. "We were stationed over in Algeria. This was an older fella, claimed he'd fought with Cain in China against the Japs, but you got to believe that's horseshit."

"It's true," Slotkin said. "I heard Cain tell China stories himself. Back when we was bustin heads for United Fruit in Honduras."

"When were you and him in Honduras?" Clovis asked. He set down his plate and wiped his big handlebar moustache with a kerchief.

"Nineteen and twelve."

"I fought under Cain in the Wadai in 1912. Somebody's got their dates mixed-up."

Clovis and Slotkin were both in their mid-forties, easily the oldest among the mercs save Cain himself. Theirs was a young man's profession, one in which death was a more common outcome than retirement. During their first years as soldiers of fortune they'd been tutored under Cain's instruction—and the simple fact they were both still alive and working bore witness to the supremacy of their mentor's tactics.

"Nothin mixed up about it," Slotkin said. "When did Cain ever let a little thing like bein in two places at once stop him?"

The men laughed.

Jubal heard hoofbeats in the dark, then a low snarl and the sound of something heavy being dragged. He rose and tossed out the remaining coffee from his mug and stood waiting.

Cain appeared out of the night on Black Answer. He rode up through camp. His rope was looped and tied about his saddlehorn, taut and pulling at something unseen in the darkness.

"I brung y'all dessert," Cain said.

He kept on riding and an instant later the beast at the end of his line was visible in the glow of the fire. A black bear, the rope around her neck. The bear snarled and thrashed and fought to regain her feet, to break free into the night, but the rope held and Black Answer dragged the bear into the midst of the camp.

Everyone scrambled away, grabbing up rifles and pistols. The bear overturned the coffee pot and it spilled hissing into the fire. Cain laughed an uproarious laugh, more than a touch of the manic in its gaiety.

"Son of a bitch," Putnam said. "Are you out of your gourd, Cain?"

"Caught her prowlin around by the horses," Cain said. "Eyein supper." He turned Black Answer to face them. The bear strained at her tether, desperate to escape. For Black Answer's part the horse showed little concern at being chained to the beast, absolute trust in Cain's power and command.

"What in hades did you drag it up here for?" Putnam asked.

"Figured some of you boys might need to satisfy your carnal desires before we head up the high country. Take a poke at her, Putnam. I done loosened her up for you."

The black bear's wild eyes reflected the firelight. She turned a half-circle, staring at the men surrounding her, and let out an enraged growl.

"No takers?" Cain asked. "All right then. Mr. McKenna, would you be so kind as to put her down?"

Jubal stepped forward and drew his .45 and racked the slide. He raised the gun and fired. The bullet hit the bear between her eyes and she lumbered to the side and let out a kind of groan, then collapsed on her belly.

Dolores stood beside Hector where they'd climbed higher into the rocks. She stared down at the carcass of the beast. In the faint glow from the fire Dolores seemed an apparition hovering over that strange tableau.

"You disappoint me, Putnam," Cain said. "By the time I was your age I'd humped every she-bear I could get my rope around. Half the bear cubs in Hidalgo County had my sparklin brown eyes. You young fellas just don't have a sense of purpose."

Putnam gripped a fistful of the bear's thick dark fur. "I wouldn't mind havin me a bearskin coat."

"You don't ever want to skin a bear," Jubal told him.

"Better listen to the jefe," Cain said. "Mr. McKenna knows what he's talkin about."

"Why not?" Putnam asked.

"Because a skinned bear looks just like a man," Jubal explained. "My grandad skinned one when he was a boy and always regretted it. Said it was just like a naked bloody man."

* * *

Mosby unrolled his soogan. He took off his boots and eased himself down. The rocks surrounding his bedding emitted the ghost of the day's heat and it was pleasant lying under stars so clear and bright.

The others had spread their own bedrolls and lay sleeping. All save Cain and Jubal. The sergeant sat with his back to the dying fire and questioned Jubal, but he spoke too softly for Mosby to hear.

The earth milled slowly beneath them. A meteor went streaking across the dark and was gone as soon as Mosby glimpsed it.

He couldn't understand why Jubal had brought along the Apache girl or what had possessed Cain to allow it. They'd come for a singular purpose and that purpose was to spill blood. It made no difference where the girl claimed she could lead them—you didn't allow a good woman to join a group of fighting men out beyond the limits of civilization. It would surely lead to trouble. He couldn't think why the sergeant stood for it. The only women they'd had with them while they were chasing Villa were the whores who followed the camps.

Watching the stars cycle overhead, Mosby thought about the girl's people living up in the mountains, that anarchic land beyond surveillance and terror. He supposed they'd chosen such a life for its freedom, whatever the hardships and demands of the forest passage. He fell asleep wondering how much longer that would last for them.

CHAPTER TWO

Autumn, 1931

Ishton's baby was sick. For seven days the child had suffered fever and chills, loss of appetite, and he cried incessantly. Watching the child in such affliction troubled Ishton, but she took comfort from a truth the People lived by—strength is born of pain endured. Once her son recovered, he'd surely be stronger for all his little body had been through.

She'd named the baby Illanipi. It was the first word she'd spoken after the long and difficult birth, a year ago, when Tsaltey-koo placed the newborn in her arms at last. "Amazing," she'd whispered. Infant names were seldom retained to maturity. The day would come when he'd receive a new name, reflective of the individual qualities he'd develop in time, but for now his mother simply called the child Amazing.

Ishton rocked the sickly infant. She did her best to make him suckle, but he wasn't hungry. He fell asleep only when exhaustion overtook him. Ishton waited for the fever to break and she kept on waiting, but it didn't break, then the morning of the fifth day red dots appeared on the baby's chest.

Ishton sent Denali running to find Carnoviste, who'd gone to check his rabbit snares in the woods. Denali and his father came racing back to camp, out of breath, Illanipi's ragged wails in their ears before they reached the wickiup.

Ishton held her child through the long hours. When he soaked his blanket with sweat, she wrapped him in a fresh one and slowly rocked him. He'd been born small and frail and this new sickness threatened to prove too much for him.

Carnoviste could do nothing save watch. The chief felt a kind of helplessness he'd never known existed and all he wanted was to trade places with his son. His other wives, Tsaltey-koo and Hanlonah, brought food and water. The women urged Carnoviste and Ishton to eat and rest, but their pleas went unheeded.

Everyone in camp feared for Illanipi's life. Children stayed close by the adults, their games postponed. Such a fever and rash weren't unknown to them—most who were stricken recovered after a few weeks of illness, but the baby was still undersized and weak. If the fever failed to relent soon, Denali's little brother would die.

Soon it would be Denali's sixteenth winter and in all his life he'd never been worried like this.

He sat by the fire. He watched Tsaltey-koo and Hanlonah exit the wickiup and walk to Gouyen's dwelling. They passed behind the hide flap. After a while the wise woman emerged, carrying a bundle of herbs, the wives following her. Gouyen went to the wickiup where Ishton tended the baby. She paused outside the entrance and glanced over at the fire. The faint trace of a smile on her lips. Then she ducked inside.

It filled Denali with a dread more terrible yet. The sickness must be dire indeed for Carnoviste to accept Gouyen's help.

* * *

Moonlight spilled through the open smoke-hole at the top of the wickiup. Carnoviste stared across at Gouyen. The wise woman's gifts of Power weren't known to include healing, not as Nantan's Power had once healed the sick, but she claimed the child could be saved. "If you can heal my son," the chief said, "I promise you'll have a place of honor with our people forever."

"My Power can heal the child," Gouyen told him. "Is that what you wish?"

Carnoviste hesitated. There was a cunning light in her eyes, impossible to miss—except by a mother in desperate need.

"Of course," Ishton answered. "Please. Whatever you have to do."

"My chief?" Gouyen asked.

Carnoviste slowly nodded.

"Good," the wise woman said. She rose and handed

Carnoviste a bundle of sage. "Take this to the fire outside. Light it and bring it back to me. The smoke will cleanse the child of evil."

Carnoviste took the sage and left the wickiup.

A leather bag hung from a cord around Gouyen's neck. She removed the bag and placed it on the ground, carful to position it at the center of the dwelling.

"Give me the child," she said.

Ishton surrendered the baby. When Carnoviste returned with the burning sage, Gouyen took it from him. She held the crying child and blew bitter smoke in his face and danced a circle about her medicine bundle, chanting a sacred song Nantan had taught her.

Carnoviste and Ishton watched in silence.

After Gouyen finished, she dropped the remnants of the sage on the bare ground and stamped them out under her moccasin. Illanipi had quieted, his cries intermittent now. Gouyen stared at the child in her arms.

It surprised Carnoviste when he saw tears in the wise woman's eyes. She gazed on the child with an unmistakable look of love. Gouyen pressed her lips to his forehead in a soft kiss, then handed the baby back to his mother.

"He's healed," Gouyen told them. "The rash will be gone by morning."

"Thank you, my sister," Ishton said. "Your Power is strong."

"I thank you for my son's life," Carnoviste said.

Gouyen smiled at the chief. She stepped to the hide

flap, then looked back at Carnoviste.

"Someday soon I'll ask a gift of you," she said. "You know what it is. And you'll give it to me, or the sickness will return and your son will die."

Gouyen stepped out into the night.

"What gift did she mean?" Ishton asked.

Dread churned in Carnoviste's stomach.

* * *

The wise woman had been mistaken—

There was no healing.

Shortly after Gouyen's departure the rash began to spread. It soon covered the baby's torso and limbs and face, only the palms of his tiny hands and the bottoms of his feet remaining clear. Illanipi cried out his pain.

Carnoviste told Gouyen what had occurred. Returned to the wickiup, she set the sage afire once again and prayed over the child. By dawn he was still crying, still desperately sick, and the whole camp knew the wise woman had failed.

Denali sat around the fire with the other warriors.

"You know why this sadness has found us," Bihido said.

"Why?" Denali asked.

"Because the medicine man is gone. It never would have happened if his Power was still with us."

"He always kept the People healthy and safe," Estoni said.

"I wish I could kill whatever beast carried him away. Now we're helpless against evil. A child suffers because we don't have our medicine man."

"You speak the truth," Denali said. He lapsed into dark contemplation.

Try as she might, Ishton couldn't get Illanipi to sleep. His discomfort was too great, the depth of his need expressible only in wails. He was weaker by the day.

Carnoviste studied the labored rise and fall of his son's crimson chest. It was more than he could bear and just before first light Carnoviste groaned deep inside himself and rose and went out of the wickiup.

Denali and the others had kept a vigil around the fire all night. When they saw Carnoviste stagger into view, one of the men called to him, but the chief didn't answer, turning away and walking out toward the woods instead. Denali hesitated. Then rose and followed his father from camp.

When the sun peeked over the ridgeline, Carnoviste walked out into an open place in the midst of the pines, a hidden meadow, and Denali stayed well back in the trees and watched him unbind his long hair. Carnoviste kneeled in the grass and faced the rising sun. He began to sing his morning prayer of gratitude for the new day. His voice broke. He bowed his head. Denali saw him weep, this man whose bow no other warrior could string.

Denali looked away from what he had no right to witness. He turned and started back toward camp—

Then stopped in his tracks, listening.

Carnoviste sang.

Denali looked back across the meadow. His father kneeled with his arms raised to the returning sun and chanted his prayer of thanksgiving though the day bring only death.

Then Denali understood what he must do, what he alone might have Power to perform, whether he felt himself worthy to wield such Power or not.

* * *

Denali came to his adopted mother barefoot and with his hair unbound, carrying his medicine bundle and a small bag of hoddentin.

"I came to sing over the baby," he told her.

"You have Power?" Ishton asked. A note of cautious hope in her voice.

"Leave me alone with him."

She hesitated, reluctant to be apart from the sickly child. She rocked the baby in her arms.

"Go, woman," he told her.

Denali reached out and Ishton gave him Illanipi. She turned and stepped outside the wickiup, the hide flap closing behind her. She would see to it that no one entered until his prayers were finished.

He placed the baby on the bed of hides at the center of the wickiup. Illanipi was still crying, struggling to breathe.

Denali kneeled and set his medicine bundle down and opened the leather bundle. Inside were these sacred things—a piece of honeycomb, the eagle feather Ishton had given him, a small blue stone, and a raven's black feather. He wasn't sure what he was supposed to do and he felt no sense of Power. He tried to think of healing songs he'd heard the elders sing, but he couldn't remember how they went. So he decided just to sing whatever came to mind.

He'd entered the wickiup from the east and now he danced clockwise about the child and chanted,

"Lightning prays a healing over you,
Thunder prays a healing over you.
In the sacred circle thunder heals,
In the circle prayers like lightning shine."

Then he took the flute from the fold of his moccasin. It was a wooden flute he'd borrowed from Oblite. His own instrument, the one Dolores had given him a lifetime ago, the flute made from the hollow bones of a bird, had gone missing some time before, lost without a trace.

Denali circled about his little brother twice more and sounded the flute four times for each of the cardinal directions. He was sending a voice to Ussen for the healing of the sick.

Without warning, a sudden energy rushed through him, this flowing forth, Power rolling over him like an invisible wave, and he knew he could help his brother.

Denali kneeled and picked up Illanipi. The baby's skin hot to the touch, fever burning within. Denali cradled him in one arm. He opened the bag of hoddentin and took a pinch of the sacred pollen between his fingers, then sprinkled it on the crown of the baby's head. Illanipi cried and squirmed.

Denali held the child and danced a circle for the fourth and final time. He sang,

"Four winds that blow
Are saying with their song—
You will live,
You will live,
You will live,
You will live."

And as he sang, an electric surge passed through his body and out his fingertips. Denali felt as if his hands were on fire.

When he placed the baby down on the blanket, Illanipi's fever had broken and he'd stopped crying. His breath was strong and easy. Already Denali could see the rash fading. Illanipi curled up in the blanket and fell immediately to sleep.

Denali stepped out of the wickiup and saw Ishton and Carnoviste where they stood waiting, worry on their faces. He told them it was all right—the boy was well and would remain so when he woke.

* * *

Throughout the following days the camp celebrated Illanipi's healing and the great Power Denali had shown was his. The warriors went out hunting and returned with a pair of good-sized deer and there was much drinking of tiswin and telling old stories as the men waited for their wives to prepare the feast. Everyone save Gouyen congratulated Denali on the healing. They rejoiced to have a young warrior of Power among them. Nantan was gone, but perhaps the People weren't without a medicine man after all.

Gouyen held back her fury until it was a solid core of hatred. Someday it would come to a head between them—Denali knew there could be no other way and he swore on life itself he'd be ready when the day came.

Estoni asked after his methods, how he'd called forth Power and controlled it for the healing. Denali told him the truth. There was no commanding such Power—it didn't rise up through any strength of will or coaxing of spirits and he couldn't say if it would ever manifest again. All he could do was thank Ussen for the restoration of his brother's health.

Late on the night of the feast they held a wheel dance. It was a favorite of the young, a dance in which maidens chose their partners whomsoever they wished. Denali lined up with the other unmarried men while pairs of maidens formed a circle about the central fire. Several girls whispered of Denali's Power, of his blazing red hair. He was oblivious to their appraisal, thinking instead they whispered of their old favorite, the warrior Estoni who stood beside him.

When the drummers began their rhythm, the girls rushed the line, racing for the strongest warriors and best dancers. To his surprise Denali found himself a favorite among them, a number of girls swarming him, but it was Jacali who reached him first and won Denali as her partner. The other girls scrambled to find unchosen men. The dancers walked out to face each other in the circle around the fire. Denali saw the firelight reflected in the dark pools of Jacali's eyes, then the drummers quickened the beat and the great wheel of dancers revolved about the fire and Denali danced forward, then backward, the wheel turning and turning, Jacali's smiling face across the flames.

* * *

That night Denali lay asleep in his wickiup. He dreamed a plain of darkness—the sky electric, full of dread expectancy. A pair of fiery circles came revolving one within the other across the shadowed plain and he felt a sense as though all things were locked in a terrible inevitability. As the circles progressed he glimpsed a figure at the heart of the innermost wheel. A bear that stood on two legs. Come to kill and devour.

Denali jolted awake as thunder broke in the heavens of his dream.

* * *

Days to come he rode the high country. Riding crest and vale and sere autumn woods, his heart going out before him exultant in bloodsong, savage and free, the horse and boy rushing in the light through woven branches like light through stained glass, worshippers in a church not made with hands, and the horse's great pumping heart ardent as the boy's own drove them on with sunset coppering the rider's face and the beast's muscled flank. Riding heedless of palimpsest destiny those cordilleras where time has no dominion. He rode in the pale dying light and through the telluric dark—the sun, the red moon, and the winds all beckoning him on. And they called him captive and beloved.

CHAPTER THREE

Jubal and Cain rode ahead, leading the way through an endless oakwood. High golden grass flourished between the trees and covered the slopes and scratched at the bellies of the horses when they passed. It was late morning and they'd been on the move since first light.

The air was dead still. Then of a sudden a little vortex went swirling through the grass and seemed to linger in place a long moment before rising to trouble the high branches of the oaks and rushing off toward the east. The thought of old Wesley came unbidden to Jubal's mind. He stared where the wind had gone. Cain had noted the strange miniature whirlwind as well and now he turned Black Answer to follow in its direction.

They came to fields of corn ready for harvest, a small farm in a sparsely settled part of the sierras, and turned up the trail toward a farmhouse of crude but effective construction. Clay walls, a door cut from the halved trunk of an oak, the slanted roof covered with chips of wood. Chickens wandered the yard pecking at bugs and there was a low shed near the corral in which several cows and mules trudged, a small pen where pigs lay in the muck. Not a few among the riders paused to wonder that a man had chosen to make a life for himself in such a lonely place.

A pack of seven dogs raced out to them, barking like mad and raising the alarm. Cain and Jubal halted well before they reached the yard. A moment later the campesino stepped out of the shed holding a shotgun and stared across the yard looking them over.

"Hello," Jubal called in Spanish. "You mind if we come up to the house?"

"Go ahead," the campesino said, also in Spanish. He was a squat and well-muscled man in his middle fifties and he wore a bushy moustache. "Devils," he shouted at the yapping dogs. "Quiet!" He leaned the shotgun against the shed and cupped his hands and let out a piercing whistle. The pack turned as one and ran to their master.

Jubal and Cain rode up to the corral and unhorsed and tied their reins to the fence. The man had sat down in a rough wooden chair in the yard under the shade of an oak and he was smoking a hand-rolled cigarette and watching them.

They walked over and introduced themselves. The campesino shook their hands and said, "My name is Juan Oso."

Jubal smiled. "Juan Oso?"

"Something funny about it?"

There was a legend in that country of a half-man, half-beast called Juan Oso, the spawn of a kidnapped woman and the bear who'd stolen her away.

The man didn't appear to be joking. From the foul smell of his cigarette Jubal knew he wasn't smoking tobacco either.

"Nothing funny about it, Señor Oso," he said. "You've carved out a good place here. That's no easy thing in these mountains."

"Thank you. Sit down."

He motioned to another chair and a three-legged stool. They sat.

"Smoke?" He made an offering gesture with the yerba cigarette.

Jubal declined. Cain nodded and reached for the cigarette.

"You know that's not tobacco," Jubal said, switching to English.

"I know it," Cain told him. He took a long drag, holding the smoke in his lungs, then handed the cigarette back as he slowly exhaled.

"You hunt the Apaches," Oso said.

"You know who I am?" Jubal asked.

"Everybody in these mountains knows about you, Señor McKenna, and what those gut-eaters did to you."

"We're headed up into the high reaches. We're going after their rancheria."

"It's time these mountains had a cleansing."

"You've had trouble with Apaches?" Cain asked, surprising Jubal with a perfect Spanish, no trace of accent.

"Of course," Oso said. "They're always stealing.

Always. Last spring not far from here, a pair of Apache rode up to a farmer where he was plowing in the middle of his field. They made him unhitch the mule, then they shot him in the belly and rode off with the mule. He died a long death."

It was peaceful around the farmstead. Cool in the shade. In that moment it was hard to imagine the threat of violent death that lay over those fields as an everyday possibility.

"I rode after them with some other men," Oso said. "We put the dogs on their trail."

"Did you catch up with them?" Jubal asked.

"They had to abandon their horses and the mule. Climb up where we couldn't follow. We got the mule back before they could eat it. So I call it a victory." He took a pull on the cigarette and held it.

"What about recently?" Cain asked. "You heard anything in the last little while?"

Oso exhaled. "A couple unshod ponies passed through a few days back. I can point you where I found their tracks."

"We'd appreciate it," Jubal said.

"Do me a favor. When you find their rancheria? Don't spare even one."

* * *

Jubal and Cain rejoined the others. They led the party upcountry in the direction Juan Oso told them the unshod ponies had gone. At long stretches between them they found little farms and ranchos and Jubal stopped to make inquires at every house they came to. The campesinos had no word to share and were much troubled at this news of Apaches roving the area.

Proceeding up one of the more well-traveled paths they came upon a half-burned carreta abandoned beside the trail. The back of the cart was filled with fresh-cut wood. Cain got down and felt of the ashes. Cold.

He kneeled holding his reins, examining the tracks surrounding the carreta. Hoofprints—two ponies, both unshod, and the shod prints of a mule. The mule had drawn the carreta till the unfortunate woodcutter met with the Apaches. They'd forced him to unhitch his stock and they'd set the carreta afire and departed.

There should've been a body, the woodcutter left slain and mutilated, but there wasn't.

"The dumb son of a bitch," Cain said. "He let em take him alive."

The Apaches had led the woodcutter away on his mule.

Cain spat. "Well, I expect they learnt him a lesson. That's the kind of mistake you don't get to make twice."

"How long ago?" Jubal asked.

"Maybe two days," Cain said. He looked over at Dolores. "We're fixin to see some of your kinfolk's handywork. Let's go."

He swung up on Black Answer and they followed the tracks, the men all riding with rifles balanced athwart the pommels of their saddles. The trail led high into the mountains and so began their ascent into provinces truly perilous and wild. The open wood of oaks gave way to deep pine forests. Trees stretched like slender pillars a hundred feet in the air and dark gorges cut in all directions across the face of the sierras like gaping wounds. They startled up herds of deer and they startled flocks of wild turkeys and soon they crossed the tracks of wolves.

A thin drizzle began to fall on the canopy of pine-needles. Soft fragrant drops showered the riders below. A rapid knocking echoed in the woods and they went on a ways and encountered two large woodpeckers of a type to become extinct in those mountains in later years. Their plumage black and white, the male with scarlet crest and very beautiful. The pair were attacking a single unlucky tree.

Toadstools grew all around the shadowed floor of the pinewoods and lichen covered the lower trunks so the trees stood like green-bearded giants. Thick layers of moss englobed rocks. Everywhere creeping fungi distorted trait and feature. As though primordial unity had set about reclaiming those woods, time coiling back upon itself, tail to mouth, and they wandered some primeval period without fixed shape or form. All things rendered provisory and of no certain ends.

The showers abated. It had been a light rainfall and the tracks of the Apaches were still visible, not too badly damaged. They followed after them. They dismounted and led the horses and packmules afoot and single file up a thousand feet on a trail shaped like a Z, slender ledges clinging to sheer cliff-face. The grade was steep, hard going every step of the way. One of the horses lost his footing and went sliding on his haunches, then righted himself without harm. Nearing the top they could see the woods below like a patch of weeds. Jubal's lungs burned from the climb. Starved for breath, the air so thin. The altitude played hell with the men, forcing them to rest along the trail and curse pounding headaches. Cain and Dolores stood waiting, their breath slow and regular while some of the mercenaries were fairly gasping.

"Let's get movin, you pack of pansies," Cain said, a wide grin stretching his weathered face. "Where's your shame? Lettin a girl and a old man out pace you."

The men swore and rose to their feet. They could understand the Apache girl's easy endurance, born and bred to that high country. It was in her blood. Yet Cain, who could've grandfathered many of them present, hadn't slowed once on the trail up and still appeared indefatigable, not even winded. Cain held nothing back—he'd come to exert the last of his strength and he reveled in the glory of it. At sixty he was an old man and much was lost to him, but he was pleased to find that much remained.

When they reached the top of the ridge, they looked down on the country that lay ahead, masked in sweeping expanses of timber. Across the distance rose palaces of ancient lava and ash, gorges opening at their base to swallow the light.

They went on. After a while Cain decided to scout ahead.

"Stay with them," Cain told Jubal, "and hang back a ways. We don't know what's up there waitin on us." He gave Black Answer his spurs and rode out in advance of the main party, one hand on his rifle.

Jubal fell in beside Mosby.

"You think he's still alive?" Mosby asked. "The woodcutter."

"I sincerely hope not," Jubal said.

Mosby nodded, grim. "Me too. Why you figure they took him, stead of just killin him?"

"Because they could. And he was too big a coward to stop them. It was the worst choice he could've made, doin what they told him. Apaches don't respect cowards. If he'd fought back, they might've made it go quick for him. They won't now."

When they rounded a bend in the trail, they found Cain standing over something spawned from a nightmare. A hideous figure was staked-out, arms and legs spread-eagle, at the foot of a massive anthill. The fine soil was heaped several feet high and resembled a miniature volcano.

The riders stopped and went no farther. Jubal didn't understand what he was looking at. The naked man had no face and his genitals were like something dropped on the floor of an abattoir. Raw bloody meat. The Apaches had staked him out beside a great colony of fire ants and covered his face and genitals in wild honey and left the wretch for the ants to devour. How he must have shrieked. He seemed to wear a scarlet mask. The colony had eaten away his lips and nose. The skin where it wasn't stripped was swollen in big red whelps—pustules had risen inflamed and loathsome to the eye and burst in vile excretions, the ants still about their appalling delight, nature itself enlisted in a torture beyond the pale, these rocks and trees and the earth indifferent to agonized screams, and Jubal didn't understand what he was looking at.

"I bet that kindly stung," Cain said.

"Damn savages," Putnam swore.

Dolores was near the back of the column. She stepped her horse forward to better see what had caused the stir. Jubal started to turn his mount to block her view, then thought better of it and let her look.

She stared down at the dead man without reaction.

Cain unscrewed his canteen and took a long drink. Then he mounted back up. "Move out. Nothin we can do for him now."

"The hell there ain't," Moroni Thayne said. "We've got to at least bury the poor bastard. I'll leave a dead Apache to rot, but this man gets a proper burial."

"Ain't no time," Cain told him. "We got to be on their trail. Say a prayer for him if you want."

"He's right," Jubal said. "That's all we can do."

Putnam stared. "I'm with the Mormon—I don't care if this poor bastard was a Mexican, he deserves better. It ain't humane to leave him like this."

"Heaven and earth both of em ain't humane," Cain said. "We're all just straw dogs. You boys want revenge for your new best buddy? Then follow me. We'll settle it when we ride up on em. But we didn't come all this way to be gravediggers. Not even if it's one of us who falls. You rot where you lay. Now we ride and that's a order, hear me?"

"Yessir," Moroni and Putnam said in unison, barely audible.

Cain looked at the Mormon. "Run that by me again, son."

"Yessir," Moroni spoke up.

"All right then. Let's go after the sorry sons of bitches."

* * *

A few hours later the party halted while Cain walked the rocky terrain, searching for sign. They'd lost the trail. They were losing it frequently now, forced to backtrack and get down and search. The Apaches had sheathed the mule's hooves in rawhide like the hooves of their horses and it was increasingly hard to follow.

"Here," Cain said, kneeling over a hoofprint. "We got em."

He mounted back up and they were in pursuit once more.

After a while they reached a little seep that trickled from a seam in a near vertical slab of rock. The Apaches had watered their horses and mule there and now the hunters watered their own caballada. It was early evening. Soon they'd have no choice but to give up the chase for the night. All of them were weary and the horses badly needed a rest and so it was decided they'd make camp.

Dolores climbed down from the saddle. She started leading her horse to the pool, but Mosby stepped forward, gripping the bridle reins of his own mount, and offered to take hers.

"Thank you," she said. "But I'll water my own."

After letting the horse drink his fill, Dolores unsaddled and hobbled him in a stretch of grass. Then she turned and walked from camp, climbing a slope of broken scree where no pines grew. Without glancing back she knew Hector was watching, likely angry at her going off alone just as he'd warned her against, but she needed to get away from them all for a moment.

Dolores stood watching the sun slip behind the hogbacks they'd crossed. It sank in the west like a burning ship and the clouds glowed as though they were a pink and purple reef in a following sea of stars. Tomorrow to rise again. The People were somewhere in the sierras and they'd greet with praise the morning whose coming she dreaded. She told herself all was as it must be. How else? For all its seeming blind indifference the world was not without ultimate reckoning, even in the deeds of men, and that reckoning from time out of mind was ever one of blood for blood. She turned and made her way back down to the camp.

* * *

Dawn. Following the trail again. Soon they came upon the burned-out mescal cooking pits. Cain walked his horse about the comal-shaped clearing, studying the ground, an eager look in his quick eyes.

By the varying age of the tracks he could tell the pair of warriors had arrived at this camp after it had already been quit. A fair-sized group of families had camped there and cooked the mescal, an Apache delicacy harvested from agave that grew in rocky outcrops in the pines. They'd moved on before the warriors came. The larger band's trail was plain to follow, the poles of a travois dragging a groove in the earth, heading northwest, and now the warriors were following them.

"That mule pullin the travois," Cain said. "He's about half-lame. He'll be supper here directly if he ain't careful. What do you figure, Mo? The band's tracks are three, maybe four days old. The bucks who killed the woodcutter come through two days back."

"The big bunch looks to be movin slow," Mosby said. "Bet they didn't get far before the bucks caught up with em."

"Let's hope it was a tearful reunion. Maybe they decided to camp wherever the bucks found em and throw a party, stay in one place a few days and get good and drunk."

"Reckon we can overtake em?"

"We're damn sure goin to try."

* * *

Jubal had been riding alongside Cain, lost in silence for some time. Finally Cain said, "Spit it out. I can tell by the constipated look on your face you got somethin to say."

Jubal hesitated. "We catch up with em, what happens then?"

"You don't need me to tell you. I reckon you know the answer to that, son."

"I guess I do."

"So maybe what you're really askin is can I be worthy?"

Jubal watched the trail ahead.

Cain glanced over at him. "You killed some of em the other times in the foothills, didn't you?"

"I've killed before. But first I tried to give them a choice. For whatever that's worth."

"Not a damn."

"I never thought of myself as a violent man."

"What breed are you then? A kind-hearted country squire?" Cain laughed. "Of course you are. You're the kindest hand that ever cut a throat."

"What we're headed for, it's not goin to be like in the foothills."

"It's sure as hell not."

"I don't know if I'm ready for it."

"Don't worry your mind," Cain said. "You'll do what you got to do when the time comes. Every man's a born killer. The weak ones deny it because it scares em to know the truth of their own nature. But when food gets scarce, if you turn your back on one of em, he'll cut your goozle quick as you please and take ever crumb you got. Let me ask you somethin. What was in you when you killed them Apaches?"

"Anger. Hatred."

"Hate's fine, but you got to quit the anger. Empty yourself out. Hate's just a kind of hunger. Let it gnaw at you a while, then we'll eat."

Hector stayed close to Dolores. She rode in their midst like a consecrated virgin under escort to some wilderness convent, a place of holy solitude where she'd go up and down the mountains mourning her maidenhood. Not for the first time Hector wished Jubal had forced her to remain behind. He didn't like the thought of making Dolores go against her own people. He was certain they'd yet to see the worst of what these mountains had to offer.

They followed the tracks all day until the last of the light was gone. Cain believed they were getting close and he was careful to post an extra man on watch that night as they slept.

At first light they went on. Midmorning they crossed a knuckled ridge under lowering banks of clouds, Cain leading them at a hellbent pace, determined to gain ground before the coming rain could obliterate the tracks. That noon Cain once more departed to scout ahead.

When he returned and met the company in the early evening, it was with word the Apaches had taken rest not far away. He'd spied their camp. It lay along a wide and shallow creekbed on the flank of the mountain. Lookouts were posted, but he'd gotten close enough to see they appeared to harbor no intention of moving anytime soon. The women were hanging strips of meat on drying racks, a fresh slaughter.

"What's the plan, Sergeant?" Mosby asked.

"We wait till dawn to hit em. Endicott and Putnam, y'all take the BARs now and go ahead on foot. Give the camp a wide berth, circle around to the north side. It'll be rough goin, but you can make it. Don't cross the creekbed till full dark and damn well don't muddy the water. Do me a favor and try not to sound like a pair of skeletons fuckin on a tin roof. Get set up and hunker down, then at first light we'll run at em from the south and drive em toward you."

The plan was met with approval. Endicott and Putnam removed their spurs. The company split up, the Browning gunners setting out afoot carrying the heavy rifles on shoulder-straps and each with a case of ammo. The two men stalked through the twilight pines.

"Our horses need water," Jubal said.

"The Apaches got the creek," Cain told him, "and there's no other water close. Only passable trail downstream goes right through their camp. We could take the horses upstream, but I won't risk muddyin water. Let em stay thirsty one night."

They made camp in a stand of rocks. Cain forbid the men from smoking out of caution against the scent of tobacco drifting to the Apaches. The gray clouds were breaking up in the sunset, threat of rain rescinded, a great relief for there could be seen on the mountainside tremendous boulders of uncertain footing, high on the slope above their position.

Night fell and the moon rose. Hector spread his bedroll next to Dolores's. The girl was already asleep or else pretending sleep. He sat up and stared across at Jubal and Cain huddled in the dark, their conversation whispered. The American lectured on the primacy of guerilla tactics as practiced in mountainous terrain. For the most part Jubal was silent, listening with something like recognition in his eyes. An acolyte at the foot of his master. Hearing the confirmation of dark truths long suspected but never voiced.

Hector turned on his side, facing away from them, and closed his eyes and tried his best to sleep.

"We'll let a couple squaws make it out alive," Cain said. "So they can go find the other bands and have a powwow, spread the word of what's comin for em."

"John Russell could be in that camp," Jubal said.

"How old is your boy now?"

"Almost sixteen."

"Won't be hard to spot, that red hair. He'll be the only one with a sunburn in the bunch. If he's there,

52

we'll swoop him up, but it ain't likely to be the case. Don't start thinkin rescue. That ain't why we're here."

"I know."

"What we do tomorrow determines what they do next."

"We just have to hit em hard enough," Jubal said.

"Now you comprende," Cain told him. "Make em see the cost and they'll give up the boy."

"I want your men to be damned careful choosin their targets."

"Any one of em hurts a hair on your son's head? I'll personally gut-shoot that man. They've been told and I'll tell em again."

They were silent a while. Then Jubal cursed and said, "It can't get light quick enough."

"This is the hard part. Waitin. Never did get used to it, even though it's how I spent most of my life. Just waitin around to kill or die."

They sat up listening to the night sounds. The horses cropping grass. One of the men on watch moving about.

"Does a number on you after a while," Cain said. "Your mind goin ever which way, givin you no peace. The battle's a relief when it finally comes. In a fight you ain't wonderin, what if I croak or end up a cripple? You ain't thinkin about right or wrong or anything else, you're just there while the world slows down and all your trainin takes over. Then before you know it, the whole thing's done. I welcome the battle. Hell is waitin."

* * *

After a while Jubal lay down in what he was sure would be a futile attempt at sleep. For some hours it was indeed just that, but finally he drifted away.

Cain took over from Ives on watch. He stayed awake all through the night, an easy task owing to the constant dull ache in his skull, sleep an impossibility with such pain. He grimaced and removed his Stetson. Running his fingers through his hair he felt it above his forehead, the sharp knot like the budding of a horn. He'd first seen it in the mirror one morning in Detroit. A small protuberance hidden under his hair. It had grown since then, the intensity of the headaches increasing with it. He hadn't mentioned it to Mosby, who would surely want him to consult a doctor. Cain didn't need any doctor to tell him what he already knew—his time was short.

In whatever was left him he'd make the most of his wrath.

Movement in the trees—

He picked up his rifle from where it leaned against a pine trunk and rose shouldering it, ready to raise the alarm.

Aubrey stepped out of the pines. All around the camp the spirits of the dead emerged from the trees. Slain Filipinos and Japanese and other islanders, the slain of Mexico and South America, a mute multitude surrounding the camp.

He lowered the rifle and spat.

The old ghosts whispered the secret, the shadow that had stalked him through every war.

The son is the father's secret revealed.

Pain pulsed in his skull. He sat back down with the Winchester across his lap and ignored the host of lost spirits and after a while they were gone, the woods empty once again.

Just as the east began to edge with blue, Cain gave his weapons a final check. He topped off the .30-30 and holstered the Colt 1911, cocked and locked. A Bowie knife was sheathed in his boot. He made sure the Remington derringer was in its holster under his left shirtsleeve. It was a tiny single-shot and of no use to him that day, but he always carried the derringer as a last resort. It had saved his life in the past and might do so again. He donned a bandoleer of .30-30 rounds. The blade Wormwood hung from the belt of his holster. Lastly he removed his spurs.

Cain kneeled and shook Jubal awake.

"It's time," he said.

The men all rose and readied themselves. They left Hector and Dolores to guard the caballada and camp supplies. In the pre-dawnlight and under Cain's orders for silence they climbed afoot across the wooded slope, moving through tumbled rock and dense brush where no horse could go, heading for the creekbed and the camp of the enemy. Jubal gripped his own .30-30, coatpockets stuffed full of rounds.

They reached the edge of the trees and paused in the deep shadows watching the camp begin to wake. Women stepped out from brush arbors made of branches and vines. They started their day in the clearing beside the creek, facing the east and kneeling in prayer. Cain noted one of the squaws carried a rifle slung over her shoulder. A relic dating back to the Apache Wars. Staked within the camp were two mules and two horses, the only livestock.

Cain led them on a slow approach, taking advantage of the cover provided by clumps of boulders, moving in close. A light breeze at their backs drifted toward the camp.

Of a sudden the old mule began to bray, alert to their presence.

Cain charged. He raised the Winchester and squeezed off a round. The squaw with the antiquated rifle slumped over where she'd kneeled praying. The other women were instantly on their feet, shouting in Apache, one of them going for the dead squaw's rifle.

Cain ran all-out. Jubal stormed after him, Moroni Thayne and the mercs following them.

A pair of young braves dashed to the horses with pistols in hand. An older warrior gave them covering fire, dropping to a knee and raising a lever-action rifle, the best of the camp's weapons. He fired at the mercenaries while the braves jerked the picket-pins free. Each of the braves gripped the mane of his horse and swung up bareback. They rode out in a swinging arc, hoping to flank the attackers.

Women ran with babies in their arms, little children at their heels, and retreated across the creekbed, running through the wide shallow stream that flowed over the rocks. The warrior with the lever-action stayed behind. He tried to hold off the mercs, buy the women time to escape. He fired into the onrushing force.

His bullet ricocheted off a stone and sent fragments of rock flying. Clovis grunted and stumbled—a sliver piercing his thigh. He cursed and kept moving.

Jubal sighted down the barrel and pulled the trigger. A rose corsage burgeoned at the old warrior's left breast—

Flowers for the void.

* * *

Endicott and Putnam on their bellies, waiting in a stone outcrop beyond the creek. They heard the bark of gunfire from the other side. Moments later the squaws came fleeing over the water, running in their short wide skirts and carrying babies and gripping the hands of older children, splashing across the lazy current. They headed straight into a trap.

The Browning gunners held their fire. They satisfied themselves that the red-haired boy wasn't among the runners, then they allowed the ones in the lead to reach the banks. Endicott and Putnam rose shouldering the BARs. They opened up on them.

A woman's scream cut through the roaring fully automatic gunfire. Bullets sprayed the water. Women and children fell. A young boy stood frozen in the midst of the creek, his right hand torn not completely off, dangling by tendons, this look of bewildered horror across his face, and the creek flowed on around him.

The gunners emptied their magazines at the same moment, then dropped low and released the spent mags.

The wounded scrambled to their feet. They turned and staggered downstream and broke from the creek, running after the few who hadn't been cut down, all of them heading for the piñes.

Endicott and Putnam slammed in fresh mags. They rose and let loose once more, firing into the backs of the runners. The heavy build of the BARs kept the recoil light and the men held the barrels steady. Only a single squaw and three young children made it into the cover of the pines, the rest lay dead on the banks and in the water.

* * *

The pair of mounted braves galloped toward Jubal and the mercenaries from the side, leveling revolvers and snapping off wild shots. The braves were intent on drawing fire away from the women and children.

Cain followed the lead rider with his rifle barrel. He shot the horse in the head and it went from full-gallop to sudden collapse, its chest plowing the earth, the rider thrown forward over its neck. The brave attempted to gain his feet, gun still clutched in his hand. Jubal's bullet caught him in the chest.

Ives and Van Zandt took out the second horseman.

Their shots hit in the same instant and the brave spilled from the back of the horse.

In the camp a squaw ran out of a brush arbor carrying a bow and quiver. She kneeled beside a meat drying rack and nocked a flint-tipped arrow and took careful aim. She sent it flying.

The arrow caught the corner of Cain's open coat and passed through without touching him. He fired on the run. The bullet's impact spun the archer half-around and she fell draped over the drying rack.

Those now fleeing the camp heard the roar of gunfire across the creek and realized the trap. They turned and ran toward the pines and an upthrust of the ridgeside that was almost vertical. It seemed a dead end, those heights surely impossible to scale, but what other choice?

A mother ran clutching the hand of her small boy. When they reached the closest of the mules, she yanked its stake loose and threw the boy on the mule's back and slapped its haunch. The mule took off toward the pines, the boy wrapping his arms around its neck. The mother turned and bent to pick up a fallen bow.

Jubal swung his barrel toward a running squaw. He hesitated, finger on the trigger. Then the old images rose up—the attack on the trail, the hag kneeling over his wife, her blade buried in Sara's stomach, and last of all John Russell slung over the big warrior's shoulder.

Hatred turned his blood to ice.

Jubal shot the woman centermass, then levered the rifle. His mind just went. Revenge took control and it wasn't hard to continue. The hardest thing was the first, afterward it was done with less struggle, less thought, and there was only numbness.

Mosby glimpsed a flash of something bundled in a woman's arm and he had the impression of a short-barreled rifle. She was racing up a slight rise toward a stand of boulders. He took aim. The stock bucked against his shoulder. He worked the lever and aimed again but then saw the bundle spill from her arms. The baby cried in the grass.

She rose up with a bloody splotch on her hip and stumbled toward the baby. She picked him up and leaned against a boulder, starting now to sing, her eyes closed, a chant coming from deep in her throat. She was singing her deathsong so that her soul would be at peace in the moment she died.

Mosby lowered the rifle. His mind whirled in a panic and he tried to gather himself.

Then a trio of mercenaries cut loose on the mother and infant, a hail of bullets piercing them. They fell dead upon the boulder.

A pair of squaws ran with two children toward the pines and the ridgeside beyond. One of the squaws had a coil of rope around her shoulder. She turned, raising a revolver, and fired back at a pursuing mercenary.

Jubal snapped off the last round in the Winchester. It clipped the squaw just before she disappeared into the trees with the others. He set out after them, feeding rounds into the rifle's loading gate on the run, and

Mosby and Van Zandt accompanied him out of the camp.

Once in the shadowed woods they moved in a three-man wedge, cautious, alert. Blood on the carpet of pine-needles. They followed the trail a distance, then it vanished. Jubal realized the squaw was gathering the blood in her hands as she ran and scattering it out into the undergrowth.

"Hold up," he said.

They paused while he scanned the ground. There—a few small drops. They went on through the pines, finding the droplets every three or four yards.

They came upon them where the woods gave way to the steep rise of bare stone ridge. In desperation the Apaches had begun climbing the wall of rock, venturing up a series of narrow ledges.

The wounded squaw was nowhere in sight. Her pistol lay empty and discarded on the ground. The second woman had climbed some thirty feet to kneel on a sharp ledge, a child clinging to her back. The rope was looped and knotted around the woman's mid-section, the other end tied about the waist of a young girl who dangled between the ground and the ledge. The squaw kneeled pulling the rope up hand-over-hand, raising the child.

Jubal and the mercenaries stared up at the scene, surprised at the sheer tenacity of their prey.

Then Jubal heard movement. He pivoted—

The wounded squaw staggered out from behind a fallen boulder, blood down the side of her leg, and lunged toward them. She gripped a bone-handled knife, the blade obsidian and gleaming, and her teeth were clenched against the pain.

Jubal and the mercs all fired as one.

They stood over her body. She lay facedown with the knife still gripped in her hand.

Van Zandt spat. He turned and raised his rifle, aiming for the woman on the ledge, then Jubal's hand shot out and jerked the barrel down.

"Let em go," Jubal said.

Mosby felt intense relief, glad they'd been spared.

"Why the hell should we?" Van Zandt asked.

"So they can find the other bands," Jubal said, "and tell em what happened here today."

Mosby looked up where the woman kneeled motionless, holding the rope, the child dangling below. They were open targets without anywhere to hide. Their fate entirely out of their own hands. The woman stared down at Mosby and when he nodded, she resumed pulling up the rope, slowly raising the girl.

Mosby turned and followed Jubal and Van Zandt back through the woods.

* * *

Heading toward the ravaged camp they heard intermittent reports of coups de grâce, pistolshots echoing in the trees. When they stepped out of the pines, they saw the brush arbors burning and horror all around. Cain and the others were in the process of executing the wounded. Dead babies lay with potted heads. Their mothers' bodies were motionless under the sun.

Wherever Jubal turned, he looked from grief to grief. Cries spilled up from the killing floor. Anguish tortured the air. The last of the wounded were attempting to crawl away and hide in the long grass, but Cain went among them, cutting and thrusting with the kalis, striding through carnage like death's own avatar.

An old woman curled in a tight ball and hugged a mortal wound in her belly. Moroni Thayne drew his .45 and dispatched her with a shot to the head.

Ives approached a squaw hiding in the grass. When she saw him coming, she rose up and tried to run with a bullet hole in her foot. Ives moved to end her suffering, but Cain pointed the kalis at him and barked an order.

"Let her live," he said. "I want her for a witness, so she can go tell the rest of em." He turned to Slotkin. "Give him a hand with the squaw. Let's put on a show for her that she ain't ever goin to forget."

Ives and Slotkin went after the limping woman. She looked back over her shoulder and hobbled faster in terror, then fell and started crawling.

Ives grabbed her ankle. She whirled about and sank her teeth into his wrist. He cursed, jerked his hand away.

Slotkin used his rifle-butt like a club. The mercenaries dragged her half-unconscious back into the heart of the camp. She was the sole survivor, other than the scattered handful hiding in the woods.

The butchery was worse still along the creek where the men took trophies, docking ears and fingers, bloody gobbets strewn on the ground.

"Sergeant?" Mosby called. "Ain't you goin to put a stop to this craziness?"

Cain laughed him to scorn. "This craziness is what we come here for. That squaw with the hurt foot is my witness. She'll tell the other bands everything that happened here—and they'll know there ain't no limit to what we're willin to do."

Cain looked over at Jubal, who stood grim-faced and silent.

"Any objection to my methods, Mr. McKenna? A tad harsh for your taste? I promise you there's a sense to my madness. Apaches believe if a body's mutilated after death, the spirit has to go through eternity that way too. You understand what I'm tellin you? They believe a true thing."

"Do what you have to do," Jubal said. "But I'll be damned if I understand it."

"You'll be in good company. We're all damned soon enough."

Mosby saw Cain look off toward the woods, his eyes strangely out of focus or so it seemed, and he smiled at nothing there.

* * *

Cain saw them ringing the camp, the spirits whose forms mirrored the features of the Apaches dead on the ground. The shade of a woman with a missing ear. One of the young braves bloody and unmanned like a luckless convert in the aftermath of some botched circumcision. The silver cords that once had bound spirit to flesh were severed, only the thinnest strands remaining, taut and wildly vibrating as though under tremendous pressure. Still the dead watched in fury as the flesh that had tabernacled their eternal spark was defiled. Cain saw the old warrior staring at him with eyes like burning coals.

Cain smiled.

* * *

He sheathed Wormwood and drew the Bowie knife from his boot. He kneeled over the corpse of the old warrior. This kind had no fear of death and Cain loved him for it.

"The point ain't to kill their bodies," Cain said. "This is a war against the spirit, not the flesh. Now bring me the squaw."

Slotkin and Ives gripped the woman's arms and carried her forward to kneel facing Cain. Blood stained her face. She fixed Cain with a look of pure hatred.

"See my Power," Cain told her in Spanish. "Power over my enemy."

He gripped a fistful of the warrior's long hair, raising the corpse's head, and ran his blade about the scalp, then rose and pressed a boot to the warrior's shoulder and jerked the hair. The scalp came free with a sickening pop. Cain raised it in a clenched fist, gory and dripping, and tossed it at the squaw's knees.

"Hate is my Power," he said. His face was masked in profound sangfroid. He could see Aubrey's ghost watching in the clearing and he turned from that spirit and met Jubal's eyes across the grass. "Stay hungry," he told him. "Keep your hate on a chain. Give it just enough rage to feed on, little crumbs, like you'd starve a dog before a fight. Then turn it loose. When you're really hungry, there's no such thing as bad food."

Mosby watched, at first uncomprehending, then in mounting dread and revulsion as Cain plunged his knife into the warrior's side and made a cut below the ribs. Cain inserted his hand deep into the gore. Feeling out the liver. He wrenched the organ free and held it in his bloodstained hand and smiled at the squaw.

Jubal and Moroni Thayne turned away, sick to their stomachs.

Cain brought the liver to his mouth and bit into it. Tasted salty bile. He chewed the unholy flesh and ate of death unto death, war unto war.

* * *

As Cain did sup he also watched the spirit of the old warrior. Tortured and maimed, the old one howled silent terror. Silver threads stretched between his shade and the bloody scalp, between his shade and the organ on which Cain dined. Those thin strings almost reached their breaking point, ready to snap at any moment, but they pulled with a hideous strength at the warrior's spirit, unrelenting. His shade was sucked toward the scalp and liver. He struggled to break free. As Cain ate, the warrior's bright shining essence darkened, drawn into each bite, streamers that gleamed and winked before Cain swallowed them up.

The old one shed off smoke-like tendrils before Cain's watching eye. The spirit flashed and dimmed, dimmed and flashed. He was trying to break loose into the woods and he reached forth his hands for his fellow spirits to aid him, but the dead squaws and braves and the little ones watched what Cain was doing and they fled in terror. The spirits retreated into the woods and the farther they ran from their flesh the more their forms were changed until they floated among the trees as glowing orbs. At last when Cain had consumed the liver entire, the remnant of the old warrior's spark broke free. Escaping into the trees its form became a lesser light among lights, one of diminished brilliance, and it disappeared from Cain's view.

Cain picked up the scalp. Its locks were entwined with strands of multi-colored lights, ancient spirits that had taken up residence there long ago, the warrior's scalp like a Medusa crown of ghosts. Hair was a dead thing that might serve as habitation for one dispossessed, suitable seat for wandering spirits. The worms of light slithered about Cain's fist. He resolved to salt and dry the scalp and carry it with him thereafter.

* * *

The men gathered before the captive squaw and filed past in a slow march, a Grand Guignol parade of such as should be nocturnes. Some of their number sported hat brims draped with severed genitalia and each paused to present the squaw a bloody scalp, Putnam bringing up the end of the line and placing about her neck a string of ears like a demonic garland.

The squaw never flinched, never revealed the slightest reaction. She stared beyond the men. Her gaze distant and unfocused, looking off at nothing.

Mosby watched in disbelieving horror. Nothing in all his years working and soldiering beside the sergeant had prepared him for what Cain unleashed. He was no stranger to war and the way of men at war, but this was a mystery to him—what had possessed the sergeant?

Jubal observed the spectacle with cold indifference.

"What the hell is this?" Moroni Thayne demanded.

Jubal only shook his head.

Moroni turned his back and hunched over, trying not to vomit.

When Cain deemed the performance finished, the mercenaries plucked their grisly plumage and went down to the creek to bathe. Bodies floated on a slow current, filaments of blood twisted in the eddies. Cain's face and arms were stained. He unbuttoned his shirt and removed it and took off his gunbelt and kneeled beside the stream. He splashed cool water on his face.

Jubal looked down where Cain kneeled along the banks and saw the great all-seeing eye tattooed across his shoulder blades. Not for the first time he wondered at the nature of the bargain he'd struck. If it had placed his soul itself at forfeit.

When Cain returned from the creek, he held a sodden handkerchief. He kneeled beside the squaw and raised the cloth to her face and she snapped at his fingers like a wild beast. Cain's left hand shot out. He clamped her jaw. He pressed the cloth to her face and cleaned away the blood in an action that was equal parts tender and brutish.

"Mo," Cain called. "Get the medical kit. That hole in her foot needs doctorin. We can't have her takin sick."

Mosby carried the kit on a strap around his shoulder. He kneeled down and opened the metal case. Cain held the squaw while Mosby cleaned out her wound and wrapped gauze around her foot.

"I don't want her anywhere near Dolores," Jubal said. "None of you say a word to Dolores about what happened here."

Cain looked up at him. "Figure it might spoil your image?"

"There's no way in hell she'd be willin to lead us to their stronghold. Not if she saw any of this."

"You sure that's the only reason to keep her in the dark?"

Jubal stared at him.

Cain grinned. "Don't worry, your secret's safe with us. Slotkin and Ives will stay here and guard the squaw while the rest of us head to camp."

* * *

They marched back toward camp where Dolores and Hector waited with the caballada. Jubal saw the girl standing on a boulder, scanning the squad of men, relief crossing her face when she spotted him. They entered camp and he found it impossible to look her in the eye.

"Where's the other two gringos?" Hector asked.

"Still back at the creek," Jubal said. "They're fine. We didn't lose anybody."

Hector gave him a slow nod. The segundo didn't need to ask what had occurred in the Apache camp—he knew it was surely bad.

Cain and Mosby mounted up. They led a pair of horses for Slotkin and Ives, a mule for the squaw to ride. Their prisoner would be freed, given the mule, a canteen, and a pack of food, then sent on her way to find another band.

The two men left camp once more and rode without speaking, taking the winding trail back to the creek. Finally Mosby looked over at Cain and broke the silence.

"What the hell was that, Sergeant? What come over you?"

Cain kept his eyes on the trail ahead.

Mosby said, "You tell me them Apaches need killin, all right, that's the job. I don't shy away from killin when it's got to be done. But I can't stand for what I seen back there, what you and the boys did to them people."

"They ain't people," Cain said.

"You tell me what they are then."

"They're dead now. Before that they was leftovers. Like monkeys are the leftovers of man and one day man'll be the leftovers of somethin else, somethin we can't even imagine. The old's got to die to make room for the new. It's nothin to piss and moan over. You ain't fixin to quit on me, are you?"

"No sir. But I got to know, why them kids? How come we got to kill little kids?"

"Don't be a half and half. What the hell were we supposed to do with em? Leave em alive for the wolves to raise? It's a mercy on the little nits. We're soldiers— or did you sign up to play mammy?"

"You a hard man. Ain't much of nothin I wouldn't do for you, Sergeant, but sometimes you a hard man."

"What I'd like to know," Cain said, "is how come you've gone so soft?"

"It wasn't just the killin. What you done to that old buck, cuttin him open and chowin down... It's like a devil flew up out of hell and got a holdt of you."

"This is hell," Cain said. "We're in it right now. And we're ever one of us the devils and the inmates both."

"I never knowed you to do anything like what you done today."

"Maybe you just didn't know me like you thought. You want to know the truth of it? I was never anything but a hired killer. Even when I wore the uniform."

"I know you, Sergeant. You ain't evil. I know there's a good man inside of you. I seen him."

The muscle in Cain's jaw started leaping uncontrollably. He reached a hand up and stilled it, pretending an urge to scratch his face.

Always before there had been a sanction for his bloodletting. Duty, honor, earning his fee. Imposing the only order he knew on the chaos that was a constant threat within and without.

Now the cord was cut. He'd severed the last of his moorings when he'd eaten of the dead Apache's liver and the world was in free fall, his soul adrift from the common fellowship of men, abandoned at last to a grand final madness.

"You ever felt split apart?" Cain asked. "Like you was a worm cut in two and the halves of you kept squirmin around, lookin for each other? For some way to put themselves back together? That's me. Just like a worm cut in half and I know there ain't no way in hell I'll ever be whole."

A look of sorrow crossed Mosby's face.

Before his friend could speak, Cain spurred Black Answer and set out ahead of him and didn't look back.

"You got to let me help," Mosby called. "You hear, Sergeant? Let me help you."

CHAPTER FOUR

It was the final night of Haozinne's sacred ordeal.

During the four days of the sunrise ceremony she must endure long intervals of fasting and dancing with little rest. It forced her to confront the darkest elements of her own inner nature. Her capacity for malevolence, her weakness of body and spirit. The ceremony would reveal the virtue of her heart. If she was strong enough, if she didn't fall in the dance despite exhaustion, then the Power of White Painted Woman, mother of the People, would infuse her being. In the end she'd know for all time the truth of her inmost self. No doubt would ever trouble her. She'd leave girlhood behind and embrace life as a woman.

Beating drums filled the camp with wild energy. The singers chanted in resonance to the drums and shook deerhoof rattles. A line of onlooking women locked arms, sisters holding each other up, and they danced forward and back and forward again, retreat and advance. Moving like an ocean under the pull of the moon.

Haozinne faced the east and danced on a deerskin. She'd trained long and hard for the ceremony, but there was a fear in her, growing with her weariness, of falling or otherwise proving herself unworthy. She hoped Ussen would bless her with the strength to continue.

Just pray, Haozinne thought. All you have to do is pray and keep on dancing.

She wore a buckskin dress adorned with beads and bright ribbons. Little bells dangled along the hem. A cut of abalone shell glimmered from her headband and an eagle feather rose out of her dark hair. She gripped a curved staff strung with bells and ribbons and as she danced Haozinne tapped the staff on the ground and the bells rang.

Haozinne danced on, sluggish but resolute. This was the single most important ceremony of her life—everything depended on its success. Afterward she'd be a grown woman and ready for marriage. The girl wiped sweat from her brow and kept moving to the rhythm of the drums and she could hear her older sister Jacali shouting encouragement from her place among the women.

There was a rattling—she heard jangling bells from the trees to the east. The mountain spirits came dancing out of the dark as if drawn to fire and song. At their heels followed the sacred clown.

In ancient days the People had lived alongside the mountain spirits or ganheh, messengers and healers. On this night the dancers would enact the spiritual world their ancestors once inhabited and all who attended the dance would receive a blessing, even the enemy among them.

The drummers' hands became a blur of motion.

The four mountain spirits circled the fire. Their bare chests were painted with animal motifs and lightning bolts and they wore breechclouts and tall moccasins. Their masks were black buckskin hoods, slits for the eyes and mouth. A great fan of wooden slats crowned their hoods, complex structures emblazoned with yellow lightning bolts, and the hanging slats struck against each other and made the distinctive sound by which the People knew the spirits drew near. The glow of the campfire shone on their headdresses. An eerie sight. Like half-recollected figures from a dream.

While the mountain spirits danced a carefully ordered series of steps, the clown stumbled after them, dancing out of step and singing behind the beat. His skin was pale and covered in ash, his moccasins worn backwards. Smaller than the rest. Like a boy among men. His mask was white and his crown took the form of a cross with a circle about it. Small bells were tied around his knees. They rang out as he danced his chaotic dance. He whirled the bull-roarer on a leather strap, spinning it faster and faster, until it produced a strange whirring-buzz.

The ragged little clown was last and least of all the dancers there, yet it was within him the greatest Power would choose to alight.

Haozinne watched them wave the long pale wands they carried. They leaped and stamped. They separated, then approached the fire from each of the cardinal directions, making wild ululating sounds.

She prayed to the Creator that he might speak to her for the good of the People.

The mountain spirits wheeled about the fire again, then the clown broke away and began his work. He moved through the People's midst bellowing his horrible laugh, the inhuman cry that long ago led them up from the dark hallowed earth. He teased children. He compelled the old ones who sat wrapped in their blankets to rise and dance with the young boys and girls. Joking loudly above the sacred songs, he made light of suffering. He went to the sick and crippled and those who despaired of life's burden and his ribald antics provoked the unfortunate to laughter, the fortunate to fear. No one could anticipate who might find himself the next victim of the clown's erratic behavior. He unbalanced the ritual proceedings, an enemy to all excess of order, and by his chaos ensured the People kept to the path their fathers had set them upon. His gift was terror and mirth.

Then he was standing before Haozinne and she could see through the openings of his mask the fire reflected in his eyes. She continued her dance and showed no sign of recognition. Just as she'd been instructed.

The clown surprised them all, as was his duty, for now he began to pray with no trace of mockery. No one had expected this, but of a sudden the clown commanded all the camp's attention and his words filled the night.

"I send a little voice, Creator.
O lean to hear my feeble voice.

76

You called forth sun and moon and earth
And made the People a sacred home.
All things belong to you.
I sing my humble gratitude.
This borrowed tongue is singing thanks,
Forgetting nothing you have made,
The grass at morning wet with dew,
The stars that shine for all to see.
I know you help us on the paths
Of peace and strife—and where they cross
That place is made a sacred place.
You set the quarters of the earth,
You are the life of living things.
Joy fills my heart to see your daughter,
A joy like waters running down the mountain
When spring has come and snows are melting.
O keep your daughter free from sorrow
And make the light of dawn her strength,
The circle of the moon her robe.
With sacred pollen she is blessed
To bring the People life again.
Your daughter's path is laid with golden pollen,
She walks in light and truth.
O let us walk beside her
And feel your song within our blood,
A song of golden pollen
To grant the People life."

Haozinne danced with new strength at the clown's

blessing. When their role in the ritual dance was finished, the mountain spirits slipped from the firelight, retreating back into the woods, and the clown joined them in the dark.

* * *

Denali took off his mask. Between his eyes a piece of abalone shell was fastened by a buckskin thong. He removed the shell and gave it and the crowned mask to Carnoviste. His father placed them on the blanket with his own hood and headdress and rolled the bundle up.

"You did well, my son," Carnoviste told him.

Bihido, Pericho, and a warrior named Ahnodia also stood removing their costumes. They started cleaning up, taking rags from a bucket of water and scrubbing away the paint and ash.

After Denali had sung healing over the baby, Carnoviste asked him to play the clown for Haozinne's sunrise ceremony. "The clown scares off sickness with his crazy laugh," Carnoviste had explained. "You have healing Power. It should be you who plays the clown." Carnoviste himself was to instruct Haozinne in the prayers and dances she must perform, a duty that should've been the medicine man's. With Nantan gone, Haozinne's mother had needed an older and respected warrior to supervise the ceremony. She'd only asked Carnoviste in reluctance after grumbling to the other women that his Power was weak.

For his part Denali had been pleased to sing a blessing over the maiden. Her sister Jacali was a true friend to him.

The warriors finished washing and dressed. Carnoviste slung a scarlet blanket over his shoulder. The vaquero's pocketwatch that Denali had presented him as a gift hung from a rawhide cord about Carnoviste's neck. They headed back toward camp to rejoin the celebration.

The social dances had begun and women were choosing partners. Denali sat down beside an elder named Itza-chu. He looked across the fire and saw Carnoviste take his place next to Ishton where she sat with Tsaltey-koo and Hanlonah. Carnoviste took the baby from Ishton and held his infant son, a look of pride and gratitude on his face. In that moment, Denali thought, who would've believed Carnoviste the furious warrior he was?

Denali looked all around at the faces bathed in firelight and it made him proud to see the beauty of his people.

Itza-chu nudged him with an elbow.

"We had a visit from a clown while you were gone," the elder said. "Best clown I ever saw."

"He probably had a good teacher," Denali said. The old man had played the clown in his youth and he'd instructed Denali in his preparations for the role.

"Only Ussen can teach laughter in dreams," Itza-chu said. "There's nothing to learn really. You have a dream and you wake up and you're a clown."

"Even so—thank you for your wisdom, Grandfather."

The elder looked pleased. "Hand me my staff, Healer. It's time I lay my head down."

* * *

Jacali looked across the fire and saw Denali with the old man. He'd played a grand clown and the words he'd spoken over her sister had stirred Jacali's heart so that she desired a dance with him. Never had she wanted to dance with a brave so much as she wanted it now. Denali wouldn't refuse her, not after what she'd done for him.

Jacali rose and started around the fire.

* * *

Denali gave Itza-chu the cane and helped him to his feet. The elder made his slow way toward his wickiup. Denali stood watching a moment, then turned back to the fire.

To find Ishton standing before him.

She smiled in her tasseled buckskins and high moccasins.

"A dance with the Healer," she said.

He hesitated. "Maybe that's not a good idea."

"And why not?"

He couldn't tell her the truth. Nantan and Gouyen's incest was the crime that led to witchcraft and perversion of Power. His knowledge of what their lust had cost the People filled Denali with great caution. And well it should—

For he felt a dull ache in his heart every time he looked on Ishton. This impossible longing, unwelcome but nonetheless real.

She was perhaps only four winters older than himself. A beautiful young woman. Of course they shared no blood, yet this lessened the taboo not at all. Ishton was his adoptive mother and the chief's favored wife. There could be no hint of impropriety between them. Denali must guard the purity of his Power or risk Nantan's own fate.

"People might think something was wrong," he told her. "I don't want anyone to say bad things about you."

"Because of a dance? What would they say?"

"I don't know. Better to be careful."

Ishton gave him a curious look, then said, "It's all right if you don't want to dance with me."

She turned to go.

Denali couldn't stop himself. He reached and grabbed her hand.

"Wait—I'll dance with you."

They joined the ring. A new dance was beginning. He glimpsed his friend Jacali turning away, stepping into the dark, her head bent low, and he wondered if she worried for her sister, but then they were swinging around the fire. The drumbeat grew more rabid with each cycle of the ring, a quickening rhythm, and looking in Ishton's eyes Denali forgot his care and the blood of the men he'd killed and the night was fine.

After a while the dancers began to disperse and the celebration died down. In the hours before dawn

Carnoviste and Haozinne retired to the ceremonial wickiup where they began the sacred prayers. For the sunrise girl the night would go on. The People slept, waiting for first light and the blessings the girl would bestow.

* * *

When the first rays shone over the ridgeline, Haozinne ducked out of the wickiup. She turned to the east and lifted her face and arms, the abalone shell on her forehead catching the dawnlight. She sang the morning song and held her palms upward as though cupping radiance like water. Sleepers woke and stepped outside to stand in the burgeoning day.

Haozinne finished her song, then Carnoviste turned to face the People. It was plain to see from his expression something was wrong. Dark news he must tell.

The girl had experienced a vision during the long dancing night. She'd told Carnoviste of the dream just before dawn and it shook him to his core.

Now he began speaking without knowing for a certainty the meaning of what he must say.

"Hear me. Ussen is listening. The sun, the winds, and darkness are all listening. Our daughter has seen an evil come to the Blue Mountains."

The entire camp was awake and standing before the sunrise girl, warriors and old ones, women with children at their hips.

Carnoviste told them of Haozinne's dream. Her spirit had been lifted up, while her body still danced below, hollow and vacant, her truest essence rising high over the sierras. She'd watched from above as a bear rose from the depths of the river. A one-eyed beast, its teeth filed to points. In its belly a ravenous hunger for dove eggs.

When the bear climbed the first ridge, a flock of magpies rushed out of the mulberry trees and swooped down on it, crying out. It swept a huge paw and emptied the sky. Then the bear crossed the following ridge and many sparrows fluttered from the pines and attacked in a whirling cloud, but wherever they pecked the bear, a mouth would yawn open and swallow up two of the birds. The bear went on, now a black mass of mouths and snapping teeth. It crossed yet another ridge and reached a rocky place near a body of water. The dove's eggs were nested in a tall pine overlooking the water. The bear began climbing the tree. Just as its claws reached into the nest Haozinne awoke, swept of a sudden back into her dancing body.

"What does it mean?" Tsaltey-koo asked from the crowd.

Carnoviste turned to Haozinne. "Tell them, daughter."

"All I know for sure," the girl told the crowd, "is the dove eggs are the People, our own band, and the bear is an evil that's come hunting us."

"The grizzly must be back," Pericho said. "It's stalking us again. What other evil could it be?"

83

"My brother's Power would protect us," Gouyen said. "If only he was still with us, we'd have nothing to fear. The People wouldn't have to be scared like rabbits."

The crowd murmured its agreement at this.

"Why does this monster hunt us?" Ishton asked.

Haozinne shook her head and stared at the ground. "I don't know," she told them.

"I wonder," Carnoviste said. "Is it because we didn't listen to Child of the Waters? We all know the story. Child of the Waters spared his enemy when he laid down his arms. This was to show the People mercy is better than revenge."

He motioned to a group of braves. "You warriors, if you ever caught your enemy sleeping, what would you do? Kill them where they lie and take your spoil. Just as I would do. Because their ways aren't the way of the People, because we learned to make ourselves deaf to their cries. As if Ussen didn't make all men brothers. I wonder if this is why the bear comes."

"Maybe you're just afraid," Gouyen spoke from the crowd. "This talk about mercy. You're getting old and slow, warrior. Maybe you want peace so no one will hurt you."

"Some of you hear weakness in my words," Carnoviste said, "because I tell you I want no more blood to stain the grass. I wish I'd listened to Child of the Waters and spared my brother when my strength was full. Maybe then I could prove to you that mercy isn't the charity of slaves. Still if any man thinks he can string my bow, let him try."

"What are we going to do?" Jacali asked.

"Don't be afraid," Carnoviste said. "Even though evil is coming, there's still hope for the People." He turned to Haozinne. "This wise and pure maiden is proof of that. I offer her my blessing and ask for hers."

He opened a little pouch and poured out a palmful of hoddentin and reached and sprinkled Haozinne with the sacred pollen. Then he kneeled and the sunrise girl opened her own bag. She touched the chief's forehead with pollen.

* * *

The People formed a long line before Haozinne and filed slowly past. She blessed each one, streaking their foreheads with yellow pollen.

When it was Denali's turn, he motioned for Ishton to go ahead and she stepped forward holding the baby. Haozinne smiled at the infant. She took him from Ishton and began singing a prayer of protection and good health.

A cry from the edge of camp.

They all turned and looked. Bihido, the warrior standing watch, was leading a woman toward them. She rode a mule, her dress torn and stained with what appeared to be dried blood. Denali recognized Chee-hash-kish, a young mother who'd gone with one of the smaller bands when they'd split up after departing Pa-Gotzin-Kay.

"They attacked," she cried out. "They killed us all, everyone but me."

* * *

Chee-hash-kish sat weeping. One of the women had given her a knife and she'd taken the blade to her tangled and filthy hair, her locks shorn in grief. She made a number of shallow cuts across her arms. Gouyen had kneeled and removed the woman's right moccasin and unbound the wound in her foot and washed it. Now the wise woman applied a poultice of herbs and wrapped it again.

Bihido and Estoni had gone with their rifles to stand lookout on the ridgetop, alert in case enemies were following Chee-hash-kish.

Carnoviste stood over the grief-stricken survivor. "Who attacked you? Who did this?"

Denali and the others gathered around.

"Yeh Yeh," she answered, speaking the name of the ancient monster. "Yeh Yeh did this."

"You need to tell me what happened," Carnoviste said.

She sobbed from deep in her chest. "They killed my baby. They killed my uncle, killed my sister and her husband. Yeh Yeh led them. He has an eye on his back and he eats people. He made me watch while he ate my uncle's liver."

She stared at Ishton where she stood holding the baby. "Yeh Yeh will eat up your baby," Chee-hash-kish told her and wept. "Then he'll spit out the bones."

Ishton looked horrified.

"Stop talking craziness," Carnoviste told her, his voice sharp.

Chee-hash-kish composed herself, wiping away the tears. Her sobbing eased. She told them how the White Eyes had found their camp two days earlier and attacked at dawn. How the man with the evil eye tattooed on his back had led them and forced her to watch all that happened. She couldn't bear to speak of what they'd done to the bodies of those she loved.

Carnoviste questioned her—was she sure they'd been White Eyes, not Mexicans? How many of them? What weapons? Her answers filled him with dread.

"My chief," Denali said. "Let's find these dogs and take their scalps."

Gouyen broke in. "Do you want to ride the ghost pony so soon, young warrior? There's too many of them and their guns never stop shooting."

"You'd just let them take our mountains?" Denali asked.

"They don't care for the Blue Mountains," she said. "That's not why they hunt us."

"Why then?"

Gouyen ignored his question. "We should look for survivors. Others might have escaped—they'll leave sign. The People don't abandon their own."

* * *

Carnoviste posted several boys to watch on the ridgeline above camp. He made sure the warriors staying behind had a good supply of ammo and he told them to keep a constant guard and make no fires in the camp. Then he hugged Ishton goodbye. It troubled him as always to leave his family in another warrior's care, but there was nothing to be done for it. He was the chief and he must help those in need.

He'd chosen his small search party. Denali and Estoni would accompany him to the scene of the massacre. Gouyen had insisted on going as well. In truth Carnoviste was grateful to have her—the wise woman's Power of Finding Enemies would ensure they didn't stumble upon the White Eye killers without warning.

Before they departed, Jacali came hand in hand with Haozinne to where Denali sat cleaning his rifle. Estoni kneeled beside him preparing his own weapons. "Were you going to leave without my sister's blessing?" Jacali asked, smiling. Before Denali could answer, Haozinne touched his cheek with pollen and began singing a prayer of protection over him.

Estoni looked from Denali to the maiden Jacali, then shook his head and rose taking up his rifle and walked away.

The quartet rode out at noon, Carnoviste and Gouyen side by side in the lead, the braves bringing up the rear.

"They were camped in the Place of the Two Dead Brothers," Carnoviste said. When Chee-hash-kish had described the camp to him, Carnoviste recognized the location. His grandfather had told him as a boy never to sleep there. The ground was witched.

"I know," Gouyen said. "They were foolish to linger in such a place, but we have bigger problems than old ghosts."

She raised a hand and they drew up. They waited while she dismounted her mule and gave her reins to Carnoviste. She went walking up the trail a distance, then stood alone and raised her arms with her palms open in front of her and prayed while slowly turning. Facing the northeast she felt a faint tingling. Her palms whitened.

"I can barely feel them," she said. "They're moving, going away from us."

"Good," Carnoviste said. "Let the White Eyes go far away."

Estoni looked at Denali. "I wish at least one of them was close. I'd cut his belly open and let the coyotes eat his guts."

Denali glanced away from the brave's cold stare.

* * *

The next morning when they reached the Place of the Two Dead Brothers, the carrion stench assailed them. Bottle flies swarmed. Coyotes and turkey vultures had outraged the corpses of the slain. Denali stared at the bodies lying hacked and brutalized, limbs and genitals severed and strewn. There wasn't a single corpse that hadn't been mutilated in some manner.

The buzzards ignored them and continued their feast. Across the camp a coyote scampered away with a hand in its mouth.

They dismounted. Estoni let his reins fall and he ran shouting at the buzzards and waving his arms. The birds rose flapping their wings and retreated a short distance.

"It's worse than Chee-hash-kish described," Gouyen said.

Denali took in the carnage. He'd known this band, played creep-and-freeze with the children, chopped wood and hauled water for the squaws. He wanted to kill the ones responsible for this, to ride out with Estoni and the other warriors and make it right.

In the ashes of the brush arbors the metal skeletons of rifles and pistols. The charred remains of bows. Fire-blackened arrowheads and knifeblades. The killers had burned every weapon, every tool.

Hundreds of shell-casings littered the ground. Carnoviste kneeled and picked up a fistful of dirt and empty cartridges. He let the earth fall from his hand and stared at the brass.

"My uncle told me what happened here," he said. "What made this a cursed place. Two brothers went out hunting alone and camped here for the night. All day they'd had no luck with game and they were hungry, nothing to eat, but they'd brought a goatskin of mescal. They sat up drinking a while. Then the elder accused his brother of causing him to miss his shot against a deer that morning, the only deer they'd seen. The younger denied it. He said it wasn't his fault his brother had a poor aim. This enraged the elder brother, who drew a knife and stabbed the young one and killed him. In the morning the killer was sorry for what he'd done. He lay beside his brother's body and stabbed himself in the heart. That night back in the main camp a deer spirit came to my grandfather in a dream. The deer spirit told him what happened and where the boys could be found. My grandfather and some other men rode out at dawn and found them here. Since then a few warriors have tried to camp in this spot, but they never stayed long. The brothers' ghosts would come up from the ground at night and act out their crime."

Carnoviste tossed the brass aside.

"Camping here was bad medicine," he said.

"It wasn't the camp that caused this," Gouyen said. "It was the White Eyes."

"Even a White Eye would have to be witched to do a thing like this."

Denali's throat was thick with sorrow and fury. "How can the People live in peace in the Other World without hands or feet? With their bodies cut apart? We should find the ones who cut them up and do the same to them."

"Listen to your son, my chief," Estoni said. "Let's take our revenge."

"My son doesn't know what he asks," Carnoviste said.

"You'll do nothing to make this right?" Estoni demanded.

"What could ever make such a thing right again, young warrior?"

"If Zunde led us, he'd die to avenge the dead."

"And our families would die with him. Go to Zunde, join his band if that's what you want. I grieve the dead, but my duty is to the living. Let's find these lost ones and help them while we can."

* * *

They watered their mules at the creek, then searched the woods for sign of survivors. Carnoviste began to fear only the woman Chee-hash-kish had escaped the slaughter, but after a while Denali found the rocks. A row of little stones and a larger pair pointing northwest. The message was simple. Five children, two women, and the direction of their journey.

The search party mounted up and rode northwest. Sometime later they came to where the refugees had sheltered for the night at the base of a ridge among boulders and mesquite. There was a dark stain on the ground, at least one of them traveling wounded.

They continued following the trail, riding in silence. Midafternoon they encountered another collection of rocks, this one pointing due west. The survivors were headed toward a spring the People often used, moving slow, blood on the trail at steady intervals now.

The sky fell to twilight and where they rode in the gloom of pine shadows the darkness was full. The searchers rode on in the direction of the spring. They were passing along the base of a wooded rise when the shape of a woman rose up at the crest.

She waved an arm. "Help us," she said in the People's tongue. "My sister is hurt."

She came staggering down toward them. When she drew close, Denali recognized her as a mother named Zi-yeh. Her hair was tangled, her buckskins filthy. She'd been lying in the brush watching their backtrail for trouble or help, whichever would come, and she looked weary and ragged.

"The White Eyes shot my sister," Zi-yeh said. "We walked with the children till she couldn't go any farther. She had to rest."

"Where are they?" Carnoviste asked.

She motioned over the rise.

"Climb up behind me, sister," Carnoviste told her.

Zi-yeh mounted the mule behind the chief. They climbed the slope and reached the top and paused there looking down on the little group of survivors. Half a dozen children stared up at them. A woman lay with a poultice pressed to her side.

"Help has come," Zi-yeh said. "Our chief has found us."

"Is your sister strong enough to ride?" Carnoviste asked.

"Tomorrow," Zi-yeh answered. She told them she'd burned the thorns from a leaf of nopal and split it and bound the fleshy sides to her sister's entrance and exit wounds.

None of them had been carrying their emergency food pouches, she confessed, shame in her voice. All they'd eaten in the days since the attack were roots and berries.

"We brought enough for all," Carnoviste said.

* * *

Denali and Estoni went to stand watch atop the rise. Taking their rifles the young warriors stalked up through the trees and each found a spot and settled in.

Down below, the survivors lay sleeping with full bellies. Carnoviste and Gouyen sat up in the darkness. Neither could sleep. When she was sure it was only the two of them awake, Gouyen spoke.

"You know who did this."

"Who?" Carnoviste asked.

"The boy's bloodfather, the White Eye who took Ishton's sister."

"How can you be sure it was him? There's more than one White Eye who'd like to see the People gone from the earth."

"He wants what was taken from him."

"So do we all."

"What if it was our camp he'd found? Your own wives and children butchered?"

"We'll be more careful," Carnoviste said. "We can move camp if we have to. The White Eye will get tired of looking for ghosts after a while and go back down

94

to his valley."

"I don't believe he will."

"Then he'll catch my arrow in his heart."

An owl went screeching over the arroyo and lighted on a pine bough. Carnoviste waited for the wise woman to comment on it, omen or portent, but she didn't speak.

"Well," he said at last. "What do you think of that? A sign?"

"The owl? You know as well as I do."

"They say it means death."

"They're right," she said.

The pair were quiet a while. Then Carnoviste rose and went to the sleeping Zi-yeh and nudged her. "Wake up, sister. I need to ask you something."

She blinked the sleep away. "What is it?"

"Did your band have any captives?"

"Two Mexican children."

"Were they taken, do you think?"

"They killed them and took their hair," Zi-yeh said.

"You can go back to sleep," he told her. "I'm sorry I woke you up."

Zi-yeh shut her eyes again.

"Even the captives," Gouyen whispered. "Nothing holds him back now. He'll kill us all. What are you going to do, warrior?"

Carnoviste stared up at the rise where Denali guarded the trail. He was quiet a long time. Then he said, "Fight for my family. The honor of that burden is better than any sign or omen."

He bent and picked up his rifle and walked out to relieve Estoni and join Denali on the nightwatch.

CHAPTER FIVE

The mercenaries rode under tattered clouds, their clothing tinged with blood and covered in dust. Weary-eyed from hard miles. They made slow progress descending the walls of pine-wooded canyons, slower time yet climbing the far slopes. There were canyons so deep their shadowed floors might conceal any number of Apache camps, but they failed to encounter any trail or sign. On occasion the woods opened themselves and Cain led them through a grassy meadow stretching out before them where wolf and bear tracks lay. Hordes of deer scattered at Cain's approach. In a single day Jubal counted as many as fifty deer and scores of wild turkeys.

The attack on the camp had alerted any hostiles to their presence in the region, so Cain eased his demands of constant stealth and gave permission for a warm supper. Putnam took down a buck and the rifleshot echoed through the canyon. He tied the carcass to the back of a mule and when they camped that night, they made a fire for the first time in a long while and had their fill of good venison.

The men's sleep proved uneasy despite their exhaustion. Those stationed on watch were hypervigilant, alert to the faintest sound from the dark reaches, but the night passed without trouble. Morning saw them heading north once again.

In the forenoon Dolores glanced back and saw a female coyote and her recently weaned pups following at a distance behind them, looking for carrion. When the party stopped to eat their ration, Dolores left a portion of her machaca on the ground for their pursuers to find. Once more in the saddle, she looked over her shoulder now and again. All through the remainder of the day the coyotes trailed after them.

Nearing sunset they halted at the edge of yet another deep slash in the mountains and sat their horses looking downcountry. A narrow stream winding through the green canyon bottom. Rude shacks and cabins. Corn tall in the fields and terraced slopes, thriving in rich volcanic soil, ready for harvest now in the fall. Cain stared out past the fields to the dark openings on the canyon wall. In those caves there yet dwelled a few inhabitants careless of sowing and reaping.

"Tarahumaras," Jubal said.

"They inclined to give us trouble?" Putnam inquired.

He shook his head. "They're peaceful."

Cain asked, "You reckon they know any Apache camps?"

"It's likely," Jubal told him. "But good luck gettin em to talk. They're a shy bunch, but they'll share supper with us and we can at least spend the night in the village."

Cain led them down the canyon wall following a trail marked with the ruts of carreta wheels. In the light of sunset they crossed through a zone where strange formations of volcanic tuff rose like pillars in the wilderness. Some standing fifty feet high, others lying toppled on the ground or else broken and leaning against their fellows. The riders weaved their way through towers of ash. Moving beneath those long narrow shadows like wanderers in a garden of sundials.

"Have you heard the news?" a voice called from among the pillars. "God is alive, captivity is led captive."

They all turned as one, the mercenaries with their hands on their weapons.

A white-haired man sat atop a broken pillar. They'd ridden right past and not one among them had glimpsed him there. He was an old man and his long white beard reached down below his collarbones. A Bible lay open on his lap, though the light was dimming, almost too faint to read. His huaraches were made from strips of old tires and he wore the simple cotton garments of the Tarahumara. His hair was wild, his face deeply seamed. A wilderness anchorite.

"Hello, friends," he said.

"And who the hell are you?" Cain asked.

"You may call me Dasein," he said in a faintly accented English. Cain recognized the subtle German in the man's voice.

"What's a Dutchman doin in these parts?"

Dasein smiled. "You have a good ear, friend. I live among the Tarahumara. These mountains are my home now. I came here much like you, perhaps. Seeking the lost."

Cain spat.

"My name's McKenna," Jubal said. He stepped Bardo to the pillar and offered up his hand. They shook.

"I know who you are," Dasein said. "All these mountains know your name. The father who searches for his son."

"We're huntin bronco camps," Cain said. "You seen any Apaches come through in the last few days?"

Dasein shook his head. "Perhaps my friends the Tarahumara have found some sign. They watch for the men of the woods."

He lowered himself from the broken pillar and jumped to the ground, spry and lively for all his white hair. "Come, friends. Join us in the village."

* * *

That night they supped with the Tarahumara, invited about the fire, and dined on boiled and roasted ears of corn. Jubal raised a gourd cup. He toasted their kindly but reticent hosts and they all drank corn beer.

The light-footed Tarahumara sat wrapped in brilliantly-colored blankets, their wide hairless faces turned to the glow of the fire. The men were thin with long arms and legs, runners' bodies, and they wore cotton breechclouts and loose-fitting shirts. The women were proud in their long skirts of bright colors and the scarves they wore over their black hair.

When Cain attempted to question an elder of the village regarding Apache movements, the old man just smiled and shook his head. Cain opened a purse of silver coins and shook them. The old man made a counter offer. In return for Cain's fine Stetson hat he'd guide them to a cave, an ancient place his tribe knew well, wherein the mummified remains of red-haired giants lay hidden alongside their strange dwarf-like companions. A forgotten race of pygmies was common talk in those mountains, though word of giants much less so. There were reports of occasional discoveries, preserved bodies small in stature, a diminutive cavefolk lost to history. Cain replied that he had no interest in mummies, goliaths or midgets either one. He inquired again if they knew the location of an Apache camp. The old man smiled and turned away.

Cain turned to Dasein. "What you said back there in the rocks, that business about God bein alive. I reckon you're some kind of holy roller? Come up here to save you a bushel of souls."

"My life isn't my own, if that's what you mean," Dasein told him. "I arrived following an understanding, deeper than the remoteness of intuition. A circumspection of concern."

"Concern for what? I reckon you'd call it penance."

"Not penance—solicitude. A clearing away of concealment. To remove the mask from my brother's face, the disguise by which he was made a stranger to himself."

"And these reds, they're your brothers. That's how you think of em."

"I am every man's brother. Bound to him and to the world by this solicitude—sometimes a standing in place for another, sometimes leaping forth, ahead down the darkened path to liberate my brother's care and return it to him. So that he might see it as it is, if only once in all his being."

"Never had much use for the Almighty myself. Reckon He thought the same about me."

"No man is ever out of the reach of His embrace."

Cain laughed. "That's exactly what I'm afraid of."

"You must have courage, friend. Dare to believe God is good." He paused a long moment. A scattered few about the fire ceased their conversation and listened, drawn to his silence. Looking into the flames he switched to a soft Spanish. "There is a lie at the root of who we are."

Dolores leaned close the better to hear.

"The first tactic of the enemy in the garden was to deceive us regarding the character of God. Hell's strategy remains the same. To make us question His goodness and through that lie sow doubt in our hearts about the truth of our identity. It's a hard thing, friends, to commune with a God you don't really love because you can't trust Him. He seems mad, doesn't He? Half of Him love, half of Him furious justice, and good luck guessing which mood He's in today. So you see that our picture of God is an idolatrous one, made in our own image, distorted beyond all recognition. Jesus Himself said no man knows the Father. Not Adam, not Moses. They didn't see Him, only glimpses darkly. Christ said I and the Father are one. If you've seen Jesus, only then have you known the true heart of the Father. The Lamb Slain from the Foundation of the World accepted that mission through His own choice. Before the birth of time, before the spirit moved on the face of the deep. In Him is reflected the likeness of the Father. There is a lie at the root of who we are, but the truth is screaming from a tree, arms stretched wide—I love you, you're created in my image, your life is worth my death. Rise up and be free."

"Sorry, Padre," Cain said. "I got no appetite for pie in the sky."

"I don't speak of some prayer to go to heaven. Hear me. His blood is speaking better things. This is the transfiguration of the whole heart. His grace shapes me to the perfect form I wore in the garden before Adam tasted of the tree. This is higher wisdom. Where the way that seems right to a man is confronted by the Way. And the eye through which you gaze is forever altered."

"If I ever get the itch to be holy, I'd sooner take up with you Mormons," Cain said, nodding to Moroni Thayne. "Seein as how your bunch are about half-Masons anyway."

"Freemasons?" Moroni asked. "How do you figure that?"

"I knew a Jack Mormon up in Nevada. Told me how old Joseph Smith gave out the Masonic code for help when the mob come to string him up. Your prophet swiped all his rituals from Masonry."

"I don't believe you," Moroni said.

"It's the truth of it. You're a Mason whether you know it or not."

"I noticed your ring, sir," Dasein told Cain. "You hold no small degree. May I ask what drew you to that craft?"

"Order," Cain said. "Masonry is order out of chaos— and that's all I'll speak on the subject." He turned the ring on his finger so that the insignia was out of view.

"How did you become introduced to this order?" Dasein pressed.

"My father."

"Was he a good man, your father?"

"He was a good man with his fists."

"We are all broken archetypes here," Dasein said. "The image our fathers were vouchsafed to represent is all too often shattered."

"I don't know a damned thing about that. I just know the son of a bitch taught me the meaning of pain and it's the best lesson I ever got. But I'd sooner park a bullet in my brain pan than thank him for the favor."

"The past, the scars that tell the story of our life, that's not who we are. In the end we are only what we choose to believe of God. The past has no hold on those

104

who walk in grace. You say your father never loved you? I say call no man your father—you have one true father in heaven. You say your mother abandoned her child? I say God gave you life. Take your eyes from things that must fall away. The name they call you by, the work you do. The accumulation of facts that constitute your illusion of an identity. All a mirage, quickly fading. Don't seek identity in what will pass away. Find it in what was from the beginning and will be forever without end. There is life through Jesus Christ, if we believe on Him, and our life is hidden now in Christ and when Christ who is our life appears, on that day, too, we will appear with Him in glory."

"That's a dandy sermon, Padre," Cain said. His voice was dull, flat. He faced away from the fire and watched the darkness as always, but his gaze seemed more distant than before. "For some of us, though, the past is a hell of a lot harder to cut loose from. I'd tell you plain what I thought of your preachin, but I don't want to offend a hermit."

"Then I'll say only what I said before," Dasein told him. "Rejoice, today in these mountains captivity is led captive. For love captures the lover and the loved."

* * *

The following morning it was decided that Dolores would join Jubal and Cain at the head of the party. They'd go in search of the main rancheria, the camp on the high plateau called Stronghold Mountain of Paradise.

"Gonna use her like a coondog," Putnam said. "Sniff the savages out."

"Or else it's a trap," Oldham said. "She's liable to lead us straight into a whole mess of Apaches."

"You can trust her," Moroni Thayne told them.

Oldham gave him a look. "How come you're so sure?"

"The girl was in love with a vaquero. The Apaches killed the boy. She's got a reason to want them taken down."

"She's still one of em."

"Dolores knows where she belongs."

"Might start to feel kinda forgetful up here."

"She won't."

Oldham spat. "Well, pardon me if I don't take your word for it."

After bidding goodbye to Dasein and departing the village they followed a northerly course. The girl rode with Jubal and Cain flanking her. At the rear of the column Hector trailed after the mercenaries.

Dolores led them among the spires. Every time they crested one ridge it was only to discover a higher one beyond it and they looked for the shape of Pa-Gotzin-Kay against the skyline. They rode through dark bowers where woodmice nested. At a hidden pool Dolores startled a flock of wildfowl into a full-throated chaos of wings and retreat.

"We're getting close," she said. She turned down a

faded game trail, the ghost of a trace, and rode deep into the woods.

"Slow down," Jubal called after her. His rifle was drawn and ready. He set Bardo to a faster pace and caught her up. "Don't go so far ahead," he cautioned.

They came upon a sudden meadow. Three mule deer looked up from their grazing and darted for the trees in sleek escaping splendor. Dolores paused. She walked her horse out into the heart of the meadow and stopped again and sat studying the ridge that loomed above the treetops. None of it familiar to her. Nothing as it should've been. She turned the horse and started back the way they'd come and the men parted to pass her through.

Pines threw shadows down the rugged slopes and hastened them on. Embracing boughs wove twilight too soon. The darkness closed around her like the arms of strangers and they quit the search for the night and set up camp.

She didn't know where she'd gone wrong, Dolores told them, but she was confident that tomorrow she'd find the plateau with little difficulty. Cain wore a bemused expression.

"Anything's possible," he said. "Give it enough time, I reckon even a blind sow finds a acorn ever once in a while."

Late in the night Dolores lay sleepless in her blankets and stared up at the stars. Old storied constellations her grandmother had pointed out for her and named, telling how each had come to be and what they meant for the People. Coyotes yowled somewhere not far away. Crying out like women possessed. Dolores wanted to lay her head against her grandmother's breast and let a long and dreamless sleep take her and never have to face the morning.

* * *

They sat their horses and watched Dolores where she stood on a jutting finger of stone, the girl staring out over the canyons and peaks. She took in the wilderness before them. Puzzling it out.

Black Answer sidled. "I got my doubts," Cain said.

"She can find it," Jubal told him. He held Bardo's reins and the reins of Dolores's mount.

"Well, she ain't had much luck so far. Makes a man wonder if the place she's got us huntin for is even real."

"Of course it's real."

"I'm glad you're so confident. Because I'm startin to think she might be takin us over the hill."

Dolores turned and started back down toward them. "I know the way now," she called.

Cain nodded. "All right then. Sigi sigi, Little Sister," he said, using a bit of old Tagalog from his time in the Philippines. "We're burnin daylight."

They rode under moss-grown outcrops of rock and they followed after the girl in what seemed more and more an aimless wandering. Nowhere did they discover evidence of any human presence save their own. The men began to complain that such a place as the girl described with woods and spring and the switchback trail its sole means of access must surely be a fantasy. She had to be leading them away from the actual rancherias.

Finally Cain looked over at Jubal. "Time to admit it," he said. "She didn't come along to help us find em. She come to make sure we never got close."

Jubal didn't answer. As for Dolores, she pretended not to understand.

Several hours later skirting the slope of a high stone upthrust, Cain sighted a crude scaffold. It stood lashed with rawhide on the peak. Ribbons fluttered in the wind. Cain halted the party and pushed his hat brim up and looked from the scaffold to the girl.

"You speak English?" he asked.

"A little," she said.

"Up there is what they call a sky burial. Reckon it's a old friend of yours?"

Dolores could see something on the platform wrapped in a thick blanket. No ravens or other eaters of the dead were present, so she judged the remains had been laid out for some time.

"Just old bones," Dolores said.

"Apaches, they're funny about them bones, ain't they?" Cain said. "Supposed to wait till mother nature strips em clean, then go hide em someplace they won't ever get found."

Dolores was silent.

Cain stared at the sky burial platform. "Yessir, bones are sacred to Apaches."

Dolores knew what was coming. She waited for it.

"Course that wouldn't be true in your case, now would it?" Cain asked. "What do you care about old dry bones? Seein as how you're leadin us after live Apaches, not on some wild goose chase. Nothin sacred about em, is there?"

"They're just bones," she said.

"Prove it for me."

"Cain—" Jubal began.

Dolores cut him off. "Give me your reata," she told the mercenary.

Cain grinned. "That's our girl."

He untied the looped reata from his saddle and handed it over. Dolores took the rope, giving Cain a cool stare, then she clapped her legs against the horse's sides and set out climbing the peak.

"What are you after with this?" Jubal asked.

"A harmless experiment is all," Cain told him. "See where her loyalties lie."

The party watched Dolores rein in and slowly walk her horse about the scaffold. Her face betrayed nothing. She tied one end of the reata around a corner pole and dismounted and looped the opposite end around the saddle horn. Holding the bridle reins she led the horse forward down the slope and slapped its flank. The horse jerked the reata taut. The platform came down in a crash of bones and baubles and dust.

Dolores untied both ends of the reata and stood coiling it. Then she mounted back up and rode down to where they waited and walked the horse up to Cain.

She tossed him the reata. "You want to play with bones? Or are you ready to find their mountain?"

"You lead the way, Little Sister," Cain told her.

* * *

Dolores rode on. She couldn't have said why she'd truly come, what her real intent had been in promising to guide them. Perhaps it was just as Cain suspected and she'd come to misdirect the expedition. Should the path to Pa-Gotzin-Kay have appeared to her at that instant she might very well have chosen to lead them on past. She told herself this. It was a comfort to think she was incapable of such betrayal, of judasing her own people, no matter what had transpired.

Yet there were darker places in her heart. Moments of naked rage when she hated them for what they'd done. For casting her out, for killing Sara and taking John Russell, and for the black change they'd wrought in Jubal. And most of all she hated them for Angel's murder, the only man Dolores believed she would ever love. In those moments she longed to see them struck down by her own hand.

Rage and love burned within her. Neither would extinguish, try as she might, and her soul was scorched earth.

Dolores fought to trace the way back in her mind, to recall the times Carnoviste led them across a hundred miles of wilderness directly to the foot of the trail. The woods had known her in those days, accepted her as kin, the mountains familiar as the lines of her grandmother's face. All afternoon she expected to crest the next rise and spot the profile of the stronghold's cliffs and ramparts, but she never did. The way was lost to her, it fled at her approach.

They were still riding at sunset, though she knew the search was finished, the mountain nowhere to be found. She was a stranger in the land. Stars appeared one by one in the fading blue, then full dark and a flood of thousands.

* * *

In the days ahead they'd discover tracks of shod and unshod mules and trail them northeast where the woods thinned out and roots of stunted pines clenched bare rock in gnarled tangles. They left the green canopy behind for basalt reaches devoid of vegetation and each night they slept in the hoofprints of the enemy. Twice they lost the trail over wind-scoured beds of stone and had to backtrack and cut for sign in long curving swaths and the final time Cain was forced to dismount and walk the ground, but his search proved fruitless. After a while he gave up and they went on without any tracks to follow. They proceeded afoot, leading the horses and packmules down ridgesides marked with boulders and scree. The peaks at sunset stood like monoliths awash in blood. The riders abandoned their blind chase with nightfall.

They broke camp as the sun rose smoking from the plains of Chihuahua. Later that morning when they found the tracks again, they were headed north and the company resumed their pursuit along the borderline.

Three times they crossed and recrossed the continental divide. Clouds below opened and closed at intervals to reveal dark chasms and distant towers. Following the trail of the Apaches along a high ridge, the sun at its zenith, they met an ancient trace that Dolores told them the Old Ones had made.

It was just a narrow washed-out foot-trail, never intended for riding, and it led through miles of rugged terrain. Jubal walked holding Bardo's reins in one hand, his rifle in the other. He looked out over the falling country and the chains of blue mountains beyond the barranca, range on range like an image caught between opposing mirrors, that infinite labyrinth rising east and west in superterranean grandeur. All beneath the azure bell where high winds sang the Anasazi requiem. Cordillera and barranca, summit and abyss, the Bavispe twisting about the riven mountains to flow through the timeless heart of the sierras.

That evening the storm hit them still on the foot-trail. Thunderheads had built with little warning and the air smelled of coming showers. A gust of wind snatched Rourke's and Mosby's hats, John B. Stetsons whirling like indignant spirits in a tempest. They got their slickers on as the rain began to fall in earnest and they kept going, nowhere to stop, no shelter on the ridge, and already water was rushing down either side of the trail.

Hector walked leading his horse and a string of three packmules. They were crossing a section where the slope at the right of the trace was washed out to a near vertical drop. The mule at the rear of the train stumbled when the mud gave way beneath its hoof. The mule's eyes rolled blind white as it fell on its belly and scrambled to rise, ears flattened back, but the water was pouring down the side of the trace and it flailed in the running muck and went sliding backward off the trail.

The lead rope went taut. The falling mule shot out a foreleg and slammed its hoof into the hindleg of the next mule in line, toppling that unfortunate beast of burden so that it went plunging over the side after its fellow. Hector cursed and gripped his horse's reins as the mule directly behind him shrieked in terror and fell being dragged toward the abyss.

Then Slotkin rushed forward, Bowie in hand, and slashed the lead before it could snap or else drag the third mule off the trail with its doomed comrades. The mule righted itself and lumbered back to its feet.

In a flash of lightning Hector saw the pair of fallen mules rolling end over end down the rocky slope. The mule carrying the 81mm shells landed on its panniers and then both mules ceased to exist. The fiery burst rained rock and bits of mule flesh down the ridgeside and the roar of the explosion was lost in a peal of thunder.

Light fled their eyes, the company enveloped in the hollow cloud's dark and booming heart. The wind swept rain against their faces and carried away curses into the night. The horses clambered on through the turmoil.

Jagged wires of lightning stitched crazed patterns. The world like an apparition in the strobes, stands of acacia floating tremulous and pale, black pinnacles silhouetted in the west. Jubal led them on. Lightning struck a rock on the ridge no more than a hundred yards away and the horses went rearing and shrieking, the men struggling to hold their reins. Smoke and electricity heavy in the air.

Cain looked down at the dark rushing waters. He stood upon those ramparts of the world and laughed a manic laugh. He led them through the raging peals and he bellowed out his song in such a joyous madness it frightened the men more than the storm itself—

Apache May, Apache May,
My darlin's gone with Slaughter.
For Texas John did steal away
The chieftain's only daughter.

Jubal struggled to keep pace behind the singing mercenary. Fire sparked by a lightning strike burned upon a western peak like a beacon. Across the canyons to the east another flame answered the first. Signal and countersignal. He looked ahead where Cain led them up the trail and in a burst of light he saw the cliff-face and the recess within. He thought his eyes were playing tricks. Another flash and he saw it plain, a city in the opening of the cliff-face, the shape of adobe buildings.

Cain led them toward the ancient ruined city.

* * *

Wind howled through the empty homes of the Old Ones. Rain cascaded off the cliff's overhanging rim and the company led their horses through the cold silver curtain. Dolores stared up at the rounded stone watchtowers and she could feel the spirits studying their approach.

A chill ran down her back, colder than the rain and the wind. She shivered.

They hobbled the caballada amid the rubble of fallen buildings and Jubal found maple branches left piled near the ashes of an old fire, some other soul foolhardy or desperate enough to camp in those haunted quarters. He set about building a fire and soon had it burning.

They sat warming themselves. The flickering light shone on broken walls. Dolores wrapped herself in a blanket and looked up where the stone ceiling of the overhang was lost in darkness.

Putnam and Endicott were of a mind that Apaches might be hiding somewhere in the ruins and they went torch in hand to clear the standing structures one by one until they were satisfied the company was alone. Wasted effort, Dolores knew. Even in dire emergency the People would never choose to camp in the Place of the Old Ones.

Collapsed walls lay about them, rotted roofbeams visible in the rubble. A number of buildings and a pair of towers still stood, the fired adobe bricks rising to shadowed heights. A flock of swallows had sheltered in a darkened window above and they chittered in that upper story like the caged songbirds of days long dead. Shards of zoomorphic pottery littered the ground, ancient seeds spilled from broken vessels. Conical granaries made of grass and clay rose like enormous pale mushrooms.

The Apaches wouldn't set foot there for any reason. Such a place was witched. Under the floors of houses and in the refuge area outside the city the dead lay buried in secret to hide their losses from observers. Scattered throughout the ruins were human bones that bore the marks of pot polish, the Old Ones who were murdered and devoured before the Spanish arrived in their galleons.

Even so close to the fire Dolores felt cold. She looked at Cain sitting where he would always choose to sit, apart from the rest and with his back turned to the flame, darkness preserving his sight.

She hugged the blanket tighter about her and tried not to think what these stones had witnessed, what evil memories indwelled their masonry.

* * *

117

Cain woke when the rains stopped of a sudden in the night. He rose from his bed there in the shadows and looked at the circle of sleepers about the fire. Mosby stood guard, leaning against a granary, obviously fighting sleep, and Cain watched him struggle to stay alert.

Sheet lightning flashed in the far distance. The wind calm, no thunder reaching them. All quiet in the city of the dead.

Cain waited. He remembered the day the cavalry troops had ridden into Carrizal on Pershing's orders, Cain a scout, Mosby a buck private, and the Carrancistas shot Mosby. The boy lying there in the dust bleeding and wide-eyed, not a damn thing Cain could do about it, nothing but drag him out of the gunfire and try to keep the Mexicans off them until it was over. He never wanted to feel that helpless again. Mosby still had the scar on his shoulder, pale against his dark skin.

When he was sure Mosby was determined to stay awake, Cain pulled on his boots and walked over to relieve him.

"Sergeant, what you doin up?" Mosby asked.

"You go on to sleep, I'll keep a eye out."

"You don't have to do that."

"I know it. Now go on, get yourself some rest."

"Well. You sure?"

"It's a order, son."

Mosby grinned. "Yessir, Sergeant. I appreciate it."

Cain kept a lone watch in the still hours. The clouds had broken and the moon shone on the walls of the nameless city. He studied the towers surmounting the complex on either side and covering all approaches up the shelf and he admired their masonry, wondered what enemy they'd guarded themselves against.

His mind began to turn over all that Dasein had spoken. What the German had said of fathers and broken things. A quiet rage built within him until he'd sooner have welcomed the ghosts than dwell any longer on that man's words. If he'd known the truth of Cain's blood, the secret he carried, surely the hermit wouldn't have been so quick to preach.

The pulsing growth on his head sent little tremors of pain that he felt flow down his spine and out his fingertips. He was the perfect watchman. Sleep no risk whatever.

After a while, to distract his mind, he went wandering through the ruins. He carried only Wormwood and he didn't bother with a torch, relying on the moonlight. The opening of that recess faced the northeast and while the moon was still low in the sky there was light by which to see.

He stepped through the open entryway of a house whose roof was still intact, rough wooden beams running across the ceiling, and he began pacing the structure off, going from room to room and counting his strides. Then he ventured back outside and stepped-off the length of the building. The counts didn't agree. Something strange there. He ducked back through the entry. After he walked to the far wall of the last room, he struck a match and held out the little flame. He could see where they'd plastered over the bricks that sealed the doorway to the little chamber beyond. Crypt of some beloved. Handprints still visible in the plaster, recorded there ages after the mason who'd fashioned that wall had vanished with the secrets of his world.

The match burned Cain's thumb—he dropped it and the light went out. He stood in darkness absolute. He began moving with his arms out-held before him, but he couldn't remember his way out of the room. His heart was actually beginning to speed up, an old man afraid of the dark, his mind bepopulating the ruins with a menagerie of unspeakable fiends, creatures hideous beyond description, each more horrific than the last with slavering jowls and needle-like fangs. A great jaw slowly unhinging to swallow him whole.

He fumbled with the book of matches and the last four spilled out.

Then he heard the clawing. Something scratching at the plaster. The sound was faint but seemed to come from inside the walled-off chamber. He stepped back. His boot-heels crunched the brittle bones of mice, kicked fragments of pottery. He started to panic, feeling ridiculous and frightened all at once. He reeled in the pitch and stumbled over a pile of debris and landed on his side. He felt around and picked up a small stone. Threw it toward the sound of the scratching. It bounced off the wall and hit the floor and he heard a rat squeal and come whining out of its nest.

Unmanned by a rat. Cain laughed at his own lack of nerves.

He rose and dusted himself and found the exit without any trouble. He stepped out of the house and caught his breath.

He retrieved fresh matches from his saddlebags and resumed his wanderings. The thoughts that had rattled him in the house were far from his mind now. Soon he came to the rear of the recess on which the city lay and faint in the moonlight he could just make out a series of markings on the stone wall. He lit a match. Figures of animals and men, sunbursts and cryptic symbols.

Out to the hillside below. Cain looked down on the remnants of terraced gardens in the moonlight. Where they'd sown and reaped together, the old and young. Work and celebration. Grandfathers and grandmothers beside them, teaching what they knew of plants and stones and stars. They wove baskets and watched the heavens.

Cain stepped to the open pit of the central kiva. He circled around until he came to the ladder, a series of old wooden rungs lashed with rawhide strips, but it held his weight and he made his descent.

Ancient walls closed around him and he struck another match. Ashes in the firepit. A rectangular ventilation shaft was set in the wall like a doorway, a low stone barrier blocking it from the firepit. On the floor a sock woven of human hair. The bones of creatures who'd fallen in over the years and trapped themselves, rabbits and mice. A salamander.

Beyond the firepit he could see a small dark circle in the floor.

It was a sipapu, the portal through which those people, whoever they'd been, were said to have ascended from the depths of the underworld. He lit a match and went to kneel over the opening. The light failed to pierce that darkness. He hadn't thought it would be so deep.

When he dropped the match into the sipapu, the blackness swallowed it whole. Like a bright coin vanishing down a well.

He tossed a pebble and listened for it to hit and he listened a long while, but there was nothing. He held another match burning directly over the hole and a cold draft like an icy breath chilled his hand and the match went out.

He kneeled there thinking about that. Why it should be. There was no sense to it. He glanced back toward the ventilation shaft, considering the possibility of a connecting tunnel, but the air was still and there was nothing to drive a current.

He reached his right hand into the opening. Tried to touch the sides of the hole. His hand passed through air, empty space.

Silence in the kiva.

He got down on his belly, reached the length of his arm into the sipapu so that his shoulder pressed against the opening. Still he couldn't touch bottom. His arm grew cold, a bone chill, and when he tried to raise up, he found that he couldn't.

What the hell was going on? He thought maybe he was having a stroke down there on the floor of the pit house with his arm stuck through a hole in the ground like a miser who'd dropped a spare penny. But a stroke was supposed to affect your left side, wasn't it? He could move his left arm just fine.

The terror he'd felt in the ruins above returned full force.

He strained with all his might and got his shoulder up off the ground. Then something wrenched his hand and he slammed down against the floor again and he thought his arm would pull free of its socket.

Ice bit his skin. He shivered, the sickly-sweet odor of decay filling his nostrils, something dead and rotting down there. Then he felt it flicking at his palm, wet and forked and rough as sandpaper. Stark fear paralyzed him. *"Come home, Teufelkind,"* his father's voice echoed in the kiva. At last the visitation he'd feared above all others called to him. A great and sourceless moonshadow fell upon Cain. *"I've been lonesome for you,"* Killcrop said. Against his will a flood of memory washed over him, each wave threatening to send him under to those depths the soul cannot bear.

* * *

His father explained everything, the dark truth laid bare at last. Called forth from its cave of unknowing and impossible to put back again.

Killcrop lay on the porch of the cabin at the river crossing, bloodied and breathing hard from the fight. The fifteen-year-old Cain stood over him. His fists ached. The twilight had passed and no light remained. Cicadas were busy at their song.

"Whenever I look at you," Killcrop told the boy, "I see Hedda. Your mater. In your eyes and in your face."

It was a connection unbroken by the grave. The boy would make some careless gesture, immediately familiar, and the shock of her beauty and loss would overwhelm Killcrop all over again. Like a revenant, the past always haunting him but out of reach forever.

Then Killcrop would begin to suspect.

If Hedda were present within him, how much more so the other? He'd examine the boy's every movement, each subtle expression, sick at heart to think what devil's echo sounded in his blood, and he'd watch for signs of his savage nature asserting itself. Apprehension would turn to obsession, but in those early days when Cain was just a babe at the breast of the Mexican wet nurse, there was no anger in Killcrop. Sorrow and fear, but nothing like the fury that would inflame him as the boy matured.

"When they rode up," Killcrop began, "I saw they

wore blue. Why should I be afraid? I thought soldiers men of honor. It must be."

The river had spilled over its banks that day, engorged with floodwaters from the night's storm far to the west. The men approached from the Texas side. They rode toward the cabin, eight riders counting the Indian scout, a few still uniformed in their regiment's blue jackets, cavalry-issue saddles on the horses, and their faces were bearded all save the scout's. Their mounts looked near exhaustion. Trembling in a lather, the end of a hard ride. It was the summer of 1869.

Killcrop had stood on the porch and watched them draw up in the yard. Their leader put his mount forward. He gave his name as Averill, of late a captain in the 4th cavalry. They'd mustered out, he said, after years protecting settlements and defending the mail against Comanche attacks and now they'd come to seek their fortune in Mexico. His manner was polite, almost refined for that country. Golden hair spilled from under his Stetson and his eyes were flashing blue.

"Would you be kind enough to take us across, sir?" Averill inquired. "For a fee, of course."

"Jawohl, Kommandant. Happy to."

Averill dismounted. He reached in his saddlebag and took out a handful of silver coins and paid the boatman fully in advance, promising a generous gratuity on completion.

The Indian scout swung out of the saddle. He was a half-breed Tonkawa, a hulking figure dressed only in a breechclout. When he approached the boatman, Killcrop took a nervous step back. Of a sudden the scout stood ramrod straight and gave a brisk salute.

"Me Tonk," he said and held the salute.

Averill grinned. "Not to worry, sir. This here is the Tonk, as you might've gathered. Our scout and unofficial mascot. He's harmless, unless you happen to be Comanche. I'd advise you to return that salute, else he's liable to stand like that all day."

Killcrop grinned. He tossed a little salute in return and the Tonkawa scout went at ease.

"Would you men like coffee?" Killcrop asked. "Mein wife can make it while you wait."

Just then Hedda stepped out the open cabin door, smiling at the strangers, pleased at the opportunity to practice her English. "Hello," she called. "Welcome to our home."

"Me Tonk," the scout yelled.

She ventured a hesitant smile. "Hello there."

"Ignore the Tonk, ma'am," Averill said. "He's a man of few words." The captain doffed his hat and introduced himself. He motioned to the little vegetable garden beside the cabin. "You keep a well-tended garden, ma'am. Not a weed to be seen."

"I pluck them up before they choke my tomatoes."

"It's a lovely plot of work."

"Thank you, Captain," Hedda said. "You men must be hungry."

"It's been sometime since we savored a woman's

cooking. We'd be truly grateful and willing to pay for your trouble."

She gave the captain her best smile, obviously charmed, and remarked it was no trouble at all.

It would take several trips to carry all the horses and packmules to the Mexican side. Averill ordered a pair of the ex-soldiers to accompany Killcrop on the first crossing, going along to guard the mounts when they reached the shore.

Averill removed his saddlebags from his horse and carried the heavy bags to the porch. He directed the Tonkawa scout and the rest to stake their horses and thereafter they settled on the porch to wait. Some rolled cigarettes while others lay with their hats over their eyes, fingers laced behind their heads, the respite not gone to waste.

Returning alone to the Texas side Killcrop saw them now sitting with plates in their laps, sipping mugs of coffee and laughing. Smoke rose from the stone chimney. He docked and led a second load of horses aboard and waved to the ex-soldiers. They waved back and he set out again.

Coming back the next time, his arms aching, Killcrop was midway between the two shores when he looked and noticed them gone from the porch.

A scream cut through the air, rising from the cabin.

He dove off the platform and started swimming.

Killcrop climbed the banks, soaked and breathing hard, and ran up the steps to the door. When he burst inside, he saw Hedda on the kitchen table, her blouse torn, blood running from her busted lip. One man held her arms, a pair of his fellows gripping her ankles and spreading her legs wide. Killcrop let out a guttural cry and rushed them.

The rifle-butt slammed into the back of his head and his world went black.

When his eyelids opened to the waking nightmare, he peered up at Averill through a fog. Hedda was begging them not to hurt him.

Blood ran down the side of Killcrop's face. He cursed them in High German.

Averill cocked a pistol. "Stand him up," he commanded.

Two men on either side of him hoisted Killcrop to his feet. He hung limp between them.

Averill pressed the pistol barrel to Hedda's left temple. Killcrop groaned.

"Behave yourself, Fritz," Averill said. "Don't force me to treat you unseemly. And boy, until you've been unseemly to by a cavalry officer, you don't know unseemly."

"Why do you do this?" Killcrop asked.

"We ran into some recent legal difficulties in relation to the contents of those bags." Averill nodded to his saddlebags on the floor. "A dispute in ownership. The kind where Mexico's the only solution. But why not have a little fun along the way? A man's got to enjoy the journey."

The ex-soldier gripping her arms said, "I'll give two-bits for first go."

"It ain't a damn auction," another said. "Should go by seniority. Ain't that right, captain?"

"Teufelspack," Killcrop shouted. "I cut your throats."

The men argued on.

"Shut up," Averill told them. "All of you shut the hell up. This special lady deserves a special touch and I think the Dutchman here likes to watch. You a watcher, Fritz?"

Killcrop cursed him.

"Let's show Fritz how the Tonk tames a white squaw."

The scout was sitting on the floor eating a plate of biscuits. He mopped honey from the plate.

"What do you say, Fritz?" Averill asked. "Ready to see the Tonk in action?"

Killcrop jerked forward, struggling to break loose. The ex-soldiers twisted his arms and slammed him back against the cabin wall. His vision danced.

"Calm yourself," Averill said. "I promise the Tonk's a gentle lover. For an Indian, anyways." He put his fingers to his mouth and whistled like a bird.

The scout looked up.

Averill motioned to the table. "Get on up there."

He rose still chewing a biscuit.

An ex-soldier said, "Dammit, Captain. I ain't goin after no Indin."

"I ain't either," his fellow said.

"Quit your moaning," Averill told them. "There's no shortage of gash where we're headed."

The scout stared at Hedda, her legs splayed on the oak table. He stepped forward, then paused and glanced at his captain.

"Me Tonk?"

"You Tonk," Averill said.

* * *

When it was over, they made Killcrop swim out to the ferry and pull it to shore. His skull throbbed between daggers of pain. Averill took Killcrop's shotgun from its place by the cabin door and shoved it in the pack of one of the mules and he took the coins they'd paid Killcrop and returned them to his saddlebags. Finally he ordered the men to lead the last of the packmules aboard along with Killcrop's own mule.

The boatman kneeled exhausted on the banks.

It was twilight when Averill and the ex-soldiers stepped on the platform and began pulling it across. The Tonkawa sat at the rear letting his feet trail in the water. He gave Killcrop a little parting salute.

Killcrop staggered up through the deepening shadows and into the cabin. He held her while she wept. After a while Hedda rose and poured water from a china pitcher and wet a rag and she kneeled cleaning the dried blood from Killcrop's face.

In the weeks that followed they waited for the blood to come. The last time they'd known each other was the night before the ex-soldiers arrived, lying together as man and wife and trying again for a child as they'd tried all three years of their marriage. They'd begun to suspect her womb could yield no life and now that pain was almost a welcome relief.

They waited long weeks, but the blood wouldn't come and they waited as weeks turned to months and still the blood didn't come. And so they knew. Finally she woke one morning with her stomach in a turmoil. Hedda rushed outside. Killcrop followed her and kneeled holding her hair while she was sick on the ground.

That night as they lay in the dark cabin he whispered to her, insisting the child was his and there was no other. Of course it is, she told him. The child was his, could only ever be his, and it would be born to their love. It made no difference, the seed from which the life within her sprang, love having power by its very wounding to graft unto itself all things.

* * *

Cain's arm was numb by the time the sipapu released him. Whatever held him relented of a sudden and Cain pulled his arm from the opening and rolled over on his back, rocking slowly side to side, and held his freezing limb against his chest. His heart wouldn't slow its hammering. Killcrop's shadow was gone and the kiva silent.

It was a long while before he rose. At last he stood on the floor of the ancient kiva and kicked a stone down the throat of the sipapu and heard almost instantly the thump as it struck bottom.

He climbed up the ladder one-handed. When he reached the top, there was a thin blue glow in the east and he stared out at the coming dawn. Light returning to that dark land. There seemed no life to greet it, the songbirds gone silent.

The sipapu had shown him a past he'd long thought dead. Cain once believed he'd escaped the boatman's tale, left all remnant of that life forgotten on a distant shore, but the secret had dogged his trail all these years and now it haunted him in this place of ghosts.

He turned to face the city that rose above the waste like the ruins of time itself.

CHAPTER SIX

The People broke camp.

Gouyen's Power of Finding Enemies told her the White Eyes had moved on across the river, departing to the northeast after massacring the other band. The killers were headed in the direction of empty Pa-Gotzin-Kay. Yet the wise woman desired a greater distance between them. The People all agreed she knew best and they gathered their scant possessions and set out.

Their path of retreat lay farther west, keeping well above the valley to the south. They travelled with utmost caution now. Every morning following prayers the women would count and recount the emergency rations. Each warrior slept and ate and relieved himself while his rifle was always close at hand.

At day's end when they'd ceased their travel, Denali would go walking the depths of the woods. Treading those places where only the soft fall of his moccasins broke the stillness and oaks raised knotty arms like offers of embrace.

Since his healing of the baby there had been others. Many among the band had asked his prayers. Once he'd spent a long night singing over a fevered grandmother until finally at dawn she'd emerged from her delirium and begun a slow recovery. The People called his Power strong and true. Not even Gouyen doubted his healings.

Yet the truth of it was that he no longer desired the Creator's gift. What use was healing a handful of the sick when evil itself stalked the mountains? His heart groaned in a terrible hunger to strike out at those who'd committed the slaughter at the creek. Now when he thought of the vaquero he'd killed on the raid, he was glad of it. The White Eyes had slaughtered so many of his people. At least he'd taken blood as well.

He never volunteered his opinion during band council, but he was discovering he could no longer keep quiet. Estoni and others had asked him more than once what action he thought they must take against the White Eyes. At those times he always deferred to Carnoviste, knowing his father wished to avoid the war path.

In truth he'd come to doubt the chief's wisdom. There was a fear growing within him that disaster would surely come to the People whether they searched it out or not—and for his part he wished to meet it standing fast beside his brothers.

All these questions troubled his mind while he walked the woods. He sought answers in the shadowed places, the sweet chill of the wild groves, but there were none to be found. Only stillness.

* * *

Several days' journey found them nearing the Camp of the Warm Springs where the medicine man had gone missing. Not far from the springs the honey cave waited with its secret. More than a few among them wished to remain in that place for a time—nowhere else within the arc of the river was a better camp to be found and their store of venison was dwindling as well. They needed to hunt and resupply.

Carnoviste was steadfast in his determination to continue on. He succeeded in persuading them of the need for greater distance. The band accepted the necessity of pushing farther northwest, but they demanded brief respite, a day or two in which they might linger and send a pair of warriors out to hunt game.

The lure of wild honey was also no small thing.

Ishton, all unknowing, was the first to suggest they retrieve a store of honey from the cave once more.

"Better to keep moving," Carnoviste said. "Don't gamble our lives for sweetness and a warm pool."

Darkness around the band council, the moon shrouded behind drifting clouds. They sat in shadow and dared not risk a fire.

"The White Eyes are across the river," Gouyen spoke up. She sat on a moss-grown rock, her slave boy kneeling at her feet. "We've had a long walk," Gouyen continued. "A rest can only do us good."

"It's a ghost place," Carnoviste said. "Your own brother disappeared there without a sign. What if someone else gets witched?"

"I dreamed of Nantan," she told them.

Everyone was taken aback that she would speak the name of the dead. ⋅

"Your words are careless," Carnoviste accused.

"I knew my words before I spoke them."

"Only a fool or witch invites the dead."

"Why should we fear Nantan's ghost? His Power was our shield."

"Then honor his spirit. Leave him at peace in the House of Ghosts."

"I never believed the bear killed my brother. A man with his Power? No bear could harm him. Before we left the Camp of the Warm Springs, my brother came to me in a dream. He told me to search for him in the hidden place."

Denali tensed where he sat in the council circle. He was instantly grateful for the darkness.

"I sent my slave boy to all the canyons and peaks," Gouyen went on. "We searched and searched, but I was wrong. I thought Nantan wanted me to seek him in the flesh, but the dream meant that my shadow should look for his in the Other World."

The face of the moon appeared out of clouds that parted like a veil.

Gouyen stared at the People in the moonlight, some still visibly upset she'd dared to speak the name, and her eyes settled at last on Denali.

"We have our Healer with his Power over the hive. Let's take our small joys where we may still find them.

The People deserve something sweet to cleanse the taste of these bitter days. What's sweeter than honey?"

* * *

All the band was set on savoring again the wild honey, even Carnoviste's wives and younger sons. Finally the chief relented. He feared arousing suspicion by too adamant a protest. In the end he judged the lesser danger was to send the Healer back into the cave.

* * *

A procession of women carrying ollas and buckskin bags followed the warriors up the rise. Children raced each other on the slope. Walking behind Ishton, Denali would reach out to his brother in the tsoch on her back and tease the baby, making him squeal with delight. Denali did his best to ignore Gouyen at their heels, the wise woman marching with a staff made of an ocotillo stalk.

When they reached the rim, Carnoviste laid out the rawhide cord. Denali sat his rifle in the grass and picked up the end of the cord bound to the stick.

"You should be holding the rope with us," Estoni told him. "Not breaking our backs on the other end."

"He's grown tall," Carnoviste said, "but he's still thin as a reed, light as comb."

"A young boy would be lighter."

"Afraid your strength will fail you, warrior?" Denali asked.

Estoni snorted. "I could hold you up by myself. It's just not worth the trouble. Why don't we send one of the chief's little sons?"

"Because our Healer has Power over the hive," Gouyen answered.

Denali studied the wise woman where she leaned on her staff at the cliff ledge.

"The bees wouldn't sting him last time," she said. "Let them welcome him again if his Power is true."

The sun sank low and fired the far wooded ridge with a green fire.

Carnoviste bent and picked up the rope. "Before we lose the light," he said.

* * *

When Denali dangled before the opening, he called out for them to stop. All the way down, there had been a great unease within him. Now hanging beside the cave he realized it was the silence that so disturbed him. No sound came from the dark cave mouth. Where was the hum of life? The hive slept.

He took a long breath, then reached out and pulled himself inside.

He stood in the dark and the quiet, letting his eyes adjust. After a while he saw the figure at rest against the comb, hundreds of bees motionless on the corpse.

Wax cells dotted the face and body. Like a strange fungal growth. Comb wrapped itself about the dead man, incorporating him into the living walls, ears and nostrils filled with confection behind layers of wax. Comb sealed his lips and the bear hide he wore had become his cerement.

A bee appeared out of the wound in the medicine man's eye. It took flight like proof of the ancient ritual of bugonia.

Denali heard Carnoviste calling, asking if all was well. He gathered himself and shouted back that he was fine, then he stepped toward the corpse.

A handful of bees stirred and flew reeling about, careening in what seemed a drunken daze. The finely-haired masses on the walls remained still, but Denali could see them moving on the body, slowly awakening to the stranger's presence.

"Don't sting," he told them, just as he'd commanded beforetime.

He stared into that hexagonal gaze.

And should he stir? A finger twitch. That head, canted to the side, righting itself of a sudden with a snap of comb, then meeting his eyes. One arm broken free, reaching out a hand in mute accusation, the mellified man staggering forward in revenge. Denali would surely throw himself out the cave opening.

He shook his head clear of demented dreams and looked about the chamber.

Time to gather honey.

The People wished to eat.

He went to the entrance and reached out and took the rope, untying the buckskin bag that was bound to the stick, and let the rope dangle free. Then he took the bag and stepped to a wall of comb, as far from the corpse as possible in the confines of the little cave.

He reached to break off a section of comb. Then stopped.

He stood in deep conflict. Carnoviste had instructed him to fill the bag and send it up. It would divert all suspicion from the cave for good. No one among them would dream their Healer capable of such madness as to serve them the sweetness of death. Not even Gouyen would believe him so willing to witch them all. It had surprised Denali when Carnoviste told him to do it—the chief caring more for his son's safety than the danger it might bring the People.

It had to be done.

Denali snapped the comb from the wall and the bees faintly stirred. The honey slowly ran down his fingers and the grooves of his palm. He rubbed his thumb and fingertip together, the golden substance between them, and thought how sweet death must taste on the tongue but so bitter in the belly.

And he thought of Ishton and all his brothers and the maiden Jacali.

Then he cast the comb from his hand and it fell at the feet of the medicine man. He would gather no death.

Once more he stared at the corpse. He stretched out a

hand, hesitated, then gripped the dead man's Izze-kloth, the cord to which the medicine bundle was tied, and when he broke the comb that bound it, a great many bees took flight all around him. Denali held the leather bag and sweat ran down his brow.

He opened the bundle and peered inside and there was his eagle bone flute, snapped in half, and there was the little skull of what could only be a bear foetus. He picked up the skull and held it on his palm a long moment, studying the strange totem. Curiously malformed. Something uncanny about its shape. But why should it be familiar?

The first bee stung his neck, a needle of sudden pain, and he dropped the skull on the cave floor.

It startled him more than it hurt, but Denali sensed he had to hurry. He threw down the medicine bundle and turned back to the entrance and reached out for the rope. Another stinger pierced his side and he shouted, "Haul me up!"

Denali straddled the stick.

A dark cloud poured forth from the entrance. Slowly he rose toward the top, hundreds of enraged bees circling him.

He gripped the rope staring up at the rim, so high above, and took their stings over and again and didn't cry out, though his grip wavered on the rope, his strength sapped, and they stung him all the more, so that he dangled there with one arm hugging the rope to him, slumped forward, and he didn't cry out, head bent low and staring down at the broken scree, so far to fall, and the great humming cloud had its way with him and still he wouldn't cry out.

* * *

By the time Carnoviste gripped his arm and pulled him up over the ledge, Denali had been stung hundreds of times.

Ishton sent Tsaltey-koo running down the slope with the baby in her arms, should the swarm continue its attack, but now the bees fled, retreating back into the mouth of the cave as if their sovereign had called them home. Ishton rushed to Denali. She began pinching his flesh about the stingers and plucking them out one by one.

"Can you breathe?" she asked.

His eyes were swollen to thin slits. He saw the crowd of panicked onlookers in the sunset featureless as shadows before him.

"I can breathe," he said. In truth he could feel a tightening about his throat like an invisible hand slowly strangling him.

"Where has your Power gone, young Healer?" Gouyen asked. She stepped toward him.

He turned in the direction of her voice and saw her like a tree walking. "There's a sickness in the hive," he choked out. "The comb was black and rotten. The honey was bad."

"You tasted of it?"

He shook his head.

"Then how do you know it's bad?"

Now he could only whisper. "I saw it wasn't good for the People to eat."

His eyes had swollen fully shut now, darkness his world entire.

CHAPTER SEVEN

The company rode through the mountain pass, high rock walls above them on either side radiating the day's heat, echoing hoofclops of horses and packmules. Dolores halted her mount and paused there in the stone breach and look back at the sierras they were leaving behind, the world that was closed off to her. Then she turned and followed the others.

They left Carretas Pass and the high country and descended out upon the llano. A western wind swept over that arid expanse. Across the distance the trailing smoke of a train. Clusters of cattle on the grassland, keeping near the windmills that stood so far away they appeared as toys turning upon the tabletop of a miniature simulacrum.

They were headed for a stand of mountains beyond the llano and not far from the U.S. border. Reports had circulated in recent months of Apache sightings on ranches below the desolate Sierra Las Espuelas. With Dolores unable to find the trail to the stronghold mountain, Cain's objectives turned to the band said to be rustling cattle along the border. "Last word of em was six months back," Cain told the company. "Some boys from the Diamond A found their camp on Big Hatchet in New Mexico. Couple of bucks had come up from the border ridin steers, if you can believe that. These steers were in the camp when they found it, rawhide over their hooves. Apaches had run off with some horses when they seen the cowboys comin. But like I say, this was six, seven months back. It ain't no sure thing, but it's the best lead we got."

Cain led them north toward a heatshimmer on the horizon. A trembling at the edge of forever. The riders carried on, drained from constant travel and punishing trails and not least of all the long night among the ruins. To a soul their sleep had been given to strange dreams in that place. In the morning they'd agreed to avoid such dwellings thereafter should they encounter the like again.

Cain alone seemed tireless. He led them at a brisk pace, though he seemed to fall in and out of a reverie, the flatland swallowing up the riders and driving Cain deeper within himself. Twice Mosby spoke and twice Cain didn't answer. Then Mosby reached out and touched his shoulder. The sergeant turned to him with a look of unrecognition on his face, an instant before it passed and he gave a nod, returning from whatever far country his mind roved.

On the plain that night encamped at a desert well they made a small fire and took their supper. They ate without savor in the way of weary men, an unwelcome but necessary task.

A windmill revolved slowly above the stock tank, a steady creak of gears. Dolores kneeled by the murk of the pool in the earthen tank and wet a bandana and twisted the cloth, straining it out, and she washed the dust from her face and neck. She rose and stared out at the llano. Empty and blue under the moonlight. Jubal had told her that long ago the plain was an ancient seafloor. She wondered what blind creatures once swam those depths, translucent bodies at home in darkness, what such hearts as theirs felt at last when the sea had forsaken them and they lay under the sun, scattered upon the burning plain.

Rourke shifted his weight where he sat before the fire. "My ass is all chewed to hell. That saddle's hard as a rock."

"Hell," Mosby said. "I been ridin so long my ass is just one big callus."

"Mine too," Endicott told him. "I could hump the whole temperance union bare-assed in a hailstorm and not feel a thing."

Rourke shook his head. "Got to have a stiff drink just thinkin about puttin the spurs to one of them prune-faced bitties."

They laughed.

Mosby turned from the conversation and looked back at the sergeant where he stood with the caballada, patting Black Answer's side while the horse bent to crop grass. The dark form of the man and horse stood two dimensional, chimeric against the moonlit sky, and when Black Answer raised his head, Cain softly whispered something in his ear.

Cain struck a match with his thumbnail and lit a cigarette.

Mosby rose from the fire and walked out to join him. "You got another one of them smokes?"

Cain tossed him the pack. Mosby took a cigarette and leaned close and lit it from Cain's burning match and they stood smoking and looking out at the dark plain.

"I like a country you can see what's comin before it gets here," Mosby said.

Cain grunted.

They smoked. It was a long while before Cain said, "Listen, Mo. You don't need to be here for the end of this. Why don't you take that Apache girl, escort her and McKenna's Mexican back to the valley? You'll get full pay."

"I go home when you go, Sergeant."

"I ain't got no home to go back to. Neither of us do. But it ain't too late for you. Take your pay and head up to Texas, buy a piece of land and find yourself a good woman. You can still make a life."

"Come on now, Sergeant. You and me just wasn't built for that."

A ragged quality in Cain's voice now. "What we done at the creek back there, I never should've made you part of it."

"I understand you got to send a message. I know you thought it needed doin."

Cain dropped his cigarette and stamped it out under his boot-heel. "What if you'd caught a stray one and died in them mountains? My mind would just cut loose. If you got killed because of me draggin you to this godforsaken country, I couldn't stand it."

"We been in worse scrapes."

"I'm afraid, Mo."

Mosby frowned in the dark. "What you afraid of, Sergeant?"

"I'm afraid somethin bad's goin to happen."

"Apaches don't worry me none. Hellfire, I'm ready for a real fight."

"Might not be Apaches that put the hurt on us. Could be somethin worse."

"Who else is there? Ain't no hard feelins between anybody in our outfit that I know of."

"I got this sense, I can't explain it. Like there's somethin waitin on us. Bidin its time before it kills us all, our bunch and the Apaches too, kills everything that moves and just ends it."

Mosby couldn't think how to reply. The Dipper hung in the Great Bear, pointing the way north, cold as the silence around them.

"You think about what I said," Cain told him finally. "Take that girl and get out before it's too damn late."

* * *

No sound save the horses and mules cropping grass, all just as it should have been. Thinking back on it later Mosby couldn't have said what woke him in the night.

Mosby opened his eyes and saw him. Anyone's guess how long Cain had been standing over Dolores in the circle of sleepers, peering down at the girl's face as though lost in some dark contemplation.

"Sergeant?" Mosby lay in his bedding, looking up.

Cain was stripped to the waist. He held the kalis out before him, unsheathed and gleaming in the moonlight, the blade poised over Dolores's chest. Save Cain and Mosby, all others about the dying fire lay asleep. Cain's watch was the first of the night.

Mosby rose and stepped forward in his stocking feet. "Put that away," Mosby whispered. "You hear me, Sergeant? You put it away now."

Dolores stirred in her bedding as Mosby turned Cain to face away from her. She gave them a troubled look.

The men came alive. Jubal rose with his pistol ready. "What the hell's the matter?" he demanded.

Cain seemed to wake of a sudden. As though pulled from a trance. He glanced at Wormwood in his hand, puzzled how it had gotten there.

Mosby met his eyes. Saw the confusion and fear.

"The sergeant thought he seen somethin," Mosby told the others. "Out there in the grass. It was just a owl come swoopin down, huntin him a midnight snack. Ain't that right, Sergeant?"

"Yessir," Cain said. "Just a owl."

"You sure?" Jubal asked.

Cain nodded. He looked defeated, strangely frail.

"Go on, get some sleep, Sergeant," Mosby told him. "I'll take the watch from here."

Cain found the sheath near his bedroll and picked it up and sheathed the kalis. "Thank you, Mo," he said, almost too quiet to hear.

"Don't you worry about it," Mosby said. "You just need some rest is all."

* * *

They rode out with sunrise and headed northwest where creosote and nopal dotted the llano. Soon the morning's cool gave way to oppressive heat and sweat glistened on the flanks of the horses and sweat stung Jubal's eyes and soaked through his shirt. The Sierra Las Espuelas hovered rippling in a heatwave. Phantasmic above the western horizon. They could see El Medio rising to the north, the Carretas Plain separating the spectral mountains.

At noon they were riding through country owned by the Palomas Land and Cattle Company. The enormous ranch stretched along the international border from El Paso to the Sonora stateline, running some thirty miles wide north and south. The American investors who owned the ranch possessed legal title to the Espuelas, but the truth of the matter was that the mountain belonged to the Apaches. No vaquero would choose to venture there alone.

Rolling silver clouds passed before the sun and for a time the company rode under pleasant shadows. Onward toward the Espuelas. Jubal stared out across the llano where shafts of sunlight broke through gaps in the cloudcover and moved like searchbeams over the distant sierra.

Later in the day they crossed a small valley and reached the base of the mountain. Immense billows of smoke rose in the southwestern sky and drifted eastward, the product of a conflagration scorching a path of cinder and ash across the Sierra Madre. The blaze had originated not far from Colonia Oaxaca in the Bavispe Valley. Now the fire was approaching the Carretas Plain driven by strong winds, perhaps twenty-five miles from the company's position. Cain paid it no mind, though more than a few of the men cast a nervous eye on the inferno's progress.

They rode along the foot of the mountain till they came to the mouth of Las Piedras Canyon and Cain turned and rode up through the high stone corridor. The canyon bottom wound through sandstone. Heaps of bear scat, tracks of predators great and small. The walls rose to heights of three hundred feet shadowing the canyon floor and dwarfing the riders and the trees that grew from the tortured ground, pinion and silver leaf oak and scrub mesquite. A hawk watched from its nest on a ledge above.

Cain led them into the corridors of death and he set a quickened pace, this sense of urgency in him now, drawing him on. Like a traveler coming to the end of a long journey. He anticipated the possibility of lookouts on the rimrock but nonetheless took no heed, for the deep shadows of the canyon walls were sure to conceal their movement. Darkness was his shield. As for Jubal he was prepared to follow Cain wherever he led.

When they passed an off-shooting branch of the canyon, Cain spotted the tracks. He halted the company and sat his horse looking over the trail. A mule train, all of them shod. The trail emerged from the tributary of the canyon and headed up the main branch of Las Piedras.

"What you reckon, Sergeant?" Mosby asked.

"Smugglers," Cain said. "Maybe candelia wax, maybe booze. Takin a load up the Cajon Bonito."

He studied the tracks a moment longer and decided on a count. One man riding point, one on drag. Eight mules total, six of them laden with goods.

"Leastwise they'll run into any bronco Apaches before we do," Mosby said. "Give us a warnin."

"I'll take any notice we can get," Cain told him. "This is surprise country up ahead."

He led them out following the trail of the contrabandos.

The horses smelled the water before they saw it and quickened to a slow trot, hooves crushing shards of broken sandstone, and when they came on the waterhole, they startled away a coyote that had been drinking there. Thick brush about the seep. A thin trickle from a crack in moss-grown rock. The contrabandos had watered their packtrain and now the little pool was much depleted but beginning to fill again. The tracks departing the spring were fresh.

The men got down and took turns letting the horses and mules drink.

Black Answer had his fill and Cain loosed the latigo to let him blow. "Hang back," he told the others. "I'm ridin ahead. Goin to have a talk with them smugglers, find out if they seen any sign of broncos."

Cain tightened the latigo and swung up into the saddle.

"They ain't likely too eager for conversation," Mosby said.

"I'll ask em nice and polite. But if you hear me get off a shot, you come runnin."

Jubal led his horse forward. "I'm goin with you," he told Cain.

* * *

Cain and Jubal rode up the canyon, rifles drawn, gaining on the contrabandos. Hoofclops sounded on sandstone. After a while they came to a blind bend in the course of the canyon and they halted as one and sat their horses.

Impossible to see what waited beyond the bend.

They listened. Dead quiet.

Jubal looked at Cain. "What do you think?"

"I think if you stick your head out there, you're liable to get it blown clean off."

"I think maybe you're right."

"Ain't no maybe to it. They heard us comin and one of em's holed up with a rifle."

Cain swung down from the saddle and gave his horse's reins to Jubal. Pressing his back to the canyon wall he stepped toward the bend.

"Hold your fire," Cain shouted. "We ain't federales or banditos either one." He switched to Spanish. "Alto el fuego. No policia!"

Silence.

Then a voice called out in English, "Who the hell are you then?"

"We're huntin Apache camps," Cain shouted. "You goin to shoot me if I step out?"

"I ain't goin to shoot you. Come on out."

Cain laughed. "That's just what I'd say if I was plannin on gut-shootin a son of a bitch."

"Buddy, I might gut-shoot a bastard if he had it comin, but I ain't no liar."

"Spoken like a honest man." Cain stepped out into the open, bold as you please. He saw a man holding a rifle climb down from a position among a cluster of boulders. Farther up the canyon a second man stood with the mule train.

Cain turned to Jubal and nodded.

Jubal walked the horses up to Cain and got down and they stood waiting for the man with the rifle to approach. He was a big man with blond stubble on his cheeks. He went up to Cain and offered his hand.

"You can call me Roy," the contrabando said. They shook. "I figured for sure you was a federale lookin for another mordida. Already paid them suckers off once, but down here it's always more, more, more."

"There's worse things to run into than federales," Cain told him. "You're lucky we ain't a pack of bronco Apaches."

Roy shook Jubal's hand. "The broncos don't bother us none. They ain't about to risk gettin their supply cut off."

"What supply?" Jubal asked.

"Me and Pablo leave em a case on every run. Damn good tequila."

Roy explained they were headed up to the Cajon Bonito which they would follow north across the borderline. It was their sixth run and they'd never had any trouble yet. "Apaches leave us alone, long as we pay the toll."

"Where do you leave it?" Jubal asked.

"In a hollowed-out spot by a side canyon," Roy said. "If you boys are up here huntin Apaches, just the two of you, y'all got bigger huevos than me. What is it, they finally run off with too much of your cattle down there?"

"They took somethin belongs to this man," Cain told him.

"We're not alone," Jubal said. "We've got some men followin behind us."

"You're goin to need em," Roy said. "I hear plenty

156

of talk about Apaches rustlin cattle down on the plain. Rumor is they got a hide camp somewhere in the canyons and they're partnered up with an American who sells the hides that their squaws tan."

"A smuggler," Jubal said.

Roy stared at him. The rifle barrel rested on his shoulder. "Yeah. A smuggler."

Jubal held his gaze.

Roy turned his head and spat. "But I ain't the one. There's a hell of a lot more money in tequila and anyway, we all got our scruples. Even me."

"But you believe the rumor about the American?" Jubal asked.

"Hell, no. What white man would buddy up with wild Apaches? His hide would be the first one they'd stake out. But I know for a fact there's an Apache camp somewhere in these canyons. Ain't about to go huntin it though, I don't care how many head of cattle they run off with. I wish you luck. They're a damned nuisance for a cattleman. You need to kill all you can before there gets to be any more of em."

* * *

Cain and Jubal rode with the contrabandos as far as the drop-off point for the case of tequila they'd leave the Apaches. It was a small cavity in the canyon wall, in times past the den of a mountain lion by the looks of the bones scattered about the interior. The contrabandos unstrapped a case from one of the mules and left it there in the shadowed opening.

Up ahead Jubal could see a side canyon coming down from the northwest. He shook hands with Roy and Pablo and thanked them for the information they'd provided, then the smugglers continued along their way.

Jubal and Cain waited for the company to catch them up.

Half an hour later Mosby rode into view with the others following single file behind him. He halted his mount before Cain.

"You talk to em?" Mosby asked.

"Just like I told you," Cain said. "You want to know somethin all you got to do is ask polite."

"They seen any broncos?"

"Maybe pointed us in the right direction."

Cain and Jubal mounted up. They led the company through the winding course of the side canyon, riding through shadows that aspired to the mantle of night. Several miles later they reached a crude fence of ocotillo stalks lashed with rawhide and set into the earth. Cain gave Jubal a look—they were getting close.

Jubal got down and began clearing a path, pulling up the long stalks. He motioned to Hector. "Stay here with Dolores and the mules," Jubal told the segundo.

Hector and Dolores dismounted. The segundo drew his rifle from the saddle-scabbard and chambered a round while the girl began seeing to the packmules.

When the way was clear, Cain and Jubal proceeded

afoot and leading their horses, going out in advance of Mosby and the others for safety. They moved through a shadowland at the bottom of the steep-walled passage.

A quarter mile up from the fence they rounded a bend and came to where the canyon forked again, the left branch running out of sight, the right branch widening out and making a gradual ascent up the far wall of the canyon. To the right where the canyon bottom was at its widest they saw the rancheria. Half a dozen stone houses and several brush arbors. An emaciated stream trickled down a portion of the canyon bottom and through the camp.

In the open fork the shadow of the canyon wall fell short and they moved at the edge of darkness. Too close—Bardo raised his head into the light and the sun caught the silver bit in the horse's mouth and flashed.

A moment later a rifleshot cracked.

Cain swore and they ran with the horses toward a cluster of boulders. It was a section of canyon wall that had broken off long ago and fallen in a jumbled heap, many boulders the size of a small house. They took cover in the rocks. They gripped their rifles and reins and tried to keep the horses' heads low. A bullet went whining off a boulder, sending chips of rock flying, even as the echo of the first shot still roared down the branches of the canyon, and it was a long moment before the sound of the second discharge reached them.

Jubal crouched watching the rancheria. Figures emerged from the brush arbors and the curious stone houses that were unlike anything he'd seen Apaches construct. He saw them running with rifles in hand. He saw others dashing to the little corral and swinging up bareback on mules while a few head of stolen cattle stood indifferent and hungry-looking.

Another bullet struck the rocks. The horses snorted and stamped, but the men kept a tight hold on the reins.

The Apaches were retreating up a trail on the sloping far wall of the canyon, hellbent on reaching the rim. Cain watched them making their run. "We got to hit em before they get up top," he shouted. "Or else we're cooked."

They had no choice but to make a charge and attempt to gain the high ground. It was a deadly gamble—the sniper had a position somewhere along the rim and they'd be taking fire out in the open. Yet Cain reasoned the greater peril lay in allowing the other braves to reach the top and begin firing down on them en masse. He'd sooner risk the lone sniper for a chance at seizing the rimrock.

They sheathed the rifles and swung into their saddles. Black Answer and Bardo ran out from the safety of cover.

The company had heard the shots and mounted up as well. Mosby came racing around the bend, the mercenaries and Moroni Thayne hard after him.

Cain splashed through the shallow stream and charged into the rancheria. Pistol in one hand, reins in the other. Dust kicked up at Black Answer's hooves, then

160

a rifleshot rang out from above. Jubal followed where Cain led.

A line of women and children were running up the broad trail that led to the rim while a handful of braves crouched with rifles and revolvers and fired into the onrushing mercs. The braves covered the retreat of their families. Camp dogs barked and howled all in a havoc.

Jubal shot a brave and saw the man go down and then they were galloping into the midst, firing and turning the horses and firing again. Mosby and the mercenaries joined them.

Bullets ricocheted off stone. Growling curs snapped at the legs of the horses. Some of those trying to hold them off were just young boys with rifles taller than they were. A boy followed Moroni Thayne with his sights. He shot Moroni's horse and the dun fell, spilling the Mormon from the saddle, then in the next instant the boy was himself cut down, his young body trampled, spasming under the crush of hooves. Moroni scurried behind one of the little stone houses. Cow-hides were pegged-out and drying all about him. He pressed his back to the stone wall and ejected the empty magazine in his .45, then took a full mag from his belt and slammed it home. He released the locked slide and chambered a fresh round.

The braves pulled back up the high ground with the fleeing women and children.

* * *

Zunde stood aiming his .30-30 at one of the mounted White Eyes. He followed the horseman's movements with his sights. A slug exploded into Zunde's hip just as he pulled the trigger and missed. He dropped to the ground. Clenched his teeth, cursed in Spanish. When he glanced at the wound, he knew he was done.

Tactical mistakes played over in his mind, each one unforgivable. He'd had a lone sentry watching both forks of the canyon, but all along he should've kept a pair of youths posted farther out above either branch. And why had he been such a fool, allowing the women to spend their days in the subcamp below? The band slept every night in the main camp high on the rim where safety was assured, but it was a dry camp and water must be carried. The women preferred the camp below. They'd dammed the stream in the canyon bottom with rocks and mud to create the little pool and there they worked the hides of butchered cattle, pegging them out under the sun. Every day they tanned new hides which they'd trade to their friends from the reservation for weapons and ammunition and good tobacco, many fine things the sierras could never have given them.

Zunde lay wounded but still unsurrendered. He shouldered his rifle and worked the lever. He fired and levered another round and fired again and all the while singing his deathsong above the pain and the din of battle. Finally the rifle was empty. He threw it down and pulled the revolver from his belt. He waited for them to come in close.

A horse came galloping down the slope behind him. Zunde turned and through the dust he could see a brave low against the pinto's neck. Heedless of danger, like a vision of youth's reckless pride. The rider darted past, then wheeled about, slowing in front of the bleeding warrior, and Zunde saw it was his son on the horse's back.

"Grab the tail," Chatto yelled.

Zunde took hold of the horse's long tail and twisted it about his wrist. Chatto gave the mount his heels and they went dragging Zunde up the slope. A pair of White Eyes chased after them and Zunde snapped off three quick shots, firing his pistol with his free hand, teeth gritted against the pain.

Then there was the sound of fire from above.

* * *

They were cutting down the last of the braves when Cain saw Ives jolt in the saddle, then heard the report of a distant rifleshot. Ives fell backward with his boot caught in a stirrup, his horse continuing up the trail.

Half a dozen rifleshots rang out. Cain caught a glint of light, then another. There along the rim, sunlight flashing off rifle barrels. Apaches were crouched with rifles seven hundred feet above the canyon bottom. He'd believed there was only the one look-out firing down on them—and so there had been at first—yet now there were others. The snipers weren't part of the retreating band, which still hadn't reached the top, but Cain had no time to ponder their sudden appearance. The rifle fire was too heavy, too many shooters, and he knew the mercenaries could never fight their way to the rim before they'd be cut to pieces.

He turned his horse. "Shooters on the rim," he shouted and rode back down the slope. "Turn back—they got too many shooters up top."

The mercs were chasing an Apache who held the tail of a pinto pony, the horse dragging him up the slope, and then the bullets were falling all about them. Jubal and the Americans turned their horses. They galloped down the grade and through the cluster of dwellings and they were heading for the bend and the southwestern fork of the canyon. A high empty plateau divided the two forks and they needed to put it between them and the Apaches. They rode all out. Thundering hooves, shots over fading echoes. Moroni Thayne stepped out from behind one of the stone houses waving his arms. Jubal reined in, slowing, and Moroni swung on behind him. A bullet pocked the stone wall, missing Jubal's head by a hand's breadth, and he booted the horse and they were running again.

At the head of the retreat Putnam gouged his mount's sides with the Spanish rowels. They spun like evil stars on the ends of his spurs. Blood dripped from the silver points. The mercenary stiffened of a sudden, his back arching, then he fell rearward in what seemed to him the slowest of descents as if through an invisible aether thick as jelly, a small eternity staring skyward, and the white disc of the sun blazed so bright his vision dimmed all about the edges of the orb. His flesh was numb, hands unfeeling when the reins slipped free, then his boots slid slowly from the stirrups.

Rourke had no time to react. His horse was directly behind Putnam's and he saw the man's back go rigid. Then Putnam fell and tumbled off the saddle and there was nothing Rourke could do. A split second and his horse trampled over Putnam and they left the broken corpse in drifting dust. Putnam's own mount went racing down the canyon without a rider.

Now Rourke led the retreat. When a bullet struck his horse's neck, he rode on, blood pouring from the wound, the horse snorting and shaking its head, then two more shots found their target, one in the horse's chest and the other its left flank. Those pumping legs fell out from under. The horse hit the ground and its chest plowed forward in a cloud of dust. Instantly Rourke was out of the saddle and on his feet. He glanced back at the riders speeding his way full tilt. The rifleshots that had killed his mount were still sounding. He started running, glancing over his shoulder and readying himself as the first horsemen approached, only one chance to get it right, then he saw Slotkin coming up alongside him with his hand out-stretched and the stirrup empty.

Rourke made his move.

He grasped Slotkin's hand and jumped up, jamming his boot into the stirrup, and swung on behind Slotkin.

They left Rourke's downed mount writhing in blood, pain-crazed eyeballs rolling upwards in their sockets, and you could hear the beast shrieking its agony up the canyon.

Slotkin's own horse took a hit and stumbled. The left frontleg snapped. The Apache rifles thundered. When the mount went down hard on its side, Rourke fell free and rolled, but Slotkin's leg was pinned under the horse's weight. The pain was so bad Slotkin feared his own leg was broken.

Slotkin cursed. Rage and terror. Trapped like any other animal. He knew the Apaches wouldn't kill him. Not right off. They'd leave him there to struggle and suffer. Should he manage to free himself, only then would they end it with a single well-placed shot from above.

Rourke rose to his feet. He looked at Slotkin where the man lay pinned.

"Help me," Slotkin yelled.

Rourke turned and started running once more.

Slotkin screamed, "You son of a—"

The running man whirled about and flailed like a spastic. Blood misted from exit wounds. Rourke fell facedown and his run was over as the Apache rifles spoke again.

Slotkin clawed at the hard earth beneath his leg. The horse lay dying. Its breaths were strained gasps and Slotkin could hear the air blowing out its great nostrils and he kicked the horse with his good leg and cursed it and begged it to rise, but the horse wouldn't rise.

Then he looked up and saw Black Answer coming. Cain extended his hand and Slotkin thought he meant to catch him up, the sergeant not comprehending that he was pinned, and despite the impossibility of it Slotkin found himself reaching out to take the offered hand. Then he saw the pistol and the black round bore of the barrel. Slotkin smiled. Cain shot him in the head and rode on past and Slotkin fell back with a bullet in his right temple and the smile still on his lips.

The company rode down the canyon, three of their number lying dead, shots coming from on high and echoing forever.

* * *

Zunde dropped his gun midway up the slope. He gripped the horse's tail with both hands. When the pinto reached the rim, Zunde let go and lay gasping, all his strength spent. His leg was covered in blood and dust and the pain was very bad.

Chatto dismounted and dropped down beside him.

"You shouldn't have done that," Zunde told the young warrior.

"I knew that's what you'd say." Chatto shook his head. "How could I let the White Eyes kill my father?"

"My son, your warrior's heart is my pride."

"Can you stand if I help you?"

Zunde didn't answer.

More rifleshots cracked. A handful of young boys and maidens were kneeling at the cliff-edge, firing down into the canyon. Chatto had been with them on the rim, directing their work in the main camp, when the sentry had fired his warning shot.

Of the braves defending the subcamp below only Zunde and Matzus had escaped. Both were hurt. Matzus carried a bullet in his side and another had passed through his shoulder. Zunde scanned the faces of the survivors. A few women kneeled binding wounds with strips of cloth torn from a blanket. He saw his daughters with the other maidens, saw his wives helping load the mules, and he thanked Ussen they'd made it unharmed. They were safe in the main camp, protected by the heights, but they couldn't linger. This camp was dry. They kept a number of waterskins and canteens filled against the necessity of retreat and now the women were gathering water rations and taking meat from the drying racks while children held the mules.

Zunde stared across at Matzus, who sat on a rock letting his wife tend his wounds. The warriors met each other's eyes. Matzus nodded. They knew they'd only slow the retreat. Someone had to hold back the White Eyes long enough for their families to get a head start.

Zunde gripped his son's arm. "The White Eyes will try to reach the rim," he said. "They'll try to circle around and come up the other trail." He nodded toward a grandmother named Natastale where she sat pressing a bloody rag to her belly. "Get a mule. Send Natastale and Matzus to the other trail. Give them rifles and ammunition, tell them to wait in the rocks where they can guard the way up. Ask them if their hearts are strong. Ask them if they're ready to die for the People."

"Let Matzus stay and guard this trail," Chatto said. "Natastale can go and watch the other."

"Leave me your rifle," Zunde told his son.

Chatto shook his head. "You can ride. You won't slow us."

"Take them back to the Blue Mountains. Find Carnoviste and tell him what the White Eyes did here."

"We need you on the retreat. We need you to show us what to do."

"You're a warrior now, my son," Zunde said. "There's nothing left for me to teach you that you don't already know. Watch over your sisters and their mothers. And remember—this has happened today to teach the People there can be no friendship between us and coyotes. Whatever choice you make to protect your people is the right choice. Take them and go."

"There's got to be another way."

"There was never any other way. Leave me the rifle."

Chatto stared at the rim camp, a few wickiups and the cluster of stone houses their trader friends across the border had taught them to build. Some among them still insisted on sleeping in wickiups, afraid to let go of the old ways, but Chatto had embraced the life and hope they'd found there. He looked over the half-finished stone house that was his own construction. Only a short while before, he'd been using the pinto to drag choice rocks into camp, then he would dismount and heft the rocks up onto the wall and set them in place, pleased at the new skills he'd learned and proud of the work's progress. He'd dreamed of all they might accomplish there in time. Now he would build no more and he had no house forever. Chatto rose and pulled his Winchester from the pinto's saddle-scabbard and stood before his father and gave him the rifle.

"Remember, my son," Zunde told him. "The People are yours to protect."

* * *

Cain led them at a gallop back to where the canyon forked. He turned Black Answer and raced up the other branch and they covered a mile without slowing until he was confident they were no longer targets. He drew up and brought the company to a halt. The sharp rise of the mesa that divided the canyons protected them now.

Cain demanded an accounting of wounded and dead.

Three men killed—Putnam, Rourke, Slotkin. None seriously wounded. The company dismounted to inspect their horses for injuries and found them unharmed though all in a lather and much disturbed.

"Red sons of bitches," Oldham said.

Endicott spat. "They goin to pay for this. Ain't they, Cain?"

"Damn right they're goin to pay," Van Zandt said. "I

170

was in the Legion with Putnam. That man saved my life in Morocco. I want fresh scalps."

"We'll take a bushel of scalps," Cain said. "Just got to find another trail up top."

"Head back to the smugglers' drop-off spot," Jubal told them. "Maybe we can find a place where the canyon wall's not so steep. We'll make a climb for it, then circle around on the rim."

Cain shook his head. "Country's too rough that direction. Even if we found a way up, it'd take a day and a half to circle back from there."

"What other option do we have?" Jubal asked.

"There's only two ways up, far as I can see. That trail above the rancheria, which we can damn well rule out, and likely wherever this fork takes us." Cain nodded up the canyon where it rose in a gradual ascent before twisting out of view. "It's a gamble, but I'll lay odds there's a trail to the top further up this branch."

"Who the hell knows what they got waitin for us up there?" Mosby said.

"It's a gamble more ways than one. But otherwise we're stuck down here holdin our peckers while most of the broncos are makin a getaway."

Cain was determined to follow the fork wherever it led, but he wouldn't risk having the entire company taken by surprise again. He gave his reins to Mosby. He ordered them to keep back and let him go well in advance, then he started up the canyon in a kind of loping half-run, the pacing he'd learned from Apache scouts long ago. It would allow a runner to maintain speed and stamina all day with little rest. He ran with his rifle chambered and in his arms. His boots ate the distance and he didn't lose his breath.

Cain ran on.

After a while he did come to a trail that went winding up the canyon wall. Steeper and more rugged than the one the Apaches had taken, but it appeared to lead all the way out onto rimrock.

The slope had drained floodwaters during the summer storms that passed over that region and parts of the trail were narrow and littered with debris. When he neared the rim, Cain got down on his belly and crawled forward to hunker just below where the trail opened onto the mesatop. He needed a look at what was out there, but he didn't feel like getting his head blown off.

He removed his hat and hung it on the rifle barrel. Took a breath. Got ready.

He stretched his arm out and held the rifle far to the side, then raised the hat into view of anyone watching the trail from the mesa. An instant later he popped his head up and looked out across the terrain.

The rifleshot split the air. Cain's decoy Stetson went spinning off the barrel.

He dropped back down. He pressed his back to the rock and ignored the shooter and closed his eyes. He called to mind his brief glimpse of the terrain, committing it to memory. Open ground on the mesatop for a hundred yards, scrub cholla and catclaw. Then a lone stand of boulders, long and narrow like the fingers of a stone giant reaching out of the earth. The Apache had to be hiding somewhere in the rocks.

Cain retrieved his hat where it had landed on the trail. He ran a finger through the hole in the crown, then settled in to wait for the others.

Sometime later he spotted Jubal and Mosby at the head of the company on the trail below. He motioned for them to join him. The pair left their horses with the mercenaries and hiked up the steep grade.

"He's hid in a patch of rocks," Cain said. "Holdin us off while the squaws and little nits put some distance between us. I figure him for one of the wounded. Volunteered to stay and guard the trail while he's busy dyin. Hell, could even be a squaw, but she'll kill you just as dead."

"We could storm him," Jubal said. "Somebody fires a BAR into the rocks while we make a run."

"Only one at a time up here, then it's no cover till you get to the rocks. We could do it, but he'd take a couple of us with him. I wisht that damned mule hadn't gone tumblin with our mortar shells—we could just blast him out."

"We already lost too many men today," Mosby said.

"Then we wait," Cain told them. "Till it gets dark or somebody wants to take a chance he finally bled out. Whichever comes first."

CHAPTER EIGHT

Mosby stripped to the waist. He racked the slide on his .45, chambering a round, and flicked on the safety, then ejected the magazine. He took a single cartridge from the ammo box and thumbed it into the mag and slid the mag back in. Seven plus one. He hoped he'd only need the one.

They'd succeeded in provoking another shot late in the afternoon, but the stand had been silent the rest of the evening and now at full dark Mosby prepared to make his approach. He removed his boots and peeled off his socks, pulled on the pair of moccasins Cain had given him. He took off his hat and started to toss it on the ground, then Moroni Thayne reached out.

"I'll hold it for you."

"Appreciate it," Mosby said and gave him the hat.

"Good luck out there," the Mormon told him.

Mosby stepped up to Cain. The sergeant wouldn't look him in the eye and Mosby didn't understand it. He refused to let himself dwell on the deteriorating state of the sergeant's mind. They would finish the mission and go back home and he'd make sure Cain found help.

It was in Mosby to believe there was no problem that couldn't be fixed, no matter the cause, no matter the damage done. He was sure Cain could be his old self again, but they had to make it home alive.

He gave Cain a salute and held it.

Cain let out a breath. He looked up at last, though his eyes were unfocused, and returned the salute and quickly snapped it off.

Mosby got down on his belly.

Endicott sat cradling the BAR, ready to rise and empty the magazine into the boulders if Mosby drew fire. Mosby nodded at the machine-gunner, then started crawling up the trail, easing out into open terrain. Pistol in hand, cocked and locked.

It was dark enough he knew the only thing that could give him away was movement. He inched forward and paused and waited long intervals before continuing on slowly once more. Finally he'd gone some distance from the trail and he could see the black shape of the boulders against the night sky. He dragged himself on his elbows toward the left flank.

Less than nine miles to the south a ridgeline stood ablaze. The sky glowed. Stars veiled in a dull haze. The fire was moving northwest toward the mouth of Las Piedras and Mosby could smell the smoke thick on the air.

He kept crawling and tried not to think about meeting a scorpion or rattlesnake in the dark. What little vegetation to be found was thorned or spined and it cut the bare skin of his chest and stomach. He ignored a hundred little cuts.

When at last he neared the stand, he rose up and kneeled a long time listening. Nothing. Perhaps a stifled cough from within the rocks. He couldn't be sure.

He flicked the safety off and entered among the boulders. Crouching and holding the .45 close, gripped with both hands, and pausing to listen, then moving ahead on the balls of his feet. He stopped and listened. Silence complete.

He went deeper into the rocks and before he could pause again there was the Apache brave staring right at him, a fleck of starlight in his unblinking eyes, and Mosby almost jerked the trigger. The brave remained motionless. He lay dead with a rifle in his arms. He'd pressed a thick clump of cobwebs to the bullet hole in his side, a natural gauze to soak up the blood, and his right hand still rested over the bloody weavings. Another wound visible high on his left shoulder. Blood had dripped below his position and the rocks were dark and slick with emptied life.

Mosby was about to call out, let the others know they could go ahead and come up the trail. Then he heard the cough.

Somewhere ahead, deeper in the cluster. He moved forward and saw her there in the rocks above him, resting with her back against a high boulder and cradling a rifle, her legs curled beneath her. Like the warrior she'd also stained the rocks with her blood.

Mosby made no noise of any sort, but the woman turned and looked at him.

* * *

Cain kneeled staring up over the rim, watching the darkness.

A burst of light in the boulders, Mosby's .45 barked.

Cain waited. He couldn't breathe. This tightness in his chest. The silence seemed to go on forever, no further shots, but it shouldn't be taking so long—something had to be wrong. Then Mosby's voice carried over the night air, calling out the all-clear.

Cain let out a breath.

* * *

They led the horses onto the rim. Cain went to the stand of rocks leading his horse and Mosby's and carrying Mosby's boots.

"You got that sucker," Cain said.

Mosby sat barefoot on a boulder, holding the moccasins in his hand and watching the glow of the distant fire. Cain tossed him the boots.

"There was two of em," Mosby said. He pulled his socks out of a boot and slipped them on. "A buck who'd already bled out and a squaw about half-dead."

"You done good."

"I done what you asked me to."

"All right," Cain told him.

"All right," Mosby said. He pulled on his left boot.

"What I'm tryin to say, I'm relieved you got the best of em and not the other way around."

Mosby tugged on his other boot and rose. "I know what you sayin, Sergeant."

They still had to take out the Apache guarding the opposite trail. Cain told Jubal to wait with the main company, then he took Oldham and Endicott and they set out afoot through the dark with Endicott lugging the BAR.

A long while later Jubal heard a single rifleshot, then the Browning's full-auto roar.

* * *

Jubal took Moroni Thayne and went back for Dolores and Hector where they'd left them waiting with the packmules.

"Don't shoot," he called out in Spanish as they neared the place. "It's me."

Hector stepped out of the dark lowering his rifle. "Put your gun away, Little Bird," he told Dolores. "Your papa has come for us."

They led the packmules through the canyon and the rancheria's lower camp and there was no sound save hoofclops and the trickling stream. The dead lay where they'd fallen, Apache and mercenary alike. Dolores looked on those dark forms and rode past.

Jubal led them up the cleared trail and into the rim camp where there stood a barbed-wire corral and yet other stone houses. Nowhere else in their journey had they seen Apaches erect such permanent structures. The walls were made of stone and adobe, the roofs of hewn wooden beams and brush. Next to one house rested a crude sledge for the hauling of meat from the butcher's ground to the drying racks.

Jubal hailed the camp. The mercs lay about the central firepit, dry brush burning, crackling. They'd take what sleep they could while awaiting first light to begin trailing the Apaches who'd escaped. Cain on watch, his back to the light. He cradled some object in a burlap sack about the size of a bowling ball.

Moroni spat, looking over the camp. "I didn't know Indins ever lived in houses like people do. Don't that beat all?"

Jubal dismounted. "This band was givin up the old ways. Becomin somethin else."

Cain spoke from the shadows. "I'd like to meet up with the son of a bitch taught these reds to be masons."

"My guess is their middleman," Jubal said. "Whoever brokers the horses and cattle they rustle, the cowhides they tan. The one who traded em good rifles and barbed wire."

"Just a den of damn thieves," Oldham said.

Some of the men rose from their bedding to help with the packmules.

Endicott took a pair of shovels from the pack of one of

the mules. "Any of you lazy bastards feel like givin me a hand? I'm fixin to go down there and bury our boys."

"Why don't you carve em a headstone while you're at it?" Cain asked. "Engrave it with their favorite scripture."

"You expect me to leave them boys to rot?"

"Sleep while you can," Cain said. "Tomorrow we're ridin hard. You want to make things right by the dead? Rest up and be ready to put the hurt on those Apaches for what they done."

"Our boys still deserve a decent burial."

"Ground's too hard. You get a layer of dirt on em, the coyotes'll dig em up the minute you turn your back."

"I can't sleep thinkin on it. Them rottin out there, no better than Apaches."

"Don't waste your strength."

Mosby rose and took a shovel from Endicott. "I'll go," he said.

"I'll spell one of you," Moroni Thayne said.

"Much appreciated," Endicott told them.

Cain laughed and shook his head. He rubbed his hand over the burlap bundle in his lap with a curious affection. "Do what you got to do. But we ain't stoppin for a siesta tomorrow."

Mosby, Endicott, and Moroni set out with the shovels back down the trail.

Dolores walked out to the edge of the light. Littered about the camp were small obsidian nodules shaped like teardrops. The composition of the Espuelas wasn't volcanic and their presence there in such profusion was a mystery. Dolores stooped and picked up a handful and walked out to the rim. She stood over the canyon and looked to the south where flames were engulfing pines in sudden flares that vanished behind walls of smoke. A haze obscuring the stars. She let the beads slip from her hand one by one and fall down into the canyon.

* * *

All through the night Chatto led his people on the path of escape. They were mounted on mules and the little Mexican ponies they'd taken from the rim corral. Small children rode tied to their mothers and grandmothers, the wounded enduring without complaint.

Among them only two other young braves were experienced enough to be called novice warriors. The boys argued with Chatto that they should stay behind at a suitable place in the trail and pick off the White Eye scouts while the others went ahead. They were eager to attempt it. Chatto believed it would cost them their lives and serve only to slow the White Eyes, not turn them back. "Can the People spare the loss of more braves?" he asked. The boys' silence was answer enough. In the end they followed Chatto's counsel and remained with the refugees.

They would seek Carnoviste's band in the sierras and take the forest passage. He hoped to find Carnoviste at the Camp of the Warm Springs, a place they'd long favored, and he suspected it would be so. He'd seen the dried scalps bound to the saddles of the White Eyes. It meant the killers had surely ridden northeast through the sierras before coming to Las Espuelas. He reasoned that Carnoviste's band would likely have withdrawn to the southwest, the direction of the warm springs, in an effort to put distance between themselves and the killer White Eyes.

That night began the labor of a pregnant woman whose husband was killed in the attack. The White Eyes with their bearded faces like bears were stalking close behind and there could be no margin to relent, not even for the most vital demands. The gray mother of the woman's dead husband chose to stay behind with her. The others passed them by. Chatto left the women a pistol and his own canteen. As soon as the baby was born they'd start walking due south, drinking from small seasonal pools until they reached the Lake of the Mountain Spirits, where they'd wait until Chatto could meet up with Carnoviste's band and send a warrior for them.

"Keep a strong heart," Chatto told the women. "Our fathers are with us."

Some could remember the days of their youth, other slaughters, other flights like this. Weariness and hunger. Lifetimes begun in exodus, destined also to end in such. They were driven and chased from every adopted home and fear had long fallen away to exhaustion. They ran for the sake of the little ones and because survival was all they knew.

Riding in the dawnlight Chatto whispered a prayer to Ussen—

Don't let the water be dry. Just a puddle, even that will be enough.

They traveled through pain and fatigue in hope of watering the mules at the hole ahead. The mounts couldn't keep going at this pace much longer. In all his life Chatto had never asked Ussen for the gift of anything, but he asked him now.

When they reached the seep at midmorning, the shallow pool was full.

They dismounted and began filling canteens and waterskins and letting the mules drink. One of the young braves released his thirsty mule and it started for the water.

"Stop your mule," Chatto said.

The brave looked confused but quickly reached and caught the hackamore. The mule strained against his grip, desperate to get at the water, and the brave knocked a balled fist against its head. It brayed and relented.

Chatto went to the mule and kneeled. Sometime earlier he'd noticed it going lame. He picked up the right forehoof and gave it a careful inspection, then let it back down. Soon the mule would begin falling and before the journey was finished, it wouldn't rise again. Better to make use of it here and now.

"Don't let it drink," Chatto said.

The brave nodded his understanding.

Chatto went to the pool and kneeled. He filled his

cupped hands with water and brought them to his lips and drank and the water was cool flowing down his throat and cool in his belly. Ussen hadn't forgotten the People.

When they'd filled the canteens and the mules had quenched their thirst, Chatto led the lame mount into the midst of the pool. It stood in the water and bowed its head and lapped up greedy mouthfuls. Chatto and the brave drew their knives. The brave cut the mule's throat and Chatto plunged his own blade into that great thumping heart. They held the mule as it thrashed and kicked and they forced it down onto its side, blades flashing, stabbing until the mule lay still and blood spread like scarlet ink in the water. Then Chatto kneeled and cut open the mule's belly. He reached within that warm wetness and jerked loose the intestine. Like a coiled serpent full of death and waiting to strike. He cut it open and darkness spilled forth into the pool.

* * *

Cain rode ahead with the expectation of a rifleshot from every bend and rise. He'd anticipated they'd leave behind one of their number, perhaps a wounded squaw, to lie in wait and ambush the trail. Nonetheless he took little precaution, riding in the open and inviting whatever would come.

In their hurry the Apaches were taking no care to conceal their tracks, the trail crossing ridges and winding down forested valleys. Before he'd departed the mercenaries, Cain had questioned Jubal's girl. Dolores told him of a waterhole to the southwest, the refugees' likely destination.

Late in the afternoon he found the tracks of two Apache squaws afoot, splitting off from the others, and at first he believed one of the pair was walking wounded. Then he followed their trail a distance and gave closer scrutiny to the traveler's gait. Pregnant, he decided. On the verge of giving birth. After a while he came to a dry wash where a coyote scratched at the dirt.

The coyote pricked its ears at the sound of Cain's approach, then it spotted him and turned and ran vanishing in the brush. Cain stared at what its diggings had unearthed. A long pale cord severed at one end. The flat blue disc with its network of branching vessels like the Tree of Life. The coyote had caught scent of it where the midwife had tried to conceal it under the dirt and now it lay half-exposed like some secret organ of the earth.

He saw where the woman had lain giving birth. Saw the fresh tracks of the midwife and the mother, again striking out due south, away from the southwestern trail of the main party.

Cain opened his saddlebag and glanced at the burlap bundle.

"What you reckon, Chief?" he asked. "Ain't worth the detour? Maybe not. But the little nit could be a buck. I'll be damned if we let him grow up to make any more of em."

He gave Black Answer his heels and set out after the midwife and her charge.

* * *

The next morning when Jubal and the mercenaries rode up to the poisoned seep, Cain sat on a rock waiting for them. Flies buzzed over the basin of water. Black Answer stood at a distance from the pool and flicked his ear at the pests. The horse had sniffed the water before refusing to drink.

The men dismounted and led their horses to the basin and the horses flared their nostrils, smelling the pool, and turned their heads away. The men cursed the water. Jubal stared at the carnage. The dead mule lay with white maggots writhing in its wounds.

"They fouled the water," Moroni Thayne said.

"Can't slip nothin past you, can they?" Cain said. He was smoking a cigarette and he had the burlap bundle on the rock beside him.

Jubal nodded toward Black Answer, the string of trophy scalps draped over the pommel of the saddle. "By my count, that's two more than you had yesterday. You got a new pair."

"Now there's a observation."

"What happened?" Jubal asked.

"Couple squaws broke off from the others with a fresh-hatched little nit. I reckon they figured we wouldn't think they was worth chasin after. They figured wrong."

"Which way did the others go from here?"

"The main bunch is still headed southwest," Cain said.

Jubal looked out across that barren expanse where whirlwinds scoured the rocky ground.

He turned to Dolores. "Is there another waterhole that way?"

"Not for a long time," she told him. "The horses won't make it. They've got to have a drink soon."

Jubal spat. Curses rose from among the mercenaries— they'd been determined to collect more scalps in revenge for the fallen.

"She's right," Cain said. "The horses are liable to drop dead in this heat. We got to head toward water."

"Supplies are gettin low," Mosby broke in. "Need to start huntin deer pretty soon to tide us over and that's goin to slow us down some."

"What do you want to do?" Cain asked Jubal.

"I want to go after them."

"Mister Jubal," Mosby said. "I know it's a hard thing to turn loose of. But if we rode up here to draw blood, I got to say we done what we come for."

"That's the damn truth," Endicott said. "They ain't likely to forget what we cost em."

"They sure as hell ain't," Oldham agreed. "I'd have liked me a few more scalps after what they pulled on us in the canyon, but we had a good run. I'll be glad to get this horse out from under my ass."

"You and me both, bud," Endicott told him.

"Sergeant," Mosby said. "You reckon it's about time we hung it up?"

"Not my place to say," Cain told them. "The job's done when the man says it is."

All eyes turned to Jubal.

"You hit em hard," Moroni Thayne said. "You showed the Apaches what you're willin to do. They'd be crazy not to give up your boy. Hell, maybe they already done it. Maybe he's waitin for you at home right this minute."

"Wouldn't surprise me one bit," Oldham said.

Jubal looked at Cain. "What do you think?"

"Like the Mormon said, they'd be crazy to hold onto the boy. Could be they already let him go."

"You don't believe that, do you?" Jubal asked.

"No, I don't."

The men were silent.

Jubal snapped the stubs on his right hand and stood thinking. After a while he said, "We'll find the closest water, then head back toward Nácori. But not through the low country—we go back through the sierras, one last pass."

Cain looked pleased.

* * *

In the Camp of the Warm Springs Ishton sat nursing the baby when the hunting party returned. They'd brought back more than just fresh game. Following behind Carnoviste and the other hunters rode Chatto and a small party of women and children. Ishton realized Zunde and the other warriors of his band weren't present and some of the women sported bloody strips of cloth tied about their limbs. Ishton knew something terrible had happened.

Everyone rushed out to greet the newcomers, children running beside the mules and ponies, maidens quick to help the wounded down and see to their care. Ishton rose with the baby at her breast and joined the welcome. She looked for Denali among the hunters, but he was nowhere to be found and she knew he'd broken away again, pursuing his own game, his own lonesome paths. More and more he chose solitude and she didn't understand the reason for it. She worried that Denali was too much alone.

Carnoviste led a mule with the carcass of a deer slung over its back, a large buck with a broken antler. He gave the reins to Oblite, then raised an arm to quiet the crowd.

"The White Eyes attacked the camp of our friends," he said. "Many were lost. Many names will go unspoken." He looked at Chatto. "The name of this young warrior's father goes unspoken, but we can never forget his courage. Now the People have come back together. When we rise as one, what enemy can stand against us?"

Ishton watched Chatto's face while her husband spoke. A mask of stone.

"Our friends are hungry from their long journey," Carnoviste finished. "Let's feed them and give them rest."

Carnoviste gripped the buck's antler and pulled the carcass off the mule. Tsaltey-koo approached with a knife and went to work butchering the deer as Ishton withdrew with the other wives to begin preparing food.

Carnoviste embraced Chatto. "No warrior was ever more courageous than your father."

"I see Ussen's blessed you with another future warrior," Chatto said. "Life is injustice. You with so many sons while my father had to make do with only me."

"Avenge him with grandsons."

"There are plenty of widows who'll be needing a man now, that's true. Too many. We had to leave behind a pregnant widow and an old woman."

"When was this?"

"Three days ago."

"The women will follow when the baby comes?"

Chatto shook his head. "I told them to make their way to the Lake of the Mountain Spirits and we'd send a warrior after them."

It was an old camp of their people, a small lake high in the Blue Mountains.

"Why wasn't my brother Denali hunting with you?" Chatto asked. "Don't tell me he's become a maiden who doesn't hunt."

"He went up the ridge by himself," Carnoviste said. "I told him he'd find the best game below with us, but the stubborn kind never listen. Now watch him come back without anything."

"The son goes hungry who doesn't listen to his father."

"You speak truth."

They rested in the shade while the women prepared the meal.

In the days after Denali was attacked by the honeybees, Carnoviste had decided they'd linger at the springs and give the boy time to heal. There was no danger of anyone else venturing into the cave, not after witnessing how even Denali's Power failed to charm the hive. None dared suffer his brutal fate and the band believed his story of the honey gone bad. Soon they'd return to the safety of empty Pa-Gotzin-Kay, where the deer were still sick with fever and where they'd have to scrape by on whatever they could gather and grow. For now they lingered where the hunting was good and kept a constant watch all hours of the day and night.

After a while Denali returned from the ridgeside with a doe across his saddle. His face was no longer swollen where the bees had stung him, though welts remained visible on his skin and many of them continued to itch. For a time when his throat had swollen almost fully closed, he'd thought he would die. He'd lain blind and rasping while Ishton had rubbed clay over his eyes and body and slowly the healing had come, slowly his eyes were opened.

He'd performed no healings since the bees stung him. An old woman had come to him and asked prayers over her for the fluid in her lungs and a hacking cough. He'd done as she'd asked, despite his reluctance. Days after he'd danced and prayed the cough remained with her, twice as vicious, and she struggled to breathe. It wasn't his only failure. A boy begged him to heal his pony that suffered from a painful infection of the eye. Though Denali danced and sang the pony grew gradually worse. Then the boy had gone to the wise woman. Gouyen told him to piss on his hands and rub the horse's eyes with the wetness, to do this four times daily, four days running. The boy did as he was told. On the fourth day the pony was healed and the boy thanked the wise woman for accomplishing what Denali's Power had failed to perform.

The band no longer sought the Healer's council on any matter.

He could feel Power's absence like a strange nakedness. As though he'd forgotten his own name. It troubled him—there were hard things ahead for the People and he didn't know if he could face them without Power. At those times when he despaired he remembered what Carnoviste told him. The chief had never known the gift of any great Power, yet he shouldered the weight of leadership nevertheless and he was determined to stand whether Power delivered him or not. A man acted as though Power were on him, Carnoviste said, and didn't pause to wonder if it was truly so. For one thing was certain above all—Power would never visit the man who spent his days waiting for it to come.

And so Denali sang his prayers. Whether Power returned or was lost to him forever, still he would go on singing.

Denali walked into camp leading the mule. When he spotted the new arrivals, he scanned their faces, then his gaze settled on his old friend.

"My brother," he called.

Chatto rose. "Brother," he said.

Denali gave the mule's hackamore to a boy and broke into a run. They met in the embrace of their People.

"I feared the bear ate you up," Chatto said.

"He tried. But the earth was hungrier and swallowed him."

"There's no doubt of it?"

"The bear's dead," Denali told him.

"Then it must be his spirit leading the White Eyes. They've come to the Blue Mountains to kill and devour."

"They don't need the bear's spirit to corrupt them. The White Eyes were already devils."

Chatto laughed. "You call them devils? My friend, don't look into a pool."

"I'm no White Eye. I'm of the People."

"Of course you are," Chatto said. "Forgive me, my friend."

CHAPTER NINE

"What's due south of here, Little Sister?" Cain asked Dolores.

Still at the poisoned seep. The company had mounted back up and they waited now for Cain to lead them out. The sun blazed in the cloudless vault.

"A couple little springs," Dolores said. "Pools smaller than this one. Then the hidden lake."

Cain placed his burlap prize in his saddlebag and stepped into the stirrup and swung astride Black Answer. "What hidden lake?"

"A camp we called the Lake of the Mountain Spirits."

Cain turned to Jubal. "Those scalps I took this mornin," he said. "The squaws were movin south, likely headed for that lake, I reckon."

Jubal was conscious of Dolores watching them, the cold intensity of her stare. "You think they were plannin on a rendezvous?" he asked Cain.

"Hell, there could be a whole pack of em camped there right now. Maybe the bunch that kept goin west was just leadin us on a goose chase. You want to spy out the lake?"

"Worth a look," Jubal said. "We've got to head toward water anyway."

Cain set out. When Jubal turned Bardo to follow him, he was careful to avoid meeting Dolores's eyes. He had no heart to look on the cold accounting contained in that gaze, the girl's ledgerbook an unerring record of the cost of all his commands.

* * *

Cain stayed close with the company. Over the next three days they rode south using seasonal pools, the horses drinking each one dry and never enough for the caballada entire. Certain of the packmules appeared on the verge of collapse and they had to be driven onward much against their will.

The way was long and difficult. Without Dolores there to lead them, even Cain wouldn't have stood a chance of finding their destination. When at last they neared the lake, Dolores saw the faint trace of an old trail that branched off their own, the path that led through the shadows of the trees to the lakeshore. This rush of memory came over her. Like the sudden recognition of a past life. So eager was she to walk those familiar shores that she booted her horse and left Cain lagging behind. And perhaps as well, she would wonder later, some part of her wished to herald warning of their arrival, should any unfortunate souls be waiting there.

Then Black Answer thundered after her. Cain reached

out and grabbed the girl's reins and they came to a halt before she could take the trail.

"Whoa there, Little Sister. Hold up and let's think this through."

Jubal drew up beside them and conferred with Cain. They decided on a course of action to ensure their tracks would go unseen by any scouts who might approach the lake after them. They'd eschew all existing trails leading to the water and instead cut their own path. Some of the men groaned at this proposal. The country about the lake was among the roughest they'd yet traversed. Creating such an egress would necessitate taking the caballada afoot over a sharp rise where brush grew thick and tangled from the dark volcanic soil. Cain cursed them for a pack of weak-kneed sisters. He dismounted and took Black Answer by the reins and started into the thicket. As always the men followed after him.

The mountain lake was an ancient caldera nestled within a curve of ridgeline. A teardrop hidden in a maze of volcanic peaks. Run-off from the ridgeside kept the lake full throughout the year and the water in the crater's rough circle was cool and deep.

When finally they crested out in the gathering twilight and looked down on the lake below, they saw it was indeed a hidden lake and ringed by a meadow and the sloping walls of the caldera. The scent of water came to the horses even on those heights and they nickered and stamped, straining for the downward slope. Cain directed Oldham to trade rifles with him—he gave the merc his

.30-30 and took Oldham's scoped Winchester, chambered in .45-70. Cain raised the German-made scope to his eye and glassed the lakeshore. The stone circle of a cold firepit, an old campsite without inhabitant. A mountain lion slinked through the long grass and parted the reeds at the water's edge and paused to drink. On the opposite shore a flock of quail.

"What do you see?" Jubal asked.

"Paradise. Or the closest the likes of us will ever get."

He lowered the scope and placed the rifle in his own saddle-scabbard. Oldham looked vexed at the apparently permanent trade in weapons, but he voiced no objection.

That night in the caldera they led the horses and mules single file along a game trail and watered at the lake. They placed blankets at the shoreline for the horses to stand on while they drank so their tracks wouldn't be left in the soft earth. When they'd had their fill, the men led them back along the same path to a camp they cut deep in the thicket.

Two men stood watch at all times. The night passed without alarm and the first day and the night of the first day and they kept a cold camp under cover of the trees. Waiting for what travelers would come. The Browning rested on its tripod, sighted on the trail. They watched the birds of the heavens lighting down by the water to splash their feathers in a flutter of wings. They watched great cats and foxes that tarried among the reeds. Nights alive in ceaseless chorus—a million chirping insects, the croak of countless frogs. In the trees at midnight a parliament of owls. Fireflies danced over the water, their shimmer on the polished black surface like otherworldly light in a scryer's glass. From time to time movement in the thicket. Silent things dark and sleek, betrayed solely by the flash of an eye, flecks of starlight caught in an orb cold and remote as any celestial fire.

Gray clouds of mosquitos went drifting like smoke among the trees. The company endured a misery of bloodletting, the swarm like an army of faeries gone vampiric. Dolores slapped bloody splotches on her arms and the men scratched at bites that bled and scabbed over. Only Cain was granted mercy. He could've gone naked through the cloud so disinterested were they in his strange blood. The men hung mosquito netting from the boughs, too deep within the trees to be glimpsed from the lake, and they huddled close behind those veils. The collective buzz of wings droned on and after a while Dolores imagined voices half-discernible, a conspiracy of whispered accusations, and found herself guilty of every charge.

They were quickly depleting the supply of canned goods. The company could remain at the lake only a short time until they'd be forced to start back to Nácori if they wished to travel with rations. Each morning Jubal insisted on one more day. He was sure the Apaches would come, he told them. The truth of it was that he dreaded a return to the paralysis of waiting, inaction's purgatory. So long as he remained in the sierras he was on the hunt and the hunt alone offered hope.

The morning of the third day Mosby caught the sergeant praying to the severed head.

Every dawn Cain went stalking off into the woods. His burlap bundle was nowhere to be seen since they'd come to the lake. Each time Cain returned from the depths of the woods, his manner was strange, troubled, as though he grieved some terrible loss. He'd sit staring out across the water. Eyes losing focus, hollow gaze. The same vacant expression he'd worn the night Mosby woke to see him looming over Dolores with the blade.

Mosby wasn't alone in noting the change. He'd seen Jubal fixing Cain with a long scrutinizing look. Grim evaluation.

In the predawn blue Mosby lay awake in his bedding. When Cain waved to the sentry and struck out for the woods, Mosby waited a while longer, then rose wearing the moccasins he'd borrowed from Cain's own saddlebags and parted the veil and slipped out of camp. He trailed the sergeant, staying well behind, though little caution was needed, Cain intent on his obscure purpose, all his energy directed toward whatever compelled him deeper into those woods.

Mosby saw the clearing ahead and he got down and moved in a crouch to the edge of the trees—

And there was Cain birth-naked and crazy.

The sergeant had removed his boots and clothes and hat, placing them on the ground beside his gunbelt and the kalis. He stood lowering the burlap sack with a rope where it hung from a high bough. Flies buzzed about the sack. When the bundle was eye-level, Cain reached and opened the burlap and pulled out the Apache's head. A warrior by the looks of it, though that countenance had known better days, the flesh much deteriorated. Salt rained from its black hair. Cain had taken from the company's supply of salt and filled the sack with it to partially preserve the severed head.

Cain stepped to the center of the clearing and in the breaking light he set the totem down and kneeled before it. He'd carved the crude likeness of an eye on its forehead. Now he picked a maggot from the thing's hair and crushed it between thumb and forefinger.

"You had a bug," Cain told the head.

Mosby took a handkerchief from his pocket and pressed it to his nose and mouth. He could smell it where he crouched and he realized only the stench of Cain's trophy scalps had covered the putrid reek during the time he'd kept the salted prize in his saddlebags.

Cain ran his fingers over the skull like a phrenologist feeling for telltale bumps and grooves. When at last he spoke, it was in raw anguish.

"You got to help me, Chief. I can't hold it together no more. Everything's sprung loose, my memory's all jumbled up. Like time done unraveled on me and I can't put it back right."

Cain balled a fist and struck himself a blow to the right temple. Mosby jolted. Cain hit himself over and over, kneeling before the severed head.

The undergrowth rustled close behind Mosby. He

whirled to see Jubal approaching, hunched low. So intent had Mosby been on Cain's turmoil that he hadn't heard the man until he was close enough to touch. Jubal raised a finger to his lips. Mosby gave him a slow nod.

Jubal moved up beside him and they kneeled watching Cain.

"It got twisted out of true," Cain said. "When that damn fool showed mercy on the heathen, took one into his own house and broke the order. Give me the strength to make it right, Chief. Let me hold on that long. We got to find that boy and give him peace, kill him like he was one of em by blood. It's too late for him now— he'll never be right again, never able to trust his own mind. That poor boy. Chief, why won't nobody give him peace?"

Cain kneaded his temple with the heel of his palm. "All on account of the fool who broke the order," he cried. He ran a hand through his hair and revealed the great bulging lump on his head.

Jubal rose. Mosby stared up at him and shook his head, urging him not to do it, but Jubal wouldn't be stopped. He stepped out of the trees and into the clearing.

"Cain," Jubal called.

When the sergeant turned to him, his eyes were distant. As though he stared past Jubal to some far terminus beyond those woods. Then of a sudden he registered Jubal's presence and clutched the Apache's head to himself.

"Put that damned thing down," Jubal said.

"Get away, you thief," Cain shouted. "I knew you was a thief from the start."

Mosby stepped out of the trees. "Do like he tells you, Sergeant."

"Mo," Cain said. "You hadn't ought to see this."

"You a sick man, Sergeant, but we goin to get you help."

"I ain't lettin you take the Chief from me," Cain said. He dove for Wormwood by his pile of clothes.

Jubal moved fast. He pressed his boot down on the kalis just as Cain's hand closed on the grip. Cain let go and went for his gunbelt, but Jubal had already drawn his own sidearm and he bent down and slammed the pistol-butt hard against Cain's head.

The sergeant fell back in a daze. Blood ran from a cut below his hairline.

Jubal tossed Cain's gunbelt and the kalis to Mosby. "Take him back to camp," he said. "I want him in irons."

"Mister Jubal, the sergeant's just sick is all. He ain't a bad man."

Jubal gave him a look. Then he stooped and picked up the Apache's severed head by the hair and walked past Mosby and out of the clearing.

After a while Cain's vision cleared and the world steadied around him. He wiped the blood from his head and rose staggering to his feet.

"Where'd he take the Chief?" he demanded.

"Just lay back," Mosby said. "You got to rest."

"The Chief don't belong to him."

"You can't be actin this way, Sergeant. Get a holdt of yourself."

Mosby reached out and gripped his arm, but Cain broke free of his grasp and ran out of the clearing, naked and barefoot, following the path back toward the lake.

* * *

Jubal emerged from the trees and stepped out into the tall grass about the water. He could feel the men watching from camp, all eyes on him and the grotesque thing he carried. He stepped to the edge of the water and reared his arm back, then swung out the Apache's head by the hair in a long sweeping arc and let go.

It splashed into the water. Jubal stood watching it sink, the black fan of hair spreading like a dark halo.

"What the hell did you do?" Cain yelled.

Jubal turned and saw him rush from the trees like a wild man of the woods, enraged and naked and shouting curses, calling for his rightful property.

Mosby broke out of the woods behind Cain. "Wait, Sergeant," he called.

"You merciful son of a bitch," Cain shouted at a full run.

Jubal stood waiting for him to come, waiting for the blows to land.

Cain snarled as he ran past. He charged splashing into the lake. The Apache's head had vanished. He pawed at the water, found nothing, then took a great breath and dove under. Almost a full minute later he rose up in an explosion of water and curses.

Jubal and Mosby stood side by side in the grass.

Cain let out a long thin cry like the cry of a wounded animal. "I lost you, Chief," he said. "Oh, Chief, ain't I sorry?"

Jubal turned his back on Cain and started toward camp. He could see Dolores and Hector among the mercenaries, all of them outside the tree line watching the bizarre scene.

Cain stood in the water, weeping now. As though he were the tortured spirit of the lake, condemned to haunt that lonely place.

"Come on out of there before you catch cold, Sergeant," Mosby said.

* * *

That evening at sunset Cain sat in the camp with a blanket covering his nakedness, his wrists behind his back in cold irons bound. He wore the shackles intended for rescued captives, should they encounter any who refused a return to civilization.

The men were much subdued after the revelations of that morning. They'd kept a grim silence while Mosby recounted what he'd witnessed in the woods. All save Endicott who'd found great hilarity in the detail of Cain grooming the thing's hair. He'd laughed a booming laugh. To a man they agreed the campaign had reached its close and they readied for departure at first light and the long ride back to Nácori. Now Cain was a prisoner of his own troops and Jubal had assumed command. Though the sergeant's madness was laid bare for all to see, still none among them would speak an ill word of him. Whatever he'd become, there was no question Cain was once a soldier.

He sat in silence and refused the rations Mosby offered. He stared across at Jubal.

"I ain't done with you," Cain said. "Not by a long shot. You and me got a bone to pick."

"Shut him up," Jubal told Mosby. "Or I will."

"Come on, now, Sergeant," Mosby said.

Cain grinned. "I get my hands on that boy of yours, I'm goin to make you choose. A gun to the boy's head, a gun to the girl's. Which will it be, your own blood or the red bitch?"

Dolores sat beside Hector. She watched Cain, her face registering not the slightest emotion. The men in their talk of Cain's madness had also revealed the full extent of the atrocities committed on the first raid, calling him Cannibal Cain and remarking on his appetite for Apache flesh. The knowledge had left her numb. She thought herself beyond sorrow.

Jubal rose, drawing his Bowie knife from his boot, and towered over Cain. "You lunatic, I should've killed you after the first rancheria. One more word and I'll cut out your tongue and feed it to you."

"Please, Mister Jubal," Mosby said. "He ain't himself.

206

This was a man served his country."

Jubal held Cain's gaze. Neither spoke.

Then Jubal sheathed the Bowie and turned.

"If you cut her pretty throat right here and now," Cain said, "I'll let your boy live when I find him."

Jubal pivoted, knife in hand. He grabbed Cain's jaw and started forcing his mouth open and Cain bit down on his fingers. Jubal slammed the Bowie's pommel down on his skull and still Cain wouldn't stop biting.

Mosby stepped up to them. "I can't let him be treated this way, Mister Jubal. Please, don't make me—"

The netting parted and Clovis, the sentry, passed through. Mud covered his arms and neck. The whites of his eyes gleamed in a mask of mud. All to keep the mosquitos at bay. He seemed a creature lately spawned from the murky depths of the lake itself.

Cain and Jubal ceased their struggle. Everyone stared at the sentry.

"Apaches," he told them. "Two riders."

* * *

They hid in the trees and watched the Apaches cross the meadow through the twilight. The pair of scouts were young warriors, one not much more than a boy, and they rode a pony and a mule. Jubal's heart leapt to see their youth, but appraising them through the fieldglasses his hopes were dashed. Neither of the two was John Russell. They watched the scouts approach

207

the old Apache campsite and inspect it. They spoke briefly, then the older scout dismounted and led his pony to a deadfall at the water's edge and tethered it by the hackamore and the pony lowered its head to drink.

Jubal watched the scout lie down in the soft grass with his hands behind his head. His mounted companion shook his head in apparent disgust. The resting Apache laughed.

"Gut em both in their sleep," Endicott whispered.

"Hell, yes," Van Zandt said.

Then the mounted scout turned his mule and started back the way they'd come, leaving the lake and his napping friend.

"Where are you goin, boy?" Jubal whispered.

It puzzled him. The scouts had almost certainly come to the rendezvous point to meet the pair of women with the baby—why would one man leave immediately? If the Apache had waited until dawn, Jubal would've deduced he was going back to the band's camp to inform the others that the women hadn't yet arrived. But not like this. Where was the logic in it? The scout hadn't even paused to water his mule. It made no sense—

Unless the band was nearby, perhaps en route to the lake itself, and the boy was riding to tell them it was safe to approach and make camp.

Jubal lowered the fieldglasses. Gut instinct told him he was right.

He turned to Moroni Thayne. "Get the men ready. There's a band of em comin."

CHAPTER TEN

Ishton rode a mule, the baby asleep in the cradleboard on her back, and she watched Denali turn with the advance guard around the cluster of rocks and out of sight down the slope. In the purple twilight she could see the wooded rim of the caldera rising around them. The mules smelled water and quickened their pace.

Two days earlier they'd abandoned the Camp of the Warm Springs in favor of returning to the sanctuary of Pa-Gotzin-Kay. The attack on Zunde's group convinced them all it was time to return to the old mountain, whatever desolation might await them. On the way to the stronghold they would camp at the lake and meet the women Chatto had sent there.

Estoni and the novice warrior Bishi had scouted ahead of the band. Bishi had soon returned to them on his mule and reported the Lake of the Mountain Spirits was safe and that the women who'd broken from Chatto's group weren't yet present. Carnoviste also asked Gouyen to take a reading with her Power of Finding Enemies. The wise woman told him it was clear—the White Eyes were far distant. Carnoviste made his decision. The band would camp that night at the Lake of the Mountain Spirits as in older days, better times, then the main party would leave at first light and continue their journey homeward. Only two warriors would remain behind to wait for the pair of refugees.

Behind Ishton came the line of women and children, then Carnoviste bringing up the rear guard. He'd allowed Denali and Chatto to ride point with some of the young braves.

Ishton rounded the end of the rocky outcrop and looked down on the meadow falling away to the lake. Denali and Chatto were leading their ponies to the water where Estoni's horse stood drinking. She rode down through the gloaming country.

The wise woman followed after her. The shin bones of a deer danced on a cord about Gouyen's neck at the rhythm of her horse's trot. She wore a horned buffalo cap, her shadow and the horse's shadow moving strange and chimeric across that darkening land. Like some latterday abomination in a sibyl's monstrous dream. Dark prophecy, the beast with the head of a bull and woman's breasts and the body of a stallion, auxiliary head looking forth to its place of eventual birth.

Idly she scratched at the red spot on the back of her hand, the place where the bee had stung her. Still itching despite the passage of time. She'd felt something tickling her hand when they'd stood on the ledge above the honey cave, just after a blinded Denali told her the honey wasn't good to eat. Gouyen had glanced down and seen the bee crawling on the webbing between her thumb and finger and she'd moved to flick it away. Too slow—the bee stung her and fell dead at her feet. The wise woman felt Power depart from her like a raven taking flight.

The welt had gone, but she couldn't stop scratching at the spot and so a faint rash remained.

No Power was left her. She guarded the secret of her loss, careful not to expose her weakness to Denali. She'd managed to heal the pony with its sickness of the eye when Denali had failed, but it was through no Power, only her knowledge of the old ways. She'd sooner die than see Denali usurp her brother's mantle. The People knew the Healer's Power was gone, but at all costs she couldn't allow them to discover she'd lost her own as well.

When Carnoviste asked her to use her Power of Finding Enemies, she'd hesitated, then stood with her palms out held and turned a circle. She'd felt nothing, no slightest indication. The lake was safe, she'd told the chief. As it surely was—the last time she'd felt the enemy they were far to the north. Even if the White Eyes had followed Chatto back into the sierras they'd be on the People's backtrail now, not ahead of them.

Until they reached Pa-Gotzin-Kay she must maintain the illusion of Power. Once on the Stronghold Mountain she would find a means to regain what was lost, though it require a blood sacrifice. Then she'd have her revenge.

Gouyen rode a short distance into the meadow before she drew up and watched Ishton continue on with the baby. She thought of following, helping the chief's wife make camp, and perhaps she'd be asked to hold the child. Always she'd wanted a child to hold and now she was old and her arms empty. Then she watched Ishton turn her mule toward Denali, who everyone knew was her favorite, and Gouyen turned her own mount and went up the slope away from the others.

* * *

Jubal waited with the line of mercenaries in the cover of the trees. They sat their horses, waiting for the last Apaches to round the trail and dismount at the lake. It was a sizeable band, the largest they'd encountered. He could see warriors and women and children through the fieldglasses, but it was too dark to discern their features. Against the possibility John Russell was among this band, Jubal ordered the men to refrain from using the BARs. The Brownings were in Hector's possession where the segundo guarded the caballada with Dolores. Jubal had also reiterated the standing order of every raid—they were never to fire on any light-skinned boy, even at the cost of their own lives. Jubal patted Bardo's chest and stared out across the twilight, waiting to lead the charge.

* * *

Cain sat shackled in camp under the pale netting, Mosby across from him with the shotgun on his lap. They waited for the sounds of battle to begin. The camp was empty save the prisoner and his guard—for Jubal refused to allow Cain anywhere near Dolores when he wasn't present. Hector and the girl had taken the caballada and withdrawn deeper into the woods.

Cain nodded at the shotgun. "Figure you'll need to put me down if I try to wander off?"

"It's just to keep us safe. In case a stray Indin runs up on us while you're chained."

"Then turn me loose and let me help stand watch."

Mosby shook his head. "Can't do that."

"I should be out there, Mo. Those men need me to lead em."

"All they need you to do is get well. We goin to find you a doctor back home, one who can figure out what's wrong. I seen that knot on your head. Terrible lookin thing. Like maybe somethin's growin in your skull, needs to be cut out. You got to trust me, Sergeant. Can you do that for me?"

There was a long silence. "I trust you, Mo. But if you want either of us to make it back home, you'd best tear down this damn skeeter net. When the Apaches get scattered in the fight, one of em could make it through the line and into the trees. If he spots this nettin, we'll be sittin ducks."

Mosby glanced up at the canopy of mosquito netting. They were deep enough in the trees that the netting couldn't be seen from the lake and it was unlikely an Apache would break through the line of mercenaries to reach their position. Even so, Cain's suggestion was a sound one and Mosby welcomed a return of his sharp reasoning.

"Reckon you're thinkin like a soldier again," Mosby said, pleased at the change in him. "I'd rather get skeeter bit than poked with a arrow, that's for sure."

Mosby rose still holding the shotgun. They'd draped lengths of rope over high boughs to hoist up the netting. One end of each rope was tied about a grommet in a corner of the mosquito net, the other tied to a metal stake driven into the ground. They'd covered the bottom inches of the netting in a layer of earth to seal it. Mosby went to a stake and kneeled and pulled the bowline loose and lowered that corner of the netting. Then he rose and stepped to the next stake and kneeled again. For a moment his back was to Cain.

Instantly Cain rose in a low squat and moved his shackled hands down past his buttocks, then sat and rocked back, bringing his knees to his chest, and passed the shackles under his bare feet. Now his shackled hands were in front of him. He rose and charged naked just as Mosby was rising, turning toward the sound of the rattling chains.

Cain threw up his arms and jumped. He brought down the length of chain over Mosby's head, catching his neck, then he was falling and Mosby went crashing down on top of him. Cain reared back hard.

The pale netting had fallen over them. Mosby gasped, eyes wide in shock. The shotgun had dropped from his grip. The chain dug into his throat and he couldn't breathe and he struggled trying to get a hand inside the chain, but there was no use, it was too tight, and all the while he hardly believed it was happening, that the sergeant was actually going to kill him. His other hand darted to his sidearm. He fumbled at the holster, pulled his .45. It was cocked and locked. He thumbed the safety off and brought the gun up over his head and fired a blind shot that missed Cain by an inch.

Mosby's ears rang from the shot. Cain shifted under him, worming away from the gun barrel, and Mosby bent his wrist and fired again, kicking up dirt. Cain pulled harder on the shackles. They lay writhing like wicked lovers, clandestine in the dark of the woods, and Mosby couldn't get any air. His mouth stretched open in a silent scream as the fallen netting lay over his face like a wedding veil, Mosby the bride and death the groom. Then blackness flooded his vision and there was the sensation of floating, hovering over some great depth. His hand went limp, the .45 slipped from his grasp.

* * *

Ishton chose a spot a short distance from the lake. Denali saw to her mule, staking it near the water to drink, while Ishton took the baby from the tsoch and spread a blanket on the ground. She placed Illanipi on the blanket. She took out a clay olla from her pack and reached inside and took up a handful of animal fat mixed with crushed roots. She began rubbing it over the baby's skin to keep away the mosquitos. The flying insects buzzed all about, but the People's blood had built up a great tolerance for them. Those few bites their grease and ointments failed to prevent were hardly noticed.

The breeze off the water was cool on Ishton's skin. The moon had yet to rise and stars were appearing in the sky and on the surface of the lake. Across the meadow women prepared meals and laid out bedding.

"This was always a happy place for our people," Ishton said. "My sister loved this camp."

"Do you miss her?" Denali asked.

"Very much. But I'm pleased to have so brave a son as you."

"You're not old enough for me to be your son."

"It makes no difference. You're the son of the chief and I'm his wife. So you're my son and you have my love."

"And you have mine," Denali told her.

She smiled.

Denali hesitated. What did it matter now with no Power to corrupt, no Power to lose? Then he said, "If the chief weren't my father, still you'd have it."

There was a silence.

"I see," Ishton said at last.

"Would you love me still?"

Ishton was aware of the others, how close they were, a few of the wives making camp nearby and perhaps listening, always quick to spread their talk.

Finally she said, "It would make Jacali very happy if you helped her and her mother with their mules."

Denali watched her wrap the baby in a shawl. Her beauty in the dying light kindled such an ache within him, Denali had to turn and look away. His longing was like a wound that would never heal. Not without her touch.

"All right," he said. "I'll go to them."

"Soon it will be time for Jacali to marry. She's young, but our life is hard. She'll need a warrior to care for her. Maybe you can go on a raid and steal a pair of horses for her."

"How many horses did Carnoviste give for you?"

She smiled. "Too many."

"I don't think there could be so many horses in the world."

She stared across the meadow. "Your father's coming," she said.

Carnoviste and the other warriors were descending the slope with the last of the People.

A pistolshot barked from the trees east of the lake and there was a pause and then another shot. An instant later they heard a rush of hooves. Denali spotted the first rider coming fast out of the trees.

Denali's rifle was in the scabbard on his saddle where he'd spread his blankets by the water. He glanced toward it and back at the rider, other horsemen appearing now out of the woods to join the charge, and he saw it was hopeless.

"White Eyes," Ishton screamed.

Running maidens echoed her cry. Women and children were dashing to their mules and mounting bareback. He saw Jacali and her sister running with their mother. He saw Estoni swing up on his horse and give it his heels, riding out straight into the onrushing horsemen, a pistol in either hand, and Denali knew he was giving his life to buy them precious time. His heart filled with pride at the warrior's courage.

Ishton scooped up the baby. Denali drew his revolver from his belt and grabbed Ishton's hand and they set out running.

* * *

Waiting in the woods the line of horseman heard the shots. Jubal cursed—half the band of Apaches had yet to reach the lake and dismount.

There was no time to wonder what had gone wrong. The shots came from the direction of their own camp and he supposed Cain must have made some desperate play and forced Mosby to shoot him.

They could see the line of mounted Apaches turning west, alerted to their presence.

"Go," Jubal shouted.

He booted his horse and led the charge out of the

woods and across the twilight meadow.

He knew even if the Apaches fled back down the trail, the company would still overtake them with their fresh mounts. Only a matter of riding them down.

Then he saw the Apaches weren't turning back the way they'd come after all. Instead they were riding hard west toward the wooded slope of the caldera rim and as the first few of them reached the tree line, they jumped down from their mounts and ran afoot into the trees. He cursed again.

* * *

Carnoviste saw them galloping out of the eastern woods, saw muzzle flashes in the falling dark, and he didn't understand how it could be happening. The trail to the lake had been clear of sign, nothing save the tracks of deer and coyotes. Estoni had sent word the lake was safe. And surest of all, Gouyen had used her Power of Finding Enemies.

Carnoviste rode among the widows and orphans. Not far ahead of him were Tsaltey-koo and Hanlonah and his sons. Already at the lake, Ishton and the baby were with Denali—Carnoviste was powerless to help them.

All he could do was what he must.

He shouted for the women to turn their mounts. They'd make a run for the western slope. There wasn't time to retreat back down the trail—if they hoped to make it alive, they'd have to race the White Eyes into cover of the woods and escape afoot over the rim.

* * *

Denali ran beside Ishton toward the stand of rocks south of the lake. He kept a tight grip on his revolver. He didn't know if they could reach the boulders before the horsemen were upon them, but he hoped they'd at least make it far enough into the long grass they could drop and hide if they had to, then crawl the rest of the way. Screams and gunshots behind them. Women fell, children fell and didn't rise. One of the White Eyes broke from the others and his horse came thundering across the meadow kicking up clumps of dirt. When Denali glanced over his shoulder, he saw the rider headed straight for them.

He let go of Ishton's hand and spun to face the horseman.

The rider's pistol spat fire—three shots snapped off fast and careless. A bearded face in the muzzle flash.

Denali dropped to one knee.

The rider adjusted his aim and there was a moment's hesitation, a strange pause while Denali stared down the barrel of the man's gun and still he didn't fire. Denali entered the floating space. He watched himself raise his own pistol and cock the hammer back, the rider saying, "John Russ—" just as Denali pulls the trigger and the bullet goes speeding toward its target, the hunting spirit unmoored from Denali's body and traveling with the lead, guiding it along one true path, and the bullet cuts a groove through the man's lower lip and explodes a pair of front teeth, then bursts upward out the back of his skull in a spray of blood and bone and instantly the hunting spirit returned to Denali.

The dead man slumped in the saddle. His horse snorted in fear and swung about and raced back toward the lake.

The baby wailed.

Denali turned and saw Ishton lying facedown in the grass. Illanipi had spilled from her arms and he was crying, crawling toward his motionless mother. Denali ran to her and kneeled. It was only a small hole the bullet had made in Ishton's back. Then he turned her over and there was the awful wound of it exiting her chest. Blood covered her buckskins and blood stained the grass and blood on his hands when he held her and pressed her to him.

Her eyelids fluttered.

"Stay," he said. "Don't go."

He held her tight. Her lips against his ear, she let out a little breath. "Love you still," she whispered.

Then she was dead in his arms.

"Ishton," he cried as though he'd call her back.

The baby lay wailing.

Denali placed Ishton's body gently in the grass and she lay with her eyes open to the stars. He picked up the baby and searched him for any wound, but there wasn't any and he held his brother and wept.

When he saw the horse coming out of the dark, he ducked low in the grass and cocked the pistol. Then he recognized the rider. He rose and called out to Gouyen.

The wise woman turned and rode toward him. She glanced at the body in the grass and the baby in Denali's arms.

Bursts of gunfire sounded from the lake.

"Give him to me and climb on," Gouyen said.

Denali handed up the baby. He looked down a last time at Ishton and he was vexed for her spirit that he had to leave her body there unprotected.

"Do you want to live?" Gouyen asked. "Come on."

Denali climbed up behind the wise woman.

* * *

Carnoviste swung down from his mount. He pulled the rifle from its sleeve and slapped the horse's rump and the horse went galloping off into the dusk. The women and children were dismounting as well, jumping from their mules and darting into the woods. They had no hope of outrunning the White Eyes' fresh horses. Instead they'd go where riders couldn't easily follow, through the thick brush on the rim, then over the ridges beyond.

Gunshots rang out from the lake. The horsemen were running down those who fled in the long grass. Mules shrieked, wounded and dying.

Carnoviste feared for Ishton and his sons, everything in his blood calling for him to go in search of them, but the chief couldn't abandon the widows and orphans. He waited until the last of the children made it into the cover of the trees, then turned and followed.

* * *

Leading the charge Jubal rode with his reins in one hand, his .45 in the other, the horse under him swift and eager for what lay ahead. As if Bardo's time in those mountains had led the horse to discover his true calling, at home in the crash and din of battle.

Across the gloaming Jubal saw them fleeing camp, some running, others jumping on the backs of mules and whipping them in a frenzy. Then a warrior rode out to meet them, passing through the midst of the runners who parted at his approach, and he was slung low on the pony's back with a pistol in either hand.

Jubal kept his gun barrel aimed skyward. They were still well out of pistol range.

Then the Apache warrior was firing on them, careless shots with no chance of finding their target, and Jubal knew he'd done it to bait the mercenaries into opening up too soon and wasting ammo. "Hold fire," Jubal shouted. Too late—the men cut loose a premature barrage.

Not a bullet touched the Apache rider.

"Hold," Jubal roared.

The mercs ceased fire. They rode on, full gallop for

the lone Apache horseman, and at last when Jubal judged they were in range, he leveled his pistol and took rough aim and pulled the trigger. It missed the rider and caught the pony in the head. The pony went skidding down on its flank, throwing the rider. The brave tumbled and rolled. He staggered to his feet, both guns lost in the fall, and drew his knife from his moccasin and stepped limping forward. The brave raised his knife. He stood beating a fist against his chest in a guttural chant.

The mercenaries fired as one. The Apache staggered and swayed, the bullets piercing his torso, then dropped to his knees and watched the riders come. Bardo struck him full-force and the Apache vanished under galloping hooves. The horse flared his nostrils and didn't slow.

They overtook the runners. They fired into the backs of women fleeing into the night and they trampled children underhoof. Moroni Thayne rode chasing a pair of shadows far across the meadow. Rourke broke off from the company as well. Jubal dispatched Van Zandt and Oldham to block the trail, closing the kill zone within the caldera. The others turned their mounts and went trolling the long uncut grass for the wounded in hiding.

* * *

Denali rode behind Gouyen south up the rise. Gunshots and screams filled the night. They hadn't gone far when they saw a pair of riders moving to block off the trail that led out of the caldera. Gouyen turned her horse and the riders never spotted them, but somewhere in the darkness at their backs they heard hoofbeats thundering closer.

The baby was crying—the White Eyes would surely hear him. Gouyen drew up at the cluster of rocks. She pulled the rifle from its saddle-scabbard and handed it to Denali. She drew the pistol from her belt and pointed the horse toward the lake and slapped its rump with the pistol barrel and the horse went trotting off into the dark.

Denali approached the rocks. A pair of high boulders were leaning against each other, touching at the top and leaving a shadowed gap below. Gouyen placed the pistol in her belt and held the baby in her arms. The baby was still crying, impossible to quiet, then above his cries they heard the sound of hoofbeats again.

Gouyen squeezed into the opening between the boulders. She ducked low and fit herself as far into the cleft as she could and Denali followed after her. She stood rocking the baby in the crook of her arm, but it was no use, still he cried on. Illanipi had been sick of late with cholic. Now under the stress of the night he wasn't keeping the usual silence of the People's infants.

Finally Gouyen pressed her palm over his mouth.

Moments later Denali stared out through the gap in the rocks and saw the dark shape of a horseman ride up, blotting out the stars. The rider paused and sat his horse. Gouyen tightened her grip on the baby's mouth.

The man swore and reached in his saddlebag.

In the darkness Denali raised his pistol. If he was forced to fire, it would surely lead the others down on them. The baby struggled in Gouyen's arms—his nose was snotty and with her hand clamped over his mouth, the child couldn't breathe. She was slowly suffocating him.

The rider unscrewed the lid from a silver flask and took a long swig.

They could hear occasional shots from the lake, the wounded being executed. The smell of smoke came to them thick on the air, something burning at the camp, and Denali hoped it was strong enough to cover their scent from the White Eye's mount. The horses of the White Eyes could often detect the smell of an Apache nearby and alert their riders.

The baby was shaking in Gouyen's arms, but she kept her hand clamped tight.

The White Eye wiped his mouth with a shirtsleeve. He screwed the lid back on and placed the flask once more in his saddlebag, then turned his horse and rode out across the grassland.

Gouyen released her grip on the baby's mouth. Instantly he was wailing.

"Let me take him," Denali said.

Gouyen surrendered the baby to him. Denali rocked the child and softly chanted a song.

Looking out through the rocks they could see the fires burning around the lake. Distant figures passed before the flames. From time to time the report of a single gunshot reached them.

In Denali's arms the baby was quiet.

Gouyen stood thinking. The trees were their only hope. Any way they turned they'd have to cross a stretch of grass to reach the woods or go clambering up the rocks and expose themselves on the high ground. Shortly the moon would rise above the rim of the caldera and shine down on the lake. They didn't have much time.

She whispered to Denali what they must do and he felt the wise woman's breath warm on his skin. He nodded his understanding. They emerged from the rocky cleft and started across the meadow while they still had the darkness.

* * *

Cain moved naked through the trees. He wore only moccasins and Mosby's gunbelt and he carried Mosby's Bowie knife in hand. His wrists were still shackled, for Jubal had carried the sole key with him into battle. The bark and crack of pistol and rifle fire sounded from the lake at his back as he stalked deeper into the woods, following the trail of the caballada.

By the time he reached the place where Hector and Dolores waited with the packmules and a few horses, it was full dark. Now there were only intermittent reports of pistolshots. He moved through the underbrush on his belly like a wise old serpent. Cicadas were loud in the trees. He saw them, the segundo and the girl. They sat with their backs to a pine trunk. Silent, gripping rifles. So close he could've reached out and cut a lock of the girl's hair if he'd chosen. He gripped the length of chain between his cuffs so it wouldn't rattle. The horses and mules were cropping grass and he spotted Black Answer among them, saddled as though waiting for his arrival.

There was nothing to stop him from rising up and charging, slashing Dolores's throat.

Not now. It wasn't yet time for Little Sister Death. He wanted her to see the carnage she'd wrought at the lake, then she'd know in her heart what she deserved and he would grant her the honor of Wormwood.

Cain withdrew, pulling back into the brush. He made a semicircle of their position and approached once again, this time where the horses were picketed.

"It's over," Hector spoke in Spanish. The sounds of the battle had ceased.

"It's never over," the girl answered.

"Everything ends, Little Bird. Even this."

"Not while there's still one living."

Cain darted out of the brush. He slashed the picketline with the Bowie and swung up onto Black Answer's saddle, harrying the packmules with a shout and waving the knife. The mules scattered in a panic, chaos of hooves, then he was riding hard through the trees. Hector shouldered his rifle and fired. The shot went wide and Cain vanished, carried away on Black Answer.

* * *

Jubal sent a man to check on Mosby that everything was all right back at camp. Meanwhile he surveyed the battlefield. Several deadfall trees lay about the lake and Jubal took a can of kerosene from his saddlebag and doused the trees and set them burning on the shore. He looked at the bodies strewn in the grass, the bodies floating on the water. A few mules stood trembling and bloody. A pony lay convulsing.

Only then did he believe they'd paid the final price. On that night the Apaches were broken at last.

Jubal looked where the silver curve of the moon was partly visible over the eastern rim. He stared, puzzled, seeming to recall it being in much the same position for some time now. He was still waiting to see it rise perceptibly when he heard movement in the shallow water at the edge of the reeds.

He turned and spotted her, a squaw lying there with a wound on her hip dark and wet. She pretended death under his gaze. Motionless now. He splashed through the water and when he got close, she struck out with a knife. Jubal kicked her in the wounded place and she let out a sharp cry and lost her grip on the knife. The blade disappeared in the water.

He dragged her out of the reeds and drew his pistol and looked at her face in the firelight. Haggard and seamed. Her hair a long and tangled gray. She was an old woman without any fear in her eyes.

"Were you with them?" he asked in Spanish. "That day on the trail. Were you with them?"

She kept her head lowered.

He bent low and yanked her hair, pulling her face upward.

"Answer me. Were you one of them who cut my wife?"

She looked him in the eye. She spat.

Warm spittle ran down Jubal's cheek. He wiped his face clean and smiled at her. He struck out with the pistol and slashed the barrel across her forehead.

"Where's my son?" he screamed. "Where's John Russell?"

* * *

Denali moved through the grass holding the silent baby. The voices of the White Eyes drifted to him on the night air. He looked to the east and saw the edge of the full moon creeping over the rim and he glanced back at Gouyen following with the rifle. She was just a dark shape now, but the light that was coming fast would flood the meadow.

Already the moon shone on the lake and its blue light touched the western woods. It cast the deep shadow of the eastern rim over the meadow, but as the moon rose higher, the shadow drew back upon itself, that covering darkness retreating across the grass. Denali looked where the trees began on the eastern slope—they had no chance of making it in time before the shadows fled and left them exposed.

He stopped and placed the baby down in the grass. He closed his eyes and began singing at a level just above silence itself, a chant for Ussen alone to hear.

Gouyen caught him up. She gripped his arm.

"We have to go," she whispered. "Now."

He kept his eyes tight shut and didn't pause in his song.

Gouyen stared at the fires on the shore. When Denali finished his prayer, he opened his eyes and looked at the moon where it was poised above the rim, then he picked up the baby and they went on.

* * *

He woke gasping. He stared up at the patch of sky above the canopy, dark save a scattering of stars, and his body shook in little convulsions. Then the girl was leaning down over him, her long hair falling, and she touched her palm to his cheek and whispered something soft. She kept repeating it and after a while he realized it was a name, Mosby, Mosby, but it was longer still before he understood the name was his own. Slowly the facts that composed John Eustace Mosby's earthly life returned to him and he sank back into a sense of identity.

Dolores kneeled over him and told him everything was going to be all right. He tried to say, "Thought you was a angel," but all that came out was something between a groan and a wheeze. Mosby turned his head, coughing, and spat up on the grass.

She wet a bandana from her canteen and touched the wet cloth to his neck. How it burned. No fire so fierce.

"Let's get him on his feet," Hector spoke. "We need to find Jubal."

* * *

Dolores and Hector emerged from the woods leading what remained of the caballada—their own horses, a mule with Mosby slumped light-headed on the saddle, and two other packmules. The rest had scattered, lost in the dark of the woods.

She looked out at the lakeshore where Jubal stood between a pair of fires, his back to them, hunched over something in the grass. He was talking, but she couldn't make out the words.

She started to go to him.

Hector grabbed her wrist. "You don't want to go over there."

She watched Jubal rear back his right arm, a pistol in his hand, and bring it sweeping down, and now she needed to see. More than anything she had to see. She tried to pull free of Hector's grip, but he tightened his hold.

"Listen to me, Little—"

She slapped him across the face without thinking what she was doing. His glasses fell off and he wore a look of hurt surprise that she knew she'd remember all her life. This gentle old man who'd sooner cut off his right arm than cause her a moment's pain. He let go and bent to retrieve his glasses.

Dolores ran toward Jubal and the lake.

She stopped short. Now she could see him gripping an old woman's hair and raising his free hand, swinging down hard to strike her with the gun barrel. He stood pistol-whipping the woman, cursing her in a dull flat monotone. The woman limp at his feet. Her face a bloody pulp. Blood ran from her torn brow like a scarlet curtain over her eyes and blood poured from her torn lip. She moaned at every blow, but she wouldn't beg him to stop and all the life remaining in her was defiance.

Dolores stared dumbstruck. Then she saw Endicott striding out of the dark—

And dangling from his hand by her long black hair the severed head of Ishton her own sister.

"Looky here," the mercenary called to Jubal. "I found Cain a new good luck charm."

Dolores fell to her knees and keened like an Apache.

Jubal turned and saw her, a look on his face stricken and pale.

* * *

When they reached the cover of the trees, Denali stopped and looked back out over the meadow where the fires burned. A wailing cry pierced the night, a cry he knew too well. Somewhere along the shore a woman of the

People grieved. Where he kneeled on the wooded slope he grieved with her and though his sorrow was silence, he sorrowed no less. He rocked the baby. Then saw the shadow of the rim begin once more to draw near across the grass, the moon rising now as if unbound by lamentation and the darkness diminishing that had covered their escape. Power had been with him one last time. The wise woman tugged at his arm. He turned and they started climbing the wooded rim.

* * *

Blood dripped from the barrel of his gun. Jubal stared at Dolores as she keened on. He let go of the squaw's hair and she fell in the grass and lay still.

Hector stepped past Dolores and walked up to him. "Put it away," he said. "She's an old woman who can't even run from you."

"One like her cut my wife's throat while I watched," Jubal said.

"Too bad you weren't so brave on that day."

His eyes flashed at Hector. "Any other man who said that to me, I'd put him down right here and now."

Mosby slid from the saddle. He walked up to Dolores and dropped to a knee and touched the girl's shoulder. By the firelight you could see a ring of raw flesh around his throat. Tears in his eyes. He took Dolores's hand and rose with her and she followed him back the way they'd come.

The squaw was spitting blood and broken teeth. Jubal holstered his pistol. He stepped past Hector, then stopped. He spoke without turning. "I never wanted to kill anyone in my life," he said.

Then he walked out into the meadow.

Hector stepped behind the squaw and drew his revolver. "Forgive me, Little Mother," he said to cover the click of the hammer pulled back. He brought the barrel to her head and squeezed the trigger.

CHAPTER ELEVEN

After dawn Carnoviste hiked out of the narrow defile where the remnant of the People were hiding. He set out climbing the hillside and when he neared the crest, he bent low approaching his young sons.

Neiflint and Oblite lay studying the land they'd quit in the night. Watching for sign of riders, movement on the valley floor and the ridge beyond. They'd rubbed clay over their bodies and tied bunches of grass about their heads and in their stillness they were one with the country.

He crawled forward and lay between them. They greeted their father with the slightest of nods. He'd sent them to the hilltop before dawn and now he'd come to check on them while the others tried to sleep below. The boys looked weary. Carnoviste hoped his face didn't betray his own exhaustion—he knew they needed him to be strong.

"Anything?" he asked.

They shook their heads. He looked out over the valley. Save the wind through the treetops there was no movement anywhere. For an instant he wished Gouyen was with them to use her Power of Finding Enemies, then he remembered how her Power had failed them at so great a cost.

Already the morning grew hot. "I'll send one of the maidens to take over for you soon," he told the boys. "Stay alert for any of ours who escaped. They shouldn't be traveling in the day, but keep a watch just the same."

"How many do you think got away?" Oblite asked.

"Not many. Our People will never be the same. I don't know what kind of life you'll have now."

The Blue Mountains had given them up. The People lay murdered around the Lake of the Mountain Spirits. Only a small handful had escaped the lakeside massacre, going over the ridge in the dark. The White Eyes hadn't attempted to follow into the trees and up the slopes where they had the high ground. All night they'd crossed ledges where not even the surest mule would go, the women lifting children up sheer rock walls by ropes, not daring to rest until they'd come down the far side of the ridge and skirted the valley floor.

Carnoviste was waiting for night to come again before they could go on. When darkness fell, they'd be traveling once more, making their way back to Pa-Gotzin-Kay.

"The People will go on," Carnoviste told them. "I hope to see your brothers and their mother again."

The boys didn't speak. Because he hadn't called Denali, Illanipi, and Ishton by name they knew he thought them dead.

"Have strong hearts," he said. "There's another world that waits for us."

* * *

Passing back down through the defile Carnoviste heard a dull drone somewhere above, growing louder, and he looked up and surveyed each quarter of heaven. There—the sun glaring off silver wings. He stood watching it pass overhead. He'd never seen such a thing before and it was in him to think of it as an enormous bird, but he knew it was no bird. Others had spoken of them before. Skyboats that carried men over desert and mountain all the way to the ocean. He wanted Power to call the skyboat down to take his people away in it, carry them over grief and trouble and the pain they'd found below, alighting in the heart of a far country. He stood watching the receding plane until it was a speck in the faultless blue.

He thought of his young wife and child lying beside the water. It was a four-day journey to the Other World. If he started out now, he could be with them in four short days. Images of the slaughter came to him, faces of the dead, and the heart in him so ardent in his youth was broken now. He'd been given a promise as a child. The medicine man told him he'd never taste of death so long as he remained in the Blue Mountains. That promise was more bitter to him now than the most evil curse. What good was survival if he lived only to bear witness the destruction of all he loved? He wanted to ride the river valley and storm the first village he found, kill every White Eye and Mexican that fled before him. Everything in him urged blood and fire, blissful death, but the mountains wouldn't allow it. He had sons who needed a father, their mothers he was sworn to protect. All the braves under the age of his own sons were dead and most of the women and children with them. It was his duty to look after the widows and orphans, though he knew they blamed him for bringing death down upon them.

None of them spoke it, but they all knew the White Eyes had come to the sierras seeking Denali. The survivors kept their silence only because the boy was lost in the attack. If he were with them now, they'd rise as one and demand Carnoviste surrender him up and stop the blood—

And he'd refuse. Even the horror they'd endured couldn't persuade him to turn his back on his son, should the blood of those who'd perished stain his hands alone. If this made him a monster, then he was content to be just such a monster in a world of false-hearted women and warriors lacking all resolve.

None of it mattered, not even this final courage. He wouldn't deceive himself. Denali had surely been swept under the slaughter with the rest.

Carnoviste lowered his head and wept—

For all he had to offer his sons was death.

* * *

Jubal stirred from his slumber that morning to the smoke of the cookfire and the smell of coffee. The men were filling their mugs with the first hot coffee they'd enjoyed in a long while. They'd camped one last time in the trees with the mosquito netting raised once more and tied to the boughs.

Jubal rose from his blankets and looked out through the pale translucent netting and past the tree line. The lake was calm, empty. Ravens had found the slain Apaches. They lighted on the corpses and pecked at the eyes of the dead. A crude cross, two sticks bound with strips of rawhide, stood over Moroni Thayne's grave on the lakeshore. Their only loss in the attack. Endicott had found his body that night still in the saddle of his mount, the horse idly grazing in the grass. The Mormon had been shot through the mouth. In his rage at the discovery Endicott had gone searching the grass for Apache dead on whom he might exact bloody recompense and he'd found the dead squaw who was Dolores's sister.

The mercs had carried Moroni to the water's edge in the night and dug a lonesome grave. They left the Apache dead where they'd fallen, all save the corpse of Dolores's sister. Jubal had rebuked Endicott for the decapitation and ordered him to retrieve the body. When he'd done so, they wrapped it and the severed head in a blanket. The bundle still rested in the grass, a corner of the red blanket fluttering in the breeze.

Across the meadow Jubal saw Dolores go dragging the long branch of a deadfall. Mosby stood hunched working a shovel. She brought the stout branch to Mosby and he turned it upright and dropped the thick end down the hole he'd dug, setting a corner post, then Dolores held it straight while he shoveled dirt into the hole around it. They were making a sky burial. Jubal looked away. He spat the taste of sleep from his mouth and put on his hat and squared it.

"Mornin, sir," Van Zandt said.

"Any sign of Cain?" he asked. Van Zandt had been the last man to pull sentry duty.

"It's like he dropped off the face of the earth," the merc said. "I figure him gone for good."

"Any of you spot him," Jubal told them, "shoot to kill. Don't listen to a word out of that lunatic's mouth."

The men nodded their agreement. "That Cain," Oldham said. "Crazy as a bedbug, but one hell of a fightin man."

"What shook loose in his head?" Rourke wondered. "Reckon the devil took him?"

"I'd sooner think that Cain took the devil."

Jubal nodded at Hector, who sat sipping coffee. The segundo wouldn't meet his eyes.

Jubal stepped from the netting and went to look over the caballada. Two of the packmules they'd lost when Cain made his escape had wandered back into camp during the night. He wasn't going to send the men out to hunt for the others, not with Cain and a handful of Apache survivors loose in the woods. They had just enough supplies to make it back to Nácori.

"What's the plan, sir?" Clovis asked when Jubal returned.

"We're done. We did what we came for. They understand what I want and now they damn well know the price they'll pay if they don't give him up."

* * *

Before dawn they'd been progressing up the ridgeside in the dark when Gouyen stopped and raised a hand. Denali stood holding the baby in one arm and his free hand went to his pistol. They listened. Someone moving through the brush to their left, coming up through the pines. Gouyen shouldered her rifle.

Chatto and Jacali emerged from the trees into the moonlight, each carrying a small child, and two other children followed in their footsteps.

"My brother," Denali called.

They turned and saw them. Jacali ran staggering forward, but Chatto only stared. Denali holstered the pistol and wrapped his arm around the maiden, who leaned hard against him.

"They killed my sister," she told him. "They killed my mother too. We thought we were the only ones still alive."

She was covered in dirt and dried blood from scratches and cuts sustained during their wild flight through the brush. He could hear the exhaustion creeping through her voice.

"It's all right," he told her. "We're together now."

"Will they track us up here?"

"I can feel my Power coming back," he lied. "Strong enough to hide our path from them. They can't hurt us now."

In truth he'd called upon the last remnant of his gift when his song had stayed the moon and now all he felt was emptiness.

"Our problems are solved," Chatto mocked. There was a coil of rawhide about his shoulder, the reata he'd used to lift Jacali and the little ones up the steepest slopes. "The Healer's Power has returned. Can it raise the dead?"

"The dead wait for us in the Other World."

"Finish your big talk later," Chatto said. "Let's start moving. I want to reach that high spot before it gets light." He pointed to a gnarled finger of granite that spired up from the pines. As though it reached forth to stroke the face of the moon.

"All right, my brother," Denali said.

"Or does your great Power tell you a better way?" Chatto asked.

"I follow where you lead."

Chatto turned his back on them and set out up the slope.

* * *

In Denali's dream he didn't know how she found him.

He was running through a pass in the mountains, through the dark and the cold, and in the dream unseen figures struck out, blows from the shadows at either side, sudden pain rushing out of the black. Laughter, mad cackling. He ran the gauntlet. He didn't know what he was running toward, but he knew if he ever stopped they would kill him.

Strange music. A sound like wind through chimes, then she was standing before him, her long hair flowing, and they weren't hurting him anymore. He fell at her feet and cried out for her to give him horses, the bright ghost herd with their manes afire, so that he might trample down the enemies who'd taken her from him.

She took him by the hand, then made him rise. She counseled him in the fullness of her wisdom to place no hope in vengeance. For such a spirit having once been loosed on the world knew no limit to its bloodletting. All are one, she told him. Every man a brother. Yet there was a wound in the heart of things and a great confusion so that men forgot the original spirit and reduced themselves to the passions of the four-legs. Nonetheless all men were one in sorrow and blood. Reaching out to slay his brother, the slayer slayed himself a thousandfold, biting and tearing his own flesh in blind frenzy, and still all the blood of the centuries seemed not enough to stop the mortal clockwork or defer for the glimmering of a single golden instant the sweeping hand's next killing blow. The void waged war on flesh, wielding time as its weapon to try the substance of a man's soul whether there were not elements in him equal to the void that time could not devour. The slayer and the slain ran on in darkness, ran on until he released the one he'd reached out to destroy.

The sun rose over her right shoulder. He watched the shade of his mother recede in the dawnlight. She let go of his hand and told him to keep a strong heart and that she'd be with him, then she spoke his name and vanished.

He knew that when night fell in the world of his dream he'd be running the gauntlet again, but he wasn't alone anymore.

* * *

Gouyen stood over the circle of sleepers and stared down at the dreaming warrior. Denali lay in exhaustion, shielded from harsh morning light by the rock overhang of the spire. Chatto and Jacali lay beside him, the children sleeping at their feet.

She was a long time watching him. She rubbed the talisman in the leather bundle between her breasts, weighing a course of action. Once taken not to be undone, never again for all the heavens' turning.

He knew their ways. He knew their camps and the seasons they favored each camp and the trails they would take. Whatever happened, he'd carry that knowledge with him, perhaps one day to return seeking vengeance of his own. Letting him go might cost the People more than when they'd taken him. Better to kill him where he lay? She had her own reasons for wanting it to be so. Yet in the end her heart was still for the People and the best chance of saving them. The coyote must live.

Gouyen tried not to think about her own hand in the horror of the lake, the blood-drenched lie she'd told Carnoviste. There would come a day when she must make it right, but for now the remnant of the People needed her. She kneeled and shook Jacali and Chatto awake and cautioned them to silence. Then she rose and motioned for them to follow her down the trail.

Denali shuddered in his sleep where they'd left him.

In the little meadow below the rocky spine Gouyen stood with the maiden and young warrior. There was a natural spring that fed a pool where birds drank. Their coming had startled the jays into a winged retreat to the boughs of a great oak overlooking the meadow and the pool. Chatto and Jacali stood side by side, facing Gouyen, like a betrothed couple in a secret wedding ceremony. The old crone a woodland priestess there to perform the rites. Instead Gouyen spoke only of death. She told them what they already suspected, who hunted the People and why even now Carnoviste would allow more of their own to be slaughtered, and she told them what must be done.

Chatto stared up the slope where his brother lay dreaming.

* * *

Denali jolted awake trying to catch his breath. His arms and legs were stiff and his tongue hurt. He turned his head to the side and spat blood.

One of the young children Chatto and Jacali had rescued sat over him with a look of fear on his soft face. "You were shaking," the boy said. "I couldn't wake you up."

"It's all right," he told the boy. He felt dazed and beaten. As though he'd spent the night wrestling a spirit.

The other children still lay asleep at his feet in the warmth and light of the new day. None older than six winters and all of them orphans now.

He rose from the stones and saw Chatto come leading Jacali and Gouyen back up the slope. Trouble in his brother's eyes, plain to see even at a distance. Jacali kept her gaze on the ground, refusing to look toward him, and this sense of foreboding came over Denali like a sudden thunderhead. Waiting to burst loose dark torrents.

"What's wrong?" he asked when they approached.

Chatto looked to the wise woman. "Tell him."

"It's against Carnoviste's wishes," Gouyen said.

"Don't pretend with me, old woman. You don't care anything for the chief's wishes."

The children stirred at the anger in Chatto's voice.

Gouyen met Denali's eyes. "He's alive," she told him. "Your father lives."

"I know," Denali said. "Carnoviste has the sacred promise—he can't be killed so long as he stays in the Blue Mountains."

"Not Carnoviste. Your true father."

He hesitated. "Carnoviste is my father."

"Your bloodfather lives. The warriors showed you a scalp after we took you, remember? It was bloody and you believed it was your White Eye father's, but it was a trick. The scalp was an old one that we carried on the raid. The blood was your mother's."

"You're lying," Denali said. "Warriors don't play such tricks. That's not our way."

"Carnoviste wanted your father to live and feel the grief of the People. It was Carnoviste who thought to bring the scalp so you'd think him dead."

"Liar. You're the one who plays tricks. I know what you are."

"May all those who dwell in the House of Ghosts haunt me if I lie. Think of it. It was Matzus who pretended to take your father's scalp. A warrior who lifts a scalp must go through four days of cleansing before he has a right to dance. But wasn't Matzus there at the celebration, dancing with the widows, the night you were brought to the Stronghold Mountain? He didn't need cleansing because he took no scalp."

"How should I remember if he danced that night?"

"Of course you remember. You watched him all night. I saw how you hated him for what you thought he'd done."

It was true—Denali could still recall Matzus dancing with the widows and how his hatred had burned.

249

Chatto said, "Your bloodfather leads the White Eyes against us."

"He never stopped looking for you," Gouyen said. "You've seen how many of the People he's killed. All just to get to you. And he'll never stop killing."

"I don't believe you," Denali told them. "I'm of the People. Carnoviste is my father and my chief."

"You have to go to your bloodfather," Chatto said.

"I won't."

"For the sake of the People, you have to."

"Why do you say this to me, my brother? Don't tell me she's witched you with her lies."

"I'm not your brother, Coyote."

Gouyen spat at his feet. "Go to them. You were never one of the People."

Denali looked her hard in the eye. "I know what your brother was," he said. "I know how he turned his Power to darkness. And Chatto knows it too."

Now Jacali looked up, first at Denali, then cutting her eyes to Chatto.

"I don't know anything of it," Chatto said. "Only your wild imaginings."

"You know."

"Then tell me," Gouyen said, "what was my brother that you feared him so much?"

Denali hesitated. If Chatto wouldn't stand beside him, how could he accuse the medicine man, even in death? To claim Nantan had transformed himself into the bear would be admitting Denali had reason to want him dead. For a certainty they'd think to search the cave, the place where Denali's Power had failed, and all would be lost. To kill an immortal medicine man meant exile or death.

"You're jealous of my Power," he told Gouyen at last. "You make up wild stories because my Power is stronger than yours and you hate me for it."

"What Power?" Gouyen demanded. She rubbed her hand as though it ached. "Your Power is gone."

"The White Eyes hunt the Blue Mountains for you," Chatto said. "You know what they do to our dead. Scalp them and cut their bodies to pieces. How many more have to live in the Other World without ears or eyes before you go back where you belong?"

"I'm of the People," he said, almost a whisper.

"Then give your People mercy," Chatto demanded. "Pick that baby up and bash his head on the rocks. All these mountains have for him is more pain. If you don't have the courage to show him mercy, then I will."

Chatto kneeled and reached for Illanipi. None of the children cried, but there was quiet terror in their eyes. Denali drew his knife and touched the blade to his friend's throat.

Chatto froze. Then he slowly raised his hand and gripped Denali's own and pressed the blade tighter to his skin so that a trickle of blood ran down his neck.

"Do it before they kill us all. I don't want to see more little ones suffer. But show me the last kindness and hide my body so I can enter the Other World whole."

He began singing his deathsong.

Denali held the knife rock-steady. He looked at Jacali, but she glanced away. Finally he lowered the knife and stepped past Chatto and the wise woman and started down the trail.

"Coward," Chatto called after him.

* * *

Denali kneeled at the little pool in the meadow and reached to trouble the water. He hesitated, thinking of Jacali, an orphan now like the rest, and he thought of his brothers and all the little ones and the price was too much. His family had been taken from him and another restored in its place only to be carried away again.

He stared down at his reflection. Red hair falling below his shoulders, skin sun-darkened but still so pale. It was as though all the events of his life belonged to some other and he wasn't himself.

A flock of jays were waiting for him to leave so they could descend and bathe at the pool and he kneeled watching them. Sunlight on their wings. Shadows moving across the grass. He watched their flight like an augur bent on discerning the shape of tomorrow. Whether it might be fashioned to the force of man's will or else man's will must be bent and hammered to meet that immutable form.

A chant drifted down to him. He looked back toward the spire and listened to the wise woman chanting a bearsong. She called on the Power of the Bear to protect the people. Now he could hear a warrior's voice joining her, Chatto echoing her prayer, and then he understood how bad it was.

Denali looked into the water. He cupped his hands in the pool and brought them to his lips and drank and the water from the spring was cool on his tongue but afterward very bitter.

He rose and started back up to the spire.

The jays lighted about the water.

* * *

When Denali returned under the dark spire, he saw Gouyen clutching the medicine bundle at her neck, kneeling across from Chatto, both of them intent on their chant. Jacali sat with Illanipi in her arms, looking on, the other children gathered around her. Fear in the maiden's eyes. She understood the wise woman and Chatto were about the business of calling something up that couldn't be put back again.

Gouyen raised her head at the sound of his approach and it was then Denali saw it, her face twisting in his vision to become the face of the grizzly, teeth bared in a snarl. A flash and it was gone, her own countenance restored. In time the bear would have to feed again.

"We told you to go to him," Gouyen said. "Why did you come back?"

Chatto didn't pause in his chanting.

"To stop you from doing this thing," Denali said. "No more sacrifices for the bear. I won't let you."

"The Power of the Bear protected the People until you took it from us. It will protect us again. That's worth any price, Coyote."

"The bear only protects from the White Eyes so that it can eat us up one at a time." He shook his head at Chatto. "How can you join her in this?"

Chatto ceased his chant. "I'll do what I have to do to save my people. I honor my father."

"There's nothing left for you here, Coyote," Gouyen said. "Go back to the White Eyes or you'll bring death on us all."

Denali drew his knife. "I want to know where your Power comes from—and I want everyone to see."

He strode forward and caught her throat with his free hand, gripping it hard, though she tried to pull away, and he slashed out with the knife.

Chatto burst to his feet, drawing his own blade. He plunged it deep in Denali's side, just below the ribs, as Denali's knife severed the rawhide cord around Gouyen's neck and the medicine bundle was in his grip.

Denali gasped. He turned his head to see the look of surprise on Chatto's face, the warrior dumbstruck, shocked at his own actions, and staring at the medicine bundle Denali held.

In Denali's own eyes a mixture of sorrow and pain and something like understanding.

Chatto's hand was frozen on the grip of the knife.

"My brother—" he began, then the wise woman was on her feet and striking out with a stone in hand.

"No," Jacali shouted. The baby wailed in her arms.

Denali took the blow to his left temple. He dropped, his legs giving out, crumbling at Gouyen's feet, and the medicine bundle fell from his hand and went spilling open on the ground.

Gouyen screamed. She dropped to her knees and scrambled to grab it up, but she was too slow—Chatto and Jacali saw everything before her gnarled hand swept it back into the bag.

A small mummified foetus, dark and leathery. A pair of misshapen heads sprouting from the selfsame neck and on each hand six tiny fingers. Like something hellspawned, born of nightmare.

Gouyen clutched the bundle to her chest in an attitude equal parts tenderness and defiance. She looked at Denali where he lay silent and still, blood on his temple, the knife buried in his side, and his eyes stared unblinking.

"You did what a warrior must do," she told Chatto.

Flecks of Denali's blood marked Chatto's face. "I thought he meant to cut your throat," he said. Everything felt unreal to him. As though he'd slipped into a dreamworld. "I didn't understand," he told her.

"You acted to save the People. Never forget—you honored your father with what you did here today."

The baby was crying. Jacali wept her own hard grief. The children gripped her dress and hid their faces against her, terrified at what they'd seen.

"My brother," Chatto said. He fell down beside Denali.

"Up," Gouyen barked. "Stand like a warrior. Would your father cry over a dead coyote?" She bent and picked up the coiled reata. "Help me build a fire. We're not done here."

* * *

Dolores stared out at the shining lake where a pale spider balanced on the surface of the water. On the far shore the reeds parted at the coming of a fox that lowered its head to drink. She couldn't understand how such a place had been the scene of the evening's anguish, tranquility so easily broken. She turned and looked across the grass to where the sky burial rose holding her sister's remains and she saw that already the ravens had found it.

The horses and mules stood at the lake's edge lapping up water while the men prepared to depart. They were leaving the mountain lake and setting out for Nácori Chico.

Jubal walked up to Bardo. The horse raised his head dripping water and Jubal snapped the stumps of his fingers, then pulled on his gloves.

"They've had their fill," he said. "Let's get movin." Jubal placed his boot in the stirrup and swung up into the saddle.

"Mister Jubal," Mosby called. "You seein this?"

Jubal turned and saw where Mosby pointed to the

northeast. A column of smoke rose from a sharp peak beyond the ridgeline.

"Looks like a signal," Mosby said.

"Maybe Apaches, maybe Cain," Jubal said. He took the fieldglasses from his saddlebag and glassed the peak. Black smoke billowing up, slowly fanning out in the high west wind.

He lowered the glasses. "Somebody wants us to know they're up there."

"Maybe it ain't meant for us," Mosby said. "Might be Apaches tryin to let each other know they made it out."

"Not likely. They'd already have a place in mind, a rendezvous to meet up with other survivors. And they sure as hell got no reason to let us know there's more of em still alive."

"Then what's it for?"

Jubal was silent a moment. Then he said, "There's somethin up there they want us to see."

"If they want us up there, that's the last place we ought to go," Clovis said.

"Maybe," Jubal told him. "Except I'm goin."

"Mr. McKenna, sir," Oldham protested, "that don't hardly seem like a good idea."

"Whatever it is, I've got to see," Jubal said. "I want two volunteers with me, but understand right now, we damn well might not make it back down again."

Endicott spat. "Long as we bring the Brownings, I'm your man."

"Might be the sergeant up there," Mosby said, staring at the spire. "Maybe I can calm him down, talk some sense into him. I'll ride."

Jubal turned to Hector and spoke in Spanish. "Get Dolores home safe. Don't wait for us, go with the men back to Nácori. We'll catch up with you or we won't. Follow the river home."

"Why are you doing this?" Hector asked. "I thought it was finished."

Jubal watched the smoke. "I have to know," he said.

When Jubal rode out, Dolores turned away and stared at the spider on the water.

* * *

Jubal and the pair of mercs cut a long swath around the stone rim that encircled the caldera, bypassing the roughest country, and he led them up a series of open game trails along the spine of the far ridge, making relatively quick work of it. By the time they approached the spire that evening, the smoke had mostly died out. Jubal paused and sat his horse on the trail and watched the last of it, pale tendrils rising from a meadow just below the spire.

He got down and held out his reins to Mosby. "Give me your BAR. Both of you stay back with the horses."

"Maybe you better let us scout ahead."

"I said stay back. Don't come unless I call."

Mosby took the reins. Jubal pulled the BAR from

Mosby's saddle-scabbard and slung the rifle strap over his shoulder. He went on afoot, stalking through the woods to approach the meadow from the side, and he scrambled down a wooded decline, the smell of smoke in the air. When he crept out of the tree line, the sun was sinking low and he saw the trunks of the deadfalls still smoldering where they'd been heaped together and set ablaze.

He gripped the BAR and stood listening, waiting for movement. The stillness unbroken. He walked out and looked at the glowing ashes. It was a signal, no doubt of it now, and he knew with a bone-deep knowing that it had been meant to draw him to this place, but he didn't understand why.

A copse of trees stood to the west across the meadow. A great oak dwarfed the others, forced them to struggle for light under its shadow. The sky shone red through the upper branches, sunset bleeding through the inkblot trees, and Jubal was about to turn away when he saw the silhouette hanging from a high bough.

His son's body swayed alone and forsaken by his chosen people.

Jubal ran to him. He fell on his knees at the base of the oak. They'd drawn rawhide cords under the boy's arms and lashed him to the tree. He wore dirty buckskins and there was a wound in his side and at his temple. His hair was long and tangled and still the very shade of red as his mother's.

Jubal took off the shoulder strap and cast the rifle

259

aside. He groaned deep in his chest and bowed his head. Kneeling like an Argonaut come to a far shore, the end of a long voyage but no homecoming now forever.

"John Russell," he whispered. His breath caught in his throat. It wasn't supposed to be this way, backward of nature's design, and he didn't know how to be the orphan of his son. He reached up and held the boy's cold bare foot and he wept with his head resting against the trunk of the oak. Out in the darkness the jays were singing.

He shook with a speechless fury. Grief and rage and something worse, guilt like an open wound. He clenched a fist and reared back and struck the hard trunk, over and over, skinning his knuckles bloody on the rough bark, weeping and striking the tree.

After a long while he rose. He looked up at the bough where the bonds were tied. "I'm comin back for you," he told John Russell. Then he turned and started through the meadow in the dark to get his horse.

"You all right, Mister Jubal?" Mosby called at his approach.

"Where'd you leave the Browning?" Endicott asked.

Jubal didn't answer. He stepped up to them on the game trail and took Bardo's reins. From the look on his face the mercenaries knew well enough what he'd found and they didn't speak another word.

He returned alone to the meadow riding the horse and he drew his Bowie knife and stopped under the oak and wrapped his arm around his son's waist, then reached up with the Bowie and cut the rawhide cords and John Russell fell into his embrace. He turned the horse to ride out a distance into the meadow. Then got down and laid him in the long grass.

About the boy's neck a small leather pouch on a string. Jubal opened it and spilled out the contents onto his palm, but he didn't understand what any of it meant—two feathers, a scrap of honeycomb, a small blue stone—and he held them in his hand a long time, wondering at them. Finally he placed the items back inside the pouch. He rose and got his coat from the saddlebag and kneeled to wrap John Russell in it. He lay in the grass beside his son.

Above them a formless sky. Gray clouds drifting over the sierras, masking constellations.

He thought he could feel his mind slipping loose of its moorings, gone out far past the limits of endurance. Now the search was over, but he couldn't rest while his son remained in these mountains. He was strong enough to make one last journey, he told himself. He'd bring John Russell home to lie beside his mother and when it was finished, he'd join them.

CHAPTER TWELVE

She came down from the heights of the continental divide with a fire raging in her skull and entered the valley where the rivers meet and she came stalking down the low country through catclaw and waving sacaton. Muscles rippling under her brown fur. A vacant quality in her gaze now. She'd pause from time to time and stand stock still, growling at long-dead visitors, vanquished foes or prey she'd once known in younger days. The worst of it was seeing her cubs again. Glimpse them moving through the trees. The breath would catch in her throat and she'd go chasing after them, but always when she got close, they'd disappear, less substantial than a dream.

In her time she'd mothered thirteen cubs. All gone now, casualties of disease or the two-legs who hunted with their packs of yipping dogs and set traps with sweet-smelling potions. She'd learned to be wary of the traps and to hate them. One misstep and it was too late, those great snapping metal jaws would not unclench never unclench no matter how she tried, and she could hear her cub, howling with his leg caught in death's cold mouth, broken and bloody, as she gave up and led the others away before the two-legs came.

Time had stolen everything from her. She was alone now without a mate in the sierras entire and she hadn't been able to close her eyes or take a drink of water for two days.

Seven days earlier she'd woke to the night flier sucking at her wound. Its horrible leering face, those leathery wings spreading wide when she stirred and saw it. She swatted a huge forepaw and rose growling to her feet in the dark cavern. The night flier hissed and scampered away on its clawed feet, out through the mouth of the cave. There was a steep drop-off beside the trail and the creature was heading for it. She lumbered after it and the night flier turned its head, hissing at her, blood on pale fangs in the moonlight, then it dove off the cliff and out of sight below. A moment later she saw it rise into view, aloft on dark wings, beating away into the night.

She'd thought it was over and so she returned to sleep, but the night flier had left a sickness to incubate in her blood. Within days she'd begun to fear the water, though she ached for a drink. Her eyes burned in their sockets like twin howling suns. The world such an agony. After a while she found herself wandering the pine ridges, host to a senseless fury. She'd rise up on her hindlegs and do crazed battle with moss-grown trunks, then the fever would slacken and her enemies become trees again, nothing for it but to go on thirsting and sick for sleep.

She'd come to the land of the two-legs at a point where the smaller stream emptied its brackish water into the big river. She walked the tall grass and turned once to snap at the air before proceeding down the valley wall. Following the canal on the south side of the river she came to a field of corn, the many ears rustling, whispering, as the stalks parted to pass her through.

She ventured out into a watermelon patch. A farmhouse and barn stood across the turned earth, a single light still visible through a window. She stood watching. After a while a shadow crossed before the glass and the light went out. She growled in the dark and her forepaw crushed a watermelon and she went on.

In the barn the horses jostled in their stalls snorting and shrieking at the smell of the beast. A colt's legs trembled as though he were standing for the first time. His mother whinnied and kicked at the boards in the stall beside him and fear made its home in the heart of every living thing.

The last grizzly had come down from the mountains to die.

* * *

The Mormon boy named Gideon left the farmhouse before dawn and walked out to the barn carrying the rifle and lantern. His family still lay asleep in the house, all save his little brother, the child watching from a bedroom window.

Gideon took a halter and opened the door of his horse's stall and haltered the roan and led it out. He draped the blanket over the roan's back, then retrieved the saddle from the saddleroom and came and set it in place. He was tightening the latigo when he looked up and saw his brother standing in the barn bay. Jacob was dressed in overalls and a pair of boots. His hair was golden curls. Like Gideon's own, like their father's.

"Where do you think you're goin?" Gideon asked. He fastened the backcinch.

"With you."

"Oh, you're goin with me, huh? Is that right?"

"That's what I said."

"You got chores."

Jacob shook his head. "It's Alma Rose's turn."

"Go on back in there and get to sleep."

Jacob stood planted.

"Your scrawny ass will fall off and get caught in a trap," Gideon told him.

"No, it won't."

"Your mamma'll tan my hide she finds out I let you skip chores and go with me."

"No, she won't," Jacob said.

"Then you don't know your own momma. Go on back inside."

Jacob didn't budge.

Gideon led the roan out the barn bay past his brother. He paused, then spoke without turning.

"Well, saddle up then, dammit. We ain't got all mornin."

They rode up the valley wall onto pine slopes overlooking fields of wheat and corn. The farms were irrigated by the canal their grandfathers had carved from the earth when they'd come to this valley from Oaxaca after the flood of 1905. The Mormons who'd settled Colonia Morelos cut their fields out of a wilderness of mesquite and scrub pine. From where the boys rode they could look out across the valley in the sunrise and see adobe homes and streets of brick in the distance. The Temple that was also a schoolhouse. O. P. Brown's mill on the river. The smoke of breakfast fires drifted from the chimneys of waking houses.

It was still dark in the pine shadows when Gideon walked the horse up to the first set. The steel jaws had snapped shut on something smaller than the bear they'd laid the trap for. The No. 6 Newhouse bear trap had broken its spine. He sat the horse and leaned from the saddle, examining what they'd caught, and it took him a moment to figure out it was a coyote. Patches of fur were missing, its hind-end almost hairless.

"What is that?" Jacob asked.

"You never seen a chupacabra before?"

"It is not a chupacabra."

"Hell yes, it is. The goatsucker itself."

Jacob put his mount forward and leaned from the saddle studying the creature. "That's just a mangy coyote, dumb-ass," he said.

"Where'd you learn to talk like that?" Gideon demanded.

"I must of picked it up somewheres."

"Your mamma'll tan my hide she hears you cussin."

"I know it," the boy said.

The next set hadn't been sprung, the bait still dangling from a tree branch. The trap jaws lay gaping just as Gideon and his father had left them. They'd placed the traps on the slopes a day after the bear had wandered through their garden and frightened the horses. Each morning Gideon rode out to check them.

The third trap was gone. The rotten-smelling fish was still there, in a burlap sack tied to a branch above the place where the trap should've been. Blood and tracks in the dirt. They could see where the long thick branch they'd secured the trap to had been dragged through the brush leaving a clear trail. A foul stench in the air, far worse than the fish. The boys followed the trail perhaps ten yards through the trees, the stench growing stronger, and when they came upon the carcass, neither of them said a word. They just drew up and sat their horses staring.

A grizzly bear lay dead on the ground beside the trap. They'd not seen a grizzly in the sierras before, only black bears, but the scene was more surprising yet. The trap's jaws were open, its teeth stained with blood, bits of hair and flesh clinging to them, and the grizzly was free. Dried blood imbued the ground about the carcass and its fur was dark with it.

By the trap a great pile of organs and butchered flesh abuzz with flies.

The horses shied at the smell of death and wildness and they wanted nothing to do with the bear's dark mystery. The boys dismounted and stood patting the horses and speaking to them until they calmed.

"What happened?" Jacob asked.

"I don't know. Somebody come along and gutted it."

"Why would somebody do that?"

"How the hell should I know?"

Jacob coughed and spat. "You ever smell anything so bad in your whole life?"

"Pretty rank."

Gideon handed his little brother the roan's reins and took a bandana from his pocket and held it over his nose and mouth and stepped toward the bear.

She lay on her belly. Her eyes open, staring through him. He wanted to see her underside, where she'd been gutted, how it had been done, and he stepped closer to turn her over.

"Careful," his brother said.

"It's deader than a hammer."

"That don't mean it can't hurt you."

Gideon hunkered down on his boot-heels and breathed through the bandana. Flies swarmed around him. He reached out to push the carcass over on its side—

And the bear rose laughing a mad man's laughter.

* * *

Cain burst forth from the belly of the bear, naked and

gore-stained, like the birth of some abomination. He howled laughter. Wrists still shackled, the chain rattling when he swung the kalis.

Wormwood caught the boy's neck and bright arterial blood sprayed the air. The boy fell. The younger one was struggling to keep the panicked horses still long enough to reach the rifle on the roan's saddle. His eyes darted to Cain. When the wild man rose holding the blade, the boy gave up on the rifle and tried to step into the stirrup.

Cain fell upon him reeking of the bear.

* * *

Cain had fled the lake astride Black Answer, scorning the battle, leaving them all behind, and vanished into the woods. In the dark he'd dismounted and led the horse over the tangled rise and down the far side, then he'd swung into the saddle once more. All night he kept Black Answer at a fast clip, swift as the trails and slopes would permit and heading northeast. He rode without destination, bound for whatever lay ahead, and he rode shackled and naked like one of the damned lately escaped from hell's lower reaches and absconding on the devil's prized steeplechaser, demons hard at his heels.

By morning he still hadn't slowed to rest or water the horse nor would he that day. Racing along narrow paths Black Answer twice lost footing and twice recovered but not before very nearly plunging them both to their deaths. Cain went slaloming trails like a mad man late for an appointment with oblivion. Cold sweat drenched the horse's coat. At the dimming of day those great nostrils misted blood.

Finally that night Black Answer staggered in the trail and gave out a long thin cry and sank exhausted to his forelegs.

Cain stepped from the saddle. He turned his head and spat.

He thought they were somewhere in the mountains surrounding the Mormon community of Colonia Morelos. He searched among the saddlebags. Mosby had placed Cain's clothes and gunbelt inside along with the kalis and little Remington one-shot. He took out the neatly folded clothes and cast them to the side of the trail. Then he traded the gunbelt he wore for his own and placed the derringer in a pouch on the gunbelt and took his canteen and slung the strap around his neck, awkward with his shackled hands. He stuck the sheathed Bowie under his belt. The scoped .45-70 was still in the saddle-scabbard, Oldham preferring Cain's .30-30 in the close confines of the battle at the lake. With the sheathed kalis hanging from his belt and the big-game rifle in hand, he set out walking.

Black Answer lay dying in the trail behind him.

Cain didn't look back.

He crossed the ridgeline in the night and proceeded down the pine-wooded slopes to the valley where the

Rio Batepito fed into the Bavispe. He stopped and stood listening. A distant strangled roar. Rattling chains, then silence in the woods. He went on a ways and after a while he heard it again, the cry that something wild makes when there's no chance of escape and ultimate defeat is at hand. He stalked off through the trees in the direction of the cries.

By the time he found her the grizzly had fallen for the last time. The trap's jaws were clamped shut on her right forepaw, steel teeth biting into flesh and bone, and she lay taking shallow breaths while Cain stood over her and she didn't even realize he was there.

He looked at the trap. Five feet of chain stretched to a long branch that she'd been pulling behind her. Now the branch was caught between the trunks of two trees and she couldn't go on. She trembled where she lay. Cain kneeled and placed his palm on her head. No reaction. When he was satisfied she was too weak to move, he set the rifle aside and examined the trap. He depressed the springs and got a grip on the jaws and pulled, the bear's blood running down his hands, and spread the jaws as wide as his own chains would allow and he moved the trap to work her limb free before letting the jaws slowly close once again.

He picked up Wormwood and straddled the bear. She didn't move or make a sound. He pressed the tip of the blade to the grizzly's chest. Then plunged it deep into her heart. At the last he could hear the final breath escape her throat like a spirit drifting into the night.

He took a huge paw in his hands and pressed the bloody claws to his forehead and drew his mark.

* * *

Now he stripped the Mormon brothers down to their arcane underwear. He was surprised to find the symbols snipped into the white cloth, the square and compass on their breasts, and he stared at those familiar sigils a long time, lost in reverie.

Then Cain scalped the corpses.

The rest of the morning he lurked in the fields on the outskirts of town like one banished from the community of man, exiled for his strange appetites. He'd tied the fresh scalps to his arms with the drawstrings of the boys' temple garments. Flies buzzed all about him, delighted at the gore, but he paid them no mind. He moved in a crouch and paused to stare out through the stalks, a watcher in the corn.

Tree-lined streets, whitewashed clapboard houses. Here and there among them a few brick homes with pitched and gabled roofs. Behind picket fences the front yards and flowerbeds were carefully tended and children ran barefoot and shouting, boys in overalls and girls in calico dresses. He brought the butt of the rifle to his shoulder and closed one eye and peered through the scope. The crosshairs lingered on a young girl playing marbles with a group of boys on the sidewalk. Then he moved the scope and for a time watched an old woman asleep in her rocking chair on a porch.

At last he drew back into the corn.

Cain departed the field and followed the river until he came to the outlying farms. He crept from a barn to the side of a two-story farmhouse and ducked below the windows to crouch peeking around the corner into the backyard. A woman stood at a laundry line hanging clothes. In the garden two women in bonnets and a man with a long gray beard walked the furrows, hoes in hand.

Cain turned and went around to the front porch. He took the steps as though he were the householder himself and opened the door and stepped into the cool quiet. He moved down a hallway in his moccasins, letting the rifle hang from his neck on the strap, and he gripped the kalis at the ready. In the kitchen he paused and listened for the creak of floorboards, but there was nothing, the house empty save its lone intruder. He wandered upstairs and toured the children's rooms and wound a music box on the girl's nightstand. A lullaby played softly. Crossing the hall he stopped to study old tintypes in their frames. A line of men leaning on shovels, the canal stretching at their backs. A sad-eyed young girl posing amid the ruins of Oaxaca, those orchards and homes swept away, destroyed as surely as Tyre of old at the hands of Alexander.

Cain stood in the master bedroom and peered through the window looking down on the woman in the backyard. She was pining a man's white shirt to the line.

On the nightstand by the bed a leatherbound *Book of Mormon*. Embossed in gold script on the cover were the words *Bishop Hiram Kimball*. He left that spurious volume where it lay and turned and opened the great oak wardrobe that stood in the corner and there were the temple vestments hanging inside.

* * *

Cain rode out the barn bay astride a dun and leading a black, the kalis under the sash across his waist, pale robes flapping in the wind and bloody golden scalps dangling from his mystic green apron. The iron manacles were still tight around his wrists, but he'd used a hacksaw, discovered in the barn, to cut the chain that had bound them together.

He wore the bishop's head-covering, a kind of white turban. When he galloped past the bishop's wife at the laundry line, a puzzled look crossed her face as though she'd mistaken him for her husband. Then he charged past the workers in the garden. The bishop raised his hoe and shouted curses. Dust trailed in Cain's wake. When he crested a rise some three hundred yards distance from the farmhouse, he drew up and turned the dun. The women below stood staring up at him. The bishop was running toward the barn to get one of the remaining horses and give chase.

Cain took the .45-70 from behind his back. He worked the lever and brought the scope to his eye and found the running man in the crosshairs. He tracked him across the garden, across the backyard. Just as the bishop ducked under the laundry line, Cain fired.

The rifle bucked hard against his shoulder. The dun whinnied and stomped. He got the horse under control and raised the barrel again and scoped the country below. The bishop lay facedown in the grass. One of the women kneeled beside him, her face contorted in a scream that reached Cain in the distance faint as an echo of the past. Blood stained the white sheet fluttering on the line.

Cain turned the horse and set out along the river road.

* * *

In the morning Mosby and Endicott sat their horses in the meadow.

Jubal stood holding his reins and handed up the BAR to Mosby. John Russell's body was wrapped in a blanket and slung over Bardo's saddle.

"Head on out," Jubal told them. "Catch up with the others."

"It ain't safe, a man alone," Mosby said.

"I'm not alone. My son's with me now."

"Let's all ride together," Endicott said.

"Got to do this myself. I don't need help and I don't want company. When you catch up with the rest, don't let Hector come back for me. I'll be along when I'm ready."

Endicott shook his head, resigned to it.

Mosby nodded. "All right, Mister Jubal. Reckon you got to do what you got to do."

The pair of mercenaries started out back down the trail.

Before they'd gone a dozen feet Jubal called after them and they drew up. "One last thing," he said. "Don't tell the girl I found him. Not this way. You understand?"

"I understand," Mosby said. "She don't need to know until she got to."

* * *

When Jubal reached the lake down below, still leading Bardo, he searched the long grass. At last among the loathsome dead and the scattered remains of camp supplies he found what he was looking for, an Apache travois of pine-branches and cowhides bound with strips of buckskin. He dragged the travois to the edge of the water where Bardo stood drinking.

Flies swarmed in a feasting frenzy. Something had been at Moroni's grave, clawmarks in the soft earth. A squaw's corpse floated on the water.

Jubal fastened the harness of the travois to his horse and picked up John Russell and placed the body on the cowhides. Then he stepped into the saddle and they set out at a slow pace.

Night came and they camped in the pines. Though

Jubal slept he found no rest and he woke tired to the bone and rose and readied the travois. Then he set out again.

By midafternoon he reached the Bavispe where it flowed south and he followed it to a small village in the valley. That evening when he rode down the lone street dragging the travois, the few inhabitants of that place looked from his weary unshaven face to the boy's body in moccasins and breechclout and none among them posed any inquiry of him. The story was known to them and now its end plain for all to see.

The patrón who searched the sierras for his captive son was a tale told throughout the valley. One of the younger men present had even written a corrido describing the joven's trials in the wilderness at the hands of his captors. The villagers looked at the pale body on the travois. They removed their wide-brimmed hats and shook their heads slowly and crossed themselves. The song wasn't complete now without a final verse.

Rain streaked the darkened sky to the north. In the village the air was calm, the trees motionless. Jubal crossed the zocalo and paused to inspect a carreta which looked to have a broken axle.

An old man sent the balladeer to fetch his guitar.

Jubal called to the men. He asked if there were any other carretas in the village he might purchase. There were not, the old man said, but the one before him was easily repaired and the price of the carreta itself would go to the owner's widow, a pious woman of little means, certain to appreciate the sale. Of course there could be no thought of charging him for the repairs. Consider it a kindness on the part of the village to assist him during this time of sorrow. Only let the widow receive something to ease her own burden in life and grant them until tomorrow afternoon, then the carreta would be in fine shape.

Jubal dismounted. He opened his saddlebag and got out a handful of coins and gave them to the old man. He instructed him to see that half went to the widow, the rest for a new axle and the construction of a casket by afternoon the next day.

The old man accepted the payment. "My family would be honored for you to sleep in our home tonight," he said.

Jubal declined the offer. He motioned to a run-down stable and said he'd spent the night there with the boy.

The balladeer returned at last with his guitar. He struck the first chord as Jubal turned, leading the horse by the bridle reins down the street.

The old man asked, "Don't you want to hear your song?"

He didn't answer. The strumming of the guitar and those heroic lyrics followed him to the stable door, then a wind came howling off the clouds and stirred the dust in the street. The balladeer played a minor chord and it began to rain.

CHAPTER THIRTEEN

It was late afternoon of the following day before Jubal loaded the pine-board casket into the cart.

The men of the village had tried mending the axle, but in the end they were forced to concede that it was beyond repair. So they cut and shaped a cottonwood pole and fitted it through the center of the patched wooden wheels and added leaves of nopal as pitiful lubricant. The men deemed the cart ready at last. Jubal traded Bardo for one of the widow's mules. She protested at first, telling him the value of the horse far exceeded that of the mule and surely she would be robbing him to accept such an exchange, but he paid her no heed. He removed the spade bit from Bardo's mouth and turned the horse loose in the village corral and afterward he placed the bit in the casket at the boy's feet. He hitched the mule to the cart and climbed onto the rude box and took up the driving reins. When he set out down the muddy street, the creak of the carreta's wheels could be heard up and down the valley.

The rain left standing puddles in the road. Twice in the first hour the cart became stuck and he had to get down on his knees in the mud and dig in front of the wheels, then lead the mule by the reins until they were freed. His boots were caked and his clothes filthy. The mule slogged on through the muck, the carreta's wheels screeching and splashing.

He caught himself glancing over his shoulder from time to time. Scanning the road behind them as though expecting some laggard messenger to arrive at last, late with report that all his sorrows were nothing but a dream. Always the road was empty.

On his right he could see the river through breaks in the trees. For what remained of the afternoon he followed a course parallel to the river. The wind passed among the silted trunks of the cottonwoods along the banks and stirred the branches and by early evening he'd encountered no fellow traveler nor sign of another soul on the road.

To the west the sun would soon slip below the foothills. The creak of the cartwheels silenced the birds in the trees well in advance of his coming and there was no sound other. He looked ahead where the road curved about a rise covered with madrone and ash and he decided to rest there for the night.

* * *

Jubal drove the carreta off the road and into the madrones at the base of the rise. He set the handbrake and climbed from the box and unhitched the mule and led it down to drink at the riverbank. He'd grown accustomed to the screech of the wheels. Now in its absence the stillness seemed loud to him.

When he returned to the carreta, the sun was poised just above the hills, a thinning band of red holding back the dark. He hobbled the mule in a patch of grass.

A pair of sparrows burst from the trees on the hillside.

Jubal stepped to the carreta and reached for the gunbelt he'd left on the box. Then he turned with his pistol in hand and saw Cain step out of the madrones in his flowing white robes.

Jubal brought up the .45. Cain showed his palms, raising his hands overhead, and kept coming, to all appearances unarmed, not even with the kalis. He wore no gunbelt, carried no rifle. His wrists were manacled, the chain between them cut and dangling.

"Well, Jubela, Jubelo, Jubelum," Cain said. "What's the word?"

"What the hell kind of crazy are you?" Jubal asked.

"You got me all wrong, friend."

"What do you want?"

He was wearing a strange cloth hat, something like a turban, and there were lines of dried blood down his forehead. He kept his hands raised high as though in benediction. Like some deranged woodland priest.

He reeked of death.

Jubal let him get as far as the back of the cart before he told him to stop. "One more step and you're dead before you hit the ground," Jubal said.

"I didn't come to bring you trouble."

He held the pistol on Cain. "Why are you followin me?"

"I ain't followin you. I was camped behind the hill and I heard your cart. Might want to grease that axle."

Cain started to lower his hands.

"Keep em over your head," Jubal ordered.

He raised his hands again. "Let me make it right between you and me. I'm sorry for goin AWOL—I owed you better. You were my apprentice and a damned good one at that."

"We don't owe each other a damn thing."

Cain nodded toward the cart. "Haulin cargo, are you?"

Jubal ignored the question. "What the hell are you dressed up as?"

"Just another widow's son. How come you to be all alone out here?" Cain looked him in the eye. "Who you got in that pine box?"

"My son," Jubal said and lowered the pistol.

Cain reached in the folds of his turban and pulled the derringer, already cocked, and he leveled the little barrel as Jubal started to bring his pistol back up. Then Cain pulled the trigger.

The .41 rimfire bullet entered just below Jubal's chin and bruised his spine before exciting out the back of his neck. He twisted as he fell. His hat came off and he landed on his back staring up at Cain. He couldn't tell where he was hit, but he thought it wasn't bad, no pain at all, and then he tried to move and couldn't raise his hand. He willed himself to move, but his limbs wouldn't respond. Cain kneeled over him. Jubal couldn't even blink, his eyes fixed in what looked for all the world like a deathstare.

Cain wore a look of puzzlement. Surprised to see him motionless instead of gurgling and flailing about. He'd never seen a man die quite like that before. So suddenly from such a wound.

Cain squinted.

"You ain't playin opossum on me now, are you?" he asked.

Silence.

"Reckon we can find out right quick." Cain reached and pulled Jubal's own Bowie knife from its sheath. The blade gleamed in the twilight and Cain struck out and stabbed Jubal in the hip.

Jubal didn't move, never made the slightest sound. A fly landed on his cheek and went crawling across his open eye and up his brow.

Cain shook his head, disappointment in his eyes. "That's a rotten run of luck. I wanted to give you the pass-grip while you bled out. My apprentice to the last. But now you're too dead for a handshake, dead as old Hiram himself."

Cain looked all about, scanned the branches of the trees. As though searching out an elusive spirit. "Where you at? Already flew off? That's the quickest I ever seen the cord get cut. Your spark must've been overdue to meet the devil, I reckon. Unless you're just shy and hidin from me. Are you a shy one, spark?"

Cain rose and turned to climb the hillside. Jubal lay watching him pass through the red-hued madrones, their tortured branches flagged with cocoons of Mexican silkworms. He strained with everything in him, but he couldn't move so much as a fingertip.

After a while he saw Cain coming back down the hill, armed with pistol and rifle, the kalis at his side, and leading a pair of horses, shining yellow scalps dangling from his apron, and the full horror of it conquered Jubal's mind.

Cain staked the horses and stooped and picked up Jubal's hat. Spun it out into the brush, then kneeled beside him and raised Jubal's leg and pulled a boot off. Pitched it away, removed the other boot. He grabbed a fistful of Jubal's shirt and ripped it open.

A silent scream howled through Jubal's every synapse.

When he'd stripped him naked and thrown the clothes deep into the brush, Cain cradled Jubal's head in his lap and took up the Bowie again. He began cutting around the scalp, making crude work of it, half-careless, and Jubal felt no pain, only the pressure of the blade. Cain rose and pressed a moccasined foot to Jubal's chest. He reached down grasping his hair. When Cain jerked the scalp free, Jubal heard a sound like distant thunder.

Blood ran down his left eye, suffusing half the world.

Still there was no pain and he longed for death to come.

The mad man sheathed his knife. Jubal watched him

tie the bloody scalp to his green apron. For a moment Cain stood looking over his handywork, then bent down and grasped Jubal's limp hand.

"I'm powerful hungry," he said. "But I'm goin to save your liver for dessert. I want me a bite of your boy's heart first."

Cain pressed his thumb hard between the second and third knuckles of Jubal's hand and shook.

"Tubal-Cain," he whispered.

He let the hand fall.

Cain gripped the Bowie and turned to the carreta and the casket inside. He pulled the pine box out the back of the cart and it slammed to the ground. He kneeled and started prying open the cover with the knife, wood groaning as the nails came loose, and Jubal could only watch.

Cain got the cover off and looked inside. He stared at the boy's corpse a long time. A look not unlike tenderness in his eye. He started to reach inside the casket, then hesitated, his hand poised above the youth's long red hair, a final uncertainty, turning the knife slowly in his other hand.

An unknown substance clung to the boy's locks. Thick and golden gleaming. He wondered for a moment if the pine boards had emitted some remnant of sap—yet this had more the appearance of honey.

A faint scent in the air like fresh pollen.

When Cain gripped the boy's hair, Jubal groaned within himself.

Cain's eyes shot wide. Jubal saw him jerk his hand back as though he'd reached into a charged current and the knife fell from his grip, his face contorting in fear and confusion.

Cain rushed to the horses. He pulled the dun's stake and swung into the saddle and clapped his legs against the horse's flanks, setting out down the road as fast as the mount would carry him. He abandoned the staked black, such was his panicked haste. Twice he glanced over his shoulder as though to assure himself he wasn't pursued.

Jubal sank into the dark.

* * *

When he woke in the night, pain consumed him and he lay gasping for breath. His nerves which had been so vacant and numb were screaming now and there was blood all over him and blowflies circling. Dried blood crusted over his left eye.

Jubal was weak but determined to stand. Slowly he got up on one knee and attempted to rise, then agony shot through him from the stab wound in his hip and he dropped down again.

He went crawling naked through the grass and rocks, dragging himself to the cart. He pulled himself up against the cart and snatched his canteen from the box before collapsing back into the grass again. The flies had been at the raw flesh on his head and he knew the wound had to be cleaned. When he got the lid off, he hesitated with the canteen in his hands and steeled himself for what was coming. Then poured the water over his head. Everything burned until he thought he'd go mad with the pain.

He was completely naked save the sock on his right foot, the sole article of clothing not torn off and thrown into the brush. He took the sock and draped it over the wound on his head to protect it from the flies. He sat trembling and cold. Waiting for a measure of strength to return. After a while he understood his strength wasn't coming back and he had to act now before he was even weaker.

Finally he crawled to the base of an ancient madrone and sat resting against the trunk and prepared himself to die.

Then something remarkable happened.

Out of the shadows the boy came walking. He wore breechclout and moccasins and his red hair fell below his shoulders. It was very strange because Jubal could turn his head and see John Russell still lying in the pine-casket, but here he was standing before him.

"Don't be afraid, Papa," the boy said.

He tried to speak the boy's name, but his voice was a strangled rasp, cut off by the wound below his chin.

"Hold on," the boy told him. "Help is coming." He turned to the road and the shadows.

Jubal fought to speak. "Stay with me. I need you."

The boy looked back over his shoulder. "I'm always

with you. Your blood is my blood." Then he told him they'd meet in the darkness on the path to the Other World. Many souls wandered lost on their journey, he said, and he was going now to seek them out and guide the blind and lame to the good road God had laid for them. When it came the day for Jubal to make his own passage, he'd be there to take his hand and show him the way.

"Stay with me, John Russell."

"Don't worry, Papa. Help is coming."

Then he stepped out onto the road and Jubal watched him turn south to disappear in the night. The wind high in the madrones was cold and lonesome.

* * *

Dolores woke from the dream.

She sat up in the dark of the cabin and looked at Hector where he slept on the floor in his bedroll beside her. In the next room the Ibarras slumbered, the old couple who'd invited the travelers to stay the night and make use of their barn and corral.

She hesitated, then shook Hector awake.

"What's the matter?" He rubbed the dust of sleep from his eyes.

"I saw him," she whispered.

"Who?"

"Jubal. He was sitting under a tree and he was scalped."

"Only a bad dream, girl. Go back to sleep."

"It's a place just off the river, back the way we came. I remember passing the hill."

"We've got a long road tomorrow. You need rest. We all do."

Hector closed his eyes, instantly asleep again.

Dolores lay down and stared at the ceiling where the laths showed through broken plaster, quiet in the little farmhouse, not even the ticking of a clock. It was their second night at the old couple's. Mosby and the other men were sleeping out in the barn. Hector had decided that with Señor Ibarra's approval they'd stay a final night in the hope Jubal would catch them up tomorrow. When Mosby and Endicott had rejoined the party, they'd explained that Jubal ordered them to ride ahead. He would come alone when he was ready. Dolores sensed there was something the men were keeping from her and she'd glimpsed Mosby speaking privately with Hector about some matter, but she chose not to puzzle over it. In truth she'd come to care little whether Jubal returned from the mountains or not.

They'd waited all that day expecting to see Jubal come up the river road, but he'd never arrived. Finally Hector decided they would start out for Nácori at dawn with or without him. The segundo was intent on getting Dolores back to the ranch.

After a while she drifted to sleep once more.

Only to dream again.

She saw him bloody and naked sitting at the base of

a madrone, a miserable figure with a sock on his head. Strangely comic. Like the last feeble antics of a dying jester, bent on eliciting a cold chuckle from the court of death itself. He reached and plucked bright red berries. When he chewed them, the berries stained his lips redly. The madrones raised their flayed martyrs' limbs in the moonlight bedecked with pale regenerative weavings.

Dolores jolted awake. The vivid quality of the dream shook her to the core. She rose from her bedroll and went to the candle-holder that rested on the table and struck a match and set the candle burning. The glow shone in the cramped little room, a kitchen on one side, the entry to the bedroom covered by a hanging blanket on the other.

Hector sat up. "What now? Did you hear something outside?" He slipped on his glasses, then his hand went to the gunbelt beside him.

"I saw him again," she said. "It was so real. He needs our help."

A look of anger crossed Hector's face and for a moment she thought he might curse. Then his expression changed to one of resigned sorrow.

"Don't torture yourself over him," Hector said. "It's not worth it. I know you're worried, but you've got to quiet your mind."

Now she took up his discarded anger. "I know what I saw," she fairly shouted.

Their argument roused the old woman, who pulled aside the blanket in the doorway, come to check on the girl. Her husband called out, "What's wrong?" from the bedroom, the entire house awake now. Hector explained that a bad dream had troubled the girl's sleep. The old woman tried to soothe her as best she could. Dolores submitted to her ministrations only in great reluctance and finally she extinguished the candle with a breath and lay under her bedroll once more.

It was perhaps an hour later when she woke from the dream a third time.

Dolores rose, careful not to wake Hector, and crept to the door. She picked up her boots and gunbelt, the little revolver Jubal had given her to carry, then slipped outside into the moonlight.

* * *

Dolores took a pair of rope hackamores from where they were hanging on a corral post. She opened the gate and stepped into the corral and fitted the hackamores on two of the mules. Then she led them out and closed the gate behind her, eyeing the barn door all the while. It remained shut, the barn dark.

She mounted up bareback. Leading the second mule she headed out down the river road.

From the shadowed window of the hayloft Mosby watched the girl ride away.

* * *

293

Frogs croaked in the reeds along the river. In the hills a coyote yipped. The moon hung in the trees like ripened silver fruit.

Dolores came riding through the dark and rounded a bend in the road and saw him. Her breath caught in her throat. In the distance on the road ahead Cain sat astride a trotting dun and he was clad in pale robes. He recognized her in the same moment. A manic grin stretched across his face.

Cain drew Wormwood and gave the dun his heels. He galloped toward her waving the curved blade over his head and letting out a howl to chill the blood.

Dolores dropped the hackamore of the mule she'd been leading. She turned her own mount and clapped her legs hard against the mule's sides and raced back the way she'd come. A fear gripped her like no other she'd ever known. The killer at her heels wouldn't stop at simple murder, for he sought to devour her soul itself.

She fumbled with the gunbelt. Hooves thundered behind her, gaining on the mule, fast as her own racing heart, then she drew the revolver and thumbed back the hammer. She twisted around on the mule and snapped off a shot.

Cain never slowed. He galloped on, narrowing the distance between them, the mule no match for the dun's sweeping strides, and Dolores fired another shot that did nothing to slow his pursuit.

At last he edged up alongside her on the road, the dun neck and neck with the mule. Dolores raised the pistol and fired point blank—once, twice—and the first bullet passed through his billowing robes, then the next shot took Cain high in the left shoulder. He roared, more rage than pain, and swung the kalis.

The blade landed with a meaty crunch. It caught the mule on the side of its face and left a bloody gash. The mule let out a cry of pain and terror, then lost its footing in a deep puddle.

Dolores spilled off the mule's back. She splashed into the mud and the pistol slipped from her hand.

Cain reined in and turned the dun.

The mule was fighting to stand in the muck with blood pouring down its face, down its chest. Dolores got to her knees and scrambled to find the pistol.

Cain dismounted. "I killed your daddy tonight, Little Sister Death. He made his confession to me before he bled out. You know what Jubal told me?"

Dolores kneeled sweeping her hands through the mud.

Cain strode forward and raised the kalis high, moonlight on the slithering blade, and he stood in his robes like a backwoods serpent handler. The girl fell back and scrambled away from him on her heels.

"Jubal told me he wisht he'd strangled you the first time he ever laid eyes on you. Said you ain't worth it. He was haulin his boy's body home in a wagon when I found him. Them Apaches killed John Russell on account of you. Jubal told me how you cost him everything, how you ain't worthy of one drop of his boy's blood."

Even through the panic swirling within her, Dolores registered the news of John Russell's death, its ring of truth.

She dove to the side and attempted to scramble to her feet, but Cain was too quick for her. He kicked her hard in the belly with a moccasined foot and the wind exploded out of her. She dropped down into the muck.

"Look here," he said. "I got a present for you."

He untied the bloody scalp from his apron and tossed it at her. "I took your daddy's scalp and now I'm fixin to collect yours. Right after I kill you graveyard dead like he should've done at the start."

He struck out with Wormwood.

The rifle blast shattered the stillness of the night. Cain spun half-around, the bullet bursting through his side, through his left ribcage, and the sweeping arc of the blade missed Dolores's head by what seemed a hair's breadth.

Cain fell to his knees. The kalis slipped from his hand and vanished in the standing water.

Dolores looked down the road and saw Mosby on his horse, the rifle at his shoulder.

When he saw that Cain had fallen, Mosby spurred the mount and galloped toward them.

Dolores got to her feet. Cain was holding himself, pressing his hands over the hole in his side. Blood ran between his fingers and dripped and faded in the mire.

Mosby dismounted. He sheathed the rifle in the saddle-scabbard and stepped up to Cain.

"Kill him," Dolores shouted. "He's crazy. Kill him now."

Mosby didn't even look at her. "Shut up, girl," he said.

Cain's breaths were ragged gasps. A trickle of blood appeared at the corner of his mouth. When Cain fell forward, Mosby dropped to his knees and caught him, eased him down onto his back.

Mosby glanced at Dolores. "Go on, get out of here."

She shook her head, confused and disgusted. She looked up and down the road, but the wounded mule had run away in the struggle and the other mule was nowhere to be seen. She stepped to Cain's dun and took its reins and climbed into the saddle.

Mosby held Cain. He gripped his hand in his own. "How come it got to be this way, Sergeant? How come it got to be like this?"

Dolores pointed the dun down the river road and set out where her dream had called her.

* * *

Cain reached a hand into the muck and retrieved Wormwood. Mosby tensed, but the sergeant only turned the kalis and pressed it to his own stomach before the blade faltered in his grasp and fell again. He struggled to raise it.

"You're sick, Sergeant," Mosby said. "You don't know what you're tryin to do."

297

"Please," Cain whispered.

Mosby knew what he was requesting, the samurai death he'd spoken of through their long years together as the honorable end for a warrior. He shook his head. What good could come of it? Yet it was a hard thing to refuse Cain's last wish as he lay dying from Mosby's own bullet.

"Please, Mo," Cain choked out.

Mosby picked up the blade Wormwood, sadic, baleful, and pressed it lightly to Cain's stomach, then took the sergeant's hand and placed it on the grip.

"That's all I can do for you," Mosby said. "I can't do the other. It ain't right that you'd ask me to. Now you got to tell me, Sergeant—where do I go now? How am I supposed to be in the world? The old times are gone and I don't think they'll come again. Not like the times we knew, when we rode together lookin for a war and ever war sharpened the steel in us. These boys now, they a new kind of soldier. They got strange ways, dark turned hearts. Tell me what I'm supposed to do, Sergeant."

When Cain tried to speak, blood bubbled from his mouth.

Mosby let go of the kalis and it wavered in Cain's weakened grasp. His eyes were pleading with Mosby.

"No sir. I can't." Mosby wept, unable to do as Cain bade him.

His face was colorless, pale and cold as a winter moon. Mosby saw Cain widowed of the power in his eye that in days past had bowed the will of beasts and men.

He lay like a broken Boaz, no longer that Cain who'd charged the enemy midst at Carrizal to save Mosby the buck private, gripping a pair of pistols, reins clenched between his teeth, the sergeant who from spurs to plumed Stetson was once the image of fate's right hand.

The kalis fell. A tear ran from the corner of Cain's eye.

"All right, Sergeant," Mosby whispered. "It's all right."

Mosby took the blade Wormwood, sadic, baleful, and wrapped Cain's languid hand around the grip and held it there, the sergeant's skin cold to the touch, and Mosby took a breath. Then he plunged the blade into Cain's stomach and made the cut.

At once he was sorry he'd done it. Mosby's voice rose like a fountain of lament and he looked to see what agony he'd caused the sergeant, but the sergeant was dead.

He drew the kalis free of Cain's wound, then rose and staggered down to the river with blood dripping from the sword. With both hands he flung Wormwood wheeling under the moon, a long bright arc, and it flashed and fell, the blade Wormwood, into the midst of the water and sank.

Mosby returned and took Cain under either arm. He went dragging him through the mud down to the riverside, the wind shrill in the cottonwoods, wailing, as thin wisps of clouds passed before the face of the moon like a widow's veil. He removed his gunbelt. He bent and took up Cain again and walked out into the slow current until the water reached his chest. Standing in the river he held Cain as though he'd perform a midnight baptism of the dead.

And never again, Mosby thought, in all the world's turning would there be such a soldier as Cain had been in those true old times.

Mosby released him.

The dead man floated on the current. The dying ravenous eye within him found no more sustenance. One pale hand was outflung behind him as though he'd reach and take hold of an offered lifeline, too late now forever, and moonlight shone on the ring the dead man wore. The river would carry him through that valley of deep meadows and many happy orchards and after a time the turtles would find him and eat the skin from his eyes.

Mosby climbed onto the banks and stood watching until the corpse was a black dot on the water, then gone, In the cottonwoods the wailing died away.

* * *

Dawn was breaking in the east when she left the road and climbed the hillside among the madrones. Dolores found him lying as in her dream, naked under the selfsame tree with a sock on his head. Jubal's eyes were closed. She was afraid she was too late.

Dolores got down and tied the dun's reins to the back of the carreta. A black horse was staked nearby and a mule stood hobbled and cropping grass. She looked at the pine box open on the ground and saw her brother's body inside, but there was no time for grief or to dwell on what Cain had told her. She took a blanket from Jubal's bedroll in the back of the cart and she removed Cain's canteen from the dun's saddle. When she stepped up to Jubal, his right eye opened, showing pale white in a mask of gore. His other eye was crusted shut with dried blood. She covered him with the blanket and helped him sip from the canteen. He tried to speak, but his voice was gone.

"Everything's going to be all right," Dolores told him. "Let me help."

She pulled a bandana from her pocket and wet it with the canteen and carefully cleaned the blood from his eye. She washed the wound under his chin. Then she took the sock from his head and looked at what Cain had done. Tearing a corner from the blanket she made a covering for his bloody head.

She'd been tending to him for some time before she realized she was crying. Tears ran down her cheeks. "Oh, Papa," she said.

"Give me your hand," he croaked.

She stood up. Jubal gripped her hand and struggled to his feet. He leaned against the trunk of the madrone with the blanket about his shoulders. They stood together in the grove as the sun rose and shadows dissolved, then she led him by the hand like the faithful daughter of some blind old king, the pair of them wandering in

301

exile. She helped him to the back of the carreta and he lay down.

Dolores stooped and got the cover of the casket back in place, then picked up the front of the casket and raised it to lean against the back of the cart. She went around and pushed from behind, straining hard, and slid the casket up into the cart beside Jubal.

Dolores unhobbled the mule and hitched it to the carreta. She pulled the black's stake and tied its reins to the cart beside the dun's, then climbed up onto the box. Dew dripped from the empty silken cocoons on the branches of the madrones. She took the reins and released the handbrake and they set out down the road following the river, the clear Bavispe with its headwaters in the sierras that formed the Great Divide.

CHAPTER FOURTEEN

Carnoviste found an opening in a deep cut on the hillside, a place the rains had carved out. It was just a gap in the arroyo wall about the size of a man's head and when he looked through it, all he could see was darkness, but he could hear their collective hum. The hive abuzz in the little cave. He returned below and cut down several maples. He lashed the first trunk with a reata and tied the reata to the mule's saddlehorn and led the mule up the slope dragging the wood. Then he went back and repeated the process for the other maple trunks. He stacked them in the arroyo and on the hill directly over the chamber. When it was ready, he piled on dead brush and set the fires blazing.

Standing at the edge of the cliff he looked down below and watched a wreath of smoke rise from the entrance. After a while the bees came pouring out. A dark cloud of them drunken and droning, sluggish from the smoke. They kept coming, gathering in thick clusters in the trees and on the rocks. All night he kept the bonfire going and through the day following and another night. On the morning of the third day the smoke no longer smelled of burning maple but like molten sugar and the color of the plumes changed from gray to blue.

Carnoviste tended the inferno. It had been a full six moons since the day Neiflint and Oblite spotted the figures coming up the trail to Pa-Gotzin-Kay. Two women and a warrior leading a group of children. Oblite ran to tell him the news, then Carnoviste had saddled a mule immediately and ridden down to meet them—as he'd done with the handful of other survivors who'd reached the mountain in pairs or alone over the last days. He didn't dare allow himself to hope who they might be.

When he'd reached the switchback just above the travelers, he recognized Gouyen by her walk. Then his eyes held on the brave beside her and he wondered. As he rounded the turn he saw it was Chatto and for a moment he failed to conceal his disappointment. Jacali was with them and several weary-looking children.

Carnoviste dismounted before them.

Gouyen stepped forward holding a baby in her arms. "I've brought your son home to you," she said.

Carnoviste took Illanipi from her. "You've given me back my life." He motioned at the pair of waterskins hanging from the saddlehorn. "Drink," he told them.

Chatto got the skins and gave them first to the children. Each one drank and passed the skin to the next.

Carnoviste stared into the baby's sleeping face. "What of his mother?"

"Gone to the House of Ghosts," Gouyen said. "All I could save was the little one."

Carnoviste groaned for the love that was lost to him. "And my son the Healer?" he asked.

"Killed by the White Eyes, his body taken away."

"Denali, my son," he said. "I wish I'd died and not you."

Chatto looked away from his grief. Jacali was weeping without making a sound, though such was not the way of the People.

The baby in his arms woke and cried out. Gouyen took the wailing child and gave him to Jacali.

"Come with me, my chief," Gouyen said. Then she led Carnoviste a distance up the trail away from the others. He sat on a rock and hung his head while Gouyen stood in front of him so the others couldn't see. She spoke very low.

"You've shamed the spirits of the warriors who gave their lives for you," she told him. "And the lives of their women and children. Are their names shouted, called back from the Other World? How much blood was lost in the dirt while you kept him?" The wise woman shook her head. "I believe today you love your enemies and hate the People. I see that if the White Eye boy had lived and all of us died, nothing would please you better."

"Don't call him that, old witch. He was of the People by everything that counts."

"Whoever he was, he's lost to you now. You have to be strong. Our women are widows, they need a strong man if the People are to continue on the earth."

"Why bring more life into this pain? Is death so

hungry? I don't have anything left to give."

"You have the blood of the People which is stronger than pain and stronger than death. Whatever Power a man like you might possess is all the Power that remains. Mine is lost. It was lost before the lake."

He spat at her feet. "You told me the lake was safe."

"And I've come to ransom my words. Now stand up and ready yourself. Stand as a warrior should, then go tell the People that the Blue Mountains will never be conquered. Speak your son's name no more. Let the dead finish their journey."

They continued up the switchbacks and out onto the plateau where the remnant waited to greet them. After many embraces and tears, just before they started for the village, Gouyen approached him again.

"My chief, will you let me hold the child once more?" she asked.

Carnoviste stared at her and held Illanipi in his arms. "Why, old witch?"

"Just for a moment I want to hold him again. Then I'll trouble you no more."

Carnoviste hesitated, but something in her eyes decided it for him. Finally he held out Illanipi.

Gouyen pressed the baby close to her breast and softly rocked him. Then a kiss upon the head and she surrendered him to the chief and turned to walk away, not following the others toward the village.

Carnoviste lingered behind. "Where are you going?" he called to her.

She didn't answer until she'd gone some distance along the edge of the high red shelf, pausing at a place where that primordial tower dropped off in a straight plunge. She stood at the edge of the fall and turned and faced him. Gouyen stared directly into his eyes.

"The People are yours to protect, my chief," she said. "For my false words I pay in blood."

The wise woman chanted no deathsong, simply stepped backward, her hand cradling the medicine bundle that dangled at her breast, and cast herself from the ramparts of paradise and was gone.

Now Carnoviste stood at the edge of another cliff and watched the entrance of the chamber become a belching furnace as wax and honey ignited. Golden lava cascaded down the cliff-face to cool on the talus below. All that day the fire raged, intense heat calcining the inner walls, and the edges of the opening began to collapse, the cave falling in on itself.

At sunset he looked to the west where thin sheets of rain descended from rolling cloudbanks and shone like a sheer red veil over the peaks. An eagle rose in a slow gyre and the dying light coppered its pinions as though it flew on burning wings. He watched the eagle turn and rise above the sierras.

Then Carnoviste spoke his son's name one last time and walked down the slope to ride back and join the revenant on Pa-Gotzin-Kay.

* * *

Three days after they had returned to the ranch they buried John Russell in the family cemetery beside his mother. It was a blustery morning when Hector and the vaqueros lowered the pine box with their reatas into the open grave. Jubal stood pale and gaunt, his head wrapped in bandages, and he leaned on his cane beside Dolores, all in black, and they watched the casket descend.

The boy would lie just up the hill from Wesley's resting place. On their return to the ranch Adela had informed Jubal and Dolores that the old man passed away in his sleep the day after they'd departed out of Nácori.

Word had been sent to Moroni Thayne's family, notifying them of his death in battle, the grave by the mountain lake, and his sons grieved the loss.

Mosby and the other mercenaries lingered only long enough for John Russell's burial. Not a man among them dared look Jubal in the eye. Later that morning the mercs were preparing to ride out for their journey back to the states. They stood in front of the hacienda looking over their fresh mounts.

Dolores stepped down from the porch and went to Mosby.

"Where will you go now?" she asked.

He stood beside his horse, rocking the saddle into place, and he didn't look at her. "Texas, maybe Oklahoma," he said, then pulled the latigo and fastened the backcinch. "Reckon I might buy me a piece of land with my pay from old man Applegate. Start a farm and try livin for a change, instead of all this killin."

"I wanted to tell you before you left," she said. "Thank you for doing what you did. For saving me from him."

Now he glanced at her, then quickly away again, but she caught the look in his eye. Unmistakable, the selfsame look she'd glimpsed in so many others, most profoundly in Cain's own killer gaze, and she knew Mosby hated her.

"You don't got to thank me for a damn thing, Little Sister," he said and swung up into the saddle.

* * *

In Nácori Chico they say he never returned from the mountains, that the Apaches killed Jubal McKenna on some desolate peak high above the timberline and the snows covered his bones. It was another who came back, they say. A stranger called Juan Lazarene, a recluse who never left the ranch nor would he accept visitors. Years passed and the American newsmen and pulp writers forgot their story of the last Indian war.

Dolores cared for Jubal. She nursed him through the long healing and she knit silken skullcaps for him to wear. The skin on his head never fully grew back over naked bone and in the years to come he wore one of her caps at all times and during all kinds of work.

And for the rest of their lives they were to each other father and daughter.

EPILOGUE

August, 2003

El Paso, Texas

The old woman kneeled in front of the cedar chest at the foot of the bed. She raised the lid and took out the little buckskin dress her grandmother had sewn for her in that long ago. Her knees pained her and she gripped the bedframe and rose slowly to her feet, then sat down on the mattress.

The door to her room stood partly open. Nurses and orderlies moved up and down the hall in the fluorescent light while an old man with a walker took halting steps, his gaze cast down at his feet.

Dolores was eighty-nine years old and a widow almost a decade now. Her children were grown and busy with their families and work, but they hadn't forgotten her. She talked to Sara in California on the phone every night and Johnny would stop by after work each day to check on her, not a weekend passing when he didn't bring his own children for a visit.

Claudia, too, came to see her when she was in town, Jubal's little girl a grandmother herself now.

Jubal had been gone for over sixty years. Though his wound never truly healed he'd lived another eleven years after the scalping until one day he bumped his head on the doorframe of the old ranch house and took to bed sick. He died not long after. Many times they'd talked among themselves of what they saw that night, Dolores her series of dreams and Jubal his vision of John Russell, what the boy had told him. In those last years before he passed away Jubal spoke to her of a perfect peace.

He left the ranch to her and Claudia. Hector managed it for them and they saw that the old man was well taken care of when he couldn't climb on a horse anymore.

Claudia grew into a fine young woman and the years she spent under her father's care and tutelage were never forgotten. She went on to attend college in Arizona where she met her husband, the two of them ultimately making a home in Phoenix.

Dolores didn't think she'd ever marry, but a few years after Claudia moved away, she met an American engineer working for a petroleum company, scouting sites in the valley. They were married in Nácori. When the baby was due, they came to Texas so the child would be born in the U.S. They'd planned on returning to raise Johnny on his grandfather's ranch, but they never did go back and after Hector passed away, she and Claudia sold the land. Dolores's husband had started work for Hughes Tool. Eventually he'd become an executive at TWA and the family would live for a time in Italy, a stone farmhouse in the hill town of Perugia. Many happy days were spent there, many nights she'd rocked her children to sleep singing an Apache lullaby. When they were a little older, she told them the story of the brave young boy taken captive by the mountain people, how his father never stopped searching for him, and in her telling she would change the ending. The father carried him home at last and the boy taught the low-landers about the mountain people, taught them of the good things they did, common to all men everywhere, and so they lived in peace, those of the mountain and those of the valley. The children loved to hear the story. As she watched them grow and change she wished Jubal could have known them.

It surprised her how much she missed him. Later she'd see a movie in the '50s called *The Searchers*. She was weeping during the last scene, shocked that she would have such a reaction to a cowboy picture show, and her husband leaned over and whispered in the darkened theater, asking if she wanted to leave.

She never realized how much Jubal's loss had meant. There had been a kind of joy even in sorrow when he was with her.

"That was the end of tears," she whispered there on the bed. "No more of that."

313

For a long time she'd been feeding a quiet rage. Angry with the way things had gone in those mountains, angry at Jubal because he'd played God and proven himself a man. Behind all his love there had been a pain that time couldn't heal and the best she'd managed over the years was telling herself she'd learned not to care. In the last weeks she'd found a fresh anger as well, new cause for bitterness, confined in this place with the old and feeble-minded. She'd fallen in her own house and once in the garden, lying helpless until Johnny found her. She wasn't able to live on her own anymore, he said. The nursing facility was just a temporary measure, Johnny promised, until she could complete the physical rehab program and he managed to renovate his own house to accommodate her moving in. So she lingered in this sterile fluorescent corner of hell. She hated being near her fellow residents, the ones who smelled of age and waste, who'd allowed themselves to be robbed of pride. Their lack of dignity disgusted her.

Then one night she had the dream. In her dream she lived that day in April over again, the afternoon during spring round-up when she'd gone riding through the hills where live oak grew and the land was cut with arroyos. She felt eyes upon her. A cold gaze. Something watching, following in the brush and shadows, stalking her through the woods. She put the horse to a faster pace, glancing back over her shoulder, but there was nothing in sight. A sense of dread churned in her belly.

Of a sudden there was a crash in the undergrowth

and she heard a deep growl. The horse shared her fear and they sped down the trail rushing fast as a frightened bird, trees blurring by, the beast racing alongside them, hidden in the brambles. She heard the thin branches snapping as it charged through the undergrowth, heard it bounding along, matching the speed of the horse, and she could smell it, sweet and rotten all at once. She was afraid it would come diving out of the trees and snatch her off the horse to carry her away in its jaws. She gave the mount her heels and ducked under a low branch and they charged up the slope to emerge from the trees onto the rise overlooking the pasture and the mesa.

She could hear it calling out in the woods.

Dolores galloped down the hill and crossed onto the mesa. Jubal was standing before the fire, holding his iron. She got down and ran to him and he dropped the iron and took her in his arms. She was shaking, her voice thick when she told him a grizzly bear had tried to get her. Jubal held her tight and spoke her name just above a whisper. Then he smiled. He brushed her hair back with his rough hands, callused and seamed, those hands that were always so gentle to her. He said there were no grizzlies in the valley, but even if one had lumbered down from the hills, it made no difference, he'd never let any harm come to her. For she'd been entrusted to his care and nothing could pluck her from the embrace of his love.

When the old woman woke in bed and opened her eyes, she could still smell him, his sweat and the smoke of the branding fire on his clothes and in his hair. She'd forgotten of that day completely and now it came back to her in perfect clarity. Jubal couldn't have looked on her with an expression of more honest love than if she'd been his only child. Nothing had forced him to do so. He was the patrón of the valley and she was just an Indio girl in his household. His kindness to her had won him no respect or admiration from those around him. He didn't have to love her as though she were his own blood. Only God had seen what compassion and gentleness lived in the heart of a man capable of such rage.

All the anger she'd harbored for years vanished in a moment and in its place a sense of gratitude. She'd climbed out of bed and gone walking the halls in her nightgown and for once she could look on the unfortunates around her with changed eyes. She'd never spoken to the others in that place and she didn't like to see them, the broken and the sick. There had been times she'd cursed them in her mind for the weakness they showed. Now she no longer felt the old fear of becoming like them. The bitterness that had shielded her from what she saw in those faces was gone and she went among them.

The victim of a stroke sat in his wheelchair staring out a dirty window all day at the cars that passed in endless succession. He couldn't speak or so much as raise a spoon to his crooked lips. Dolores began feeding him at the dinner table while she ate her own meal. Soup would run down his chin and she'd reach and wipe it away. Visitors who saw them during meal-times remarked how cute they were, an old woman caring for her invalid husband, and they'd compliment her and say they hoped their own marriage was so strong when they were her age. She tried telling them once how it was, but they didn't listen.

She read to the ones who couldn't get out of bed, too sick or too long in despair, but after a while she put the books away and just told them the story. The same old story she'd told her children. She was there to greet the newly arrived, those who came with sadness and confusion in their eyes, and when the preacher came each Sunday, she traveled up and down the halls encouraging them to rise and join her in the chapel. Because she couldn't look into their hearts she tried to love them all without distinction.

Johnny came and told her the house was ready. He'd built railings on the porch steps and installed a stairlift inside that would carry her up to her bedroom. She had to tell him she wasn't going. This was where she was needed.

She wasn't seeking anyone's praise. That wasn't why she stayed. She was there only to love and that made everything simple—no one could break her heart now, no one could hurt her, because she didn't place her expectation on people. Her expectation was for the Lord. And she came to see the purpose of her life was to receive His love and once having received it to reflect that love so all might see.

Dolores went among them day by day and shared her own surprise at so simple a truth that God was good. Through long and wasted years she'd felt unworthy of the blood, the son whose death stood in place of hers, and she found there were many here like herself who'd run from the cross. Many who thought their lives, such as they were, of no worth. A great doubt had taken root in their hearts regarding the truth of their identity. No one begins as a hopeless sinner, she told them. We're all lost sons and daughters here. Then she would tell them how the Son of the Father's love had freely chosen to stand as blood ransom so that He might restore the family that was lost.

Your life lived is worth His death, she said.

That which is purchased is of the worth a man's willing to pay. And so the firstborn of the dead breathes the very breath of heaven into man once more and we inhabit the garden again.

She discovered from their eager reception that faith was simply an automatic response to a revelation of the goodness of God, correction to an image long out of true. Her new friends were moved to tears at the hope they'd found among the liminal shadows of that dark waystation.

You're never out of the reach of His embrace, she told them. For love captures the lover and the loved.

Twice in the last days she'd slipped her bonds and found herself floating above the body of a frail dark-skinned old woman. Then she was gliding out over the cantilevered houses on the hill, the electric star shining on the Franklin Mountains, and she'd taken the pass into Mexico and the sierras of her birth. Pa-Gotzin-Kay stood empty now and only foxes and wild cats walked upon it. Her spirit followed the Bavispe from its fountainhead to where it flowed down the valley and through the ranch. She drifted among the trees in the orchard, their branches dark and barren, casualties of a wasting disease, and at last she came to the great tree. A small hole in the earth at its base lay open. The likeness of the Santo Niño was gone, the image of the Child Jesus she'd placed in captivity. She looked at the highest boughs of that tree and there on the tips of the branches grew bright green buds.

Dolores sat on the bed and clutched the buckskin dress. Wrapped in its folds was the rawhide bag she'd been wearing about her neck when she was captured. Now she opened it and took out the deck of leather cards and spread them on the mattress. She'd not examined them in half a century.

She shuffled the deck and laid out four of the cards facedown and ran her fingers over them. Hesitating, lingering above a card. She reached to turn it over, then thought better of it.

Dolores remembered what she'd seen in the cards that first night at the McKenna table, sitting across from John Russell in the light of the cressetlamps. The Tree of Life whose reaching branches mirrored its great roots. Then the other card, a mystery indeed, the hive teeming with life behind the bones of the rotted bear's ribcage. Out of the eater, something sweet.

She'd come to understand the truth of what her grandmother told her—

Dolores let the cards lie unrevealed, for she knew time is born with a caul on its face.

A limb scratched at the windowpane. The nightsky was starflung, brilliant beyond the upper boughs of the tree outside her window. They were burning there in the glass, Castor and Pollux caught in the tangled branches, eternal twins that flared and faded and flared again, and she hugged the buckskin dress to her.

THE END

Made in United States
Orlando, FL
23 January 2023

28954319R10209